Dear Reader,

Clay Thornton is a confirmed bachelor with one disastrous marriage to a high-powered career woman behind him and no plans to remarry in his future. Dr. Jenna Macklin has always been too busy to think about marriage or babies.

But Mother Nature has a way of playing havoc with the best-laid plans of man or doctor. Jenna and Clay have a lot of problems to work through before they can make all the pieces of their very different lifestyles fit together into a whole.

But it wouldn't be a romance if they didn't find true love, and we wouldn't be happy if that happy-ever-after ending for Clay and Jenna didn't include a whole passel of babies in their future!

Marisa Carroll

MARISA CARROLL

is the pen name of the award-winning writing team of Carol Wagner and Marian Scharf of Deshler, Ohio. The sisters have published over thirty romance novels in the past fifteen years.

They are recipients of several industry awards including *Romantic Times Magazine* Career Achievement Award in 1991, and were finalists in the Romance Writers of America's RITA Award competition in 1992. In 1999 *Romantic Times Magazine* honored them with a nomination as one of the top storytellers of the year.

Carol and Marian were born and raised in Northwestern Ohio, pursuing careers in nursing, X-ray technology and the business community before entering the writing field in 1982.

Books by Marisa Carroll

Harlequin American Romance

Natural Attraction #127
Jenna's Choice #160
Tomorrow's Vintage #190
Come Home to Me #256
Ties that Bind #286

Harlequin Superromance

Remembered Magic #268
Gathering Place #318
Rescue from Yesterday #418
Refuge from Today #426
Return to Tomorrow #437
One to One #515
Keeping Christmas #529
Wedding Invitation #598
Marry Me Tonight #635
Peacemaker #655
The Man Who Saved Christmas #718
Megan #742
Before Thanksgiving Comes #811
Winter Soldier #841
Last-Minute Marriage #942

Anthologies

My Valentine, 1994
My Secret Admirer, 1999

Tyler

Crossroads
Loveknot

Tyler: Hometown Reunion

Unexpected Son
Mission: Children

Maitland Maternity

Baby: 101

babies
& BACHELORS USA

Marisa Carroll
Jenna's Choice

HARLEQUIN®

TORONTO • NEW YORK • LONDON
AMSTERDAM • PARIS • SYDNEY • HAMBURG
STOCKHOLM • ATHENS • TOKYO • MILAN • MADRID
PRAGUE • WARSAW • BUDAPEST • AUCKLAND

HARLEQUIN BOOKS
225 Duncan Mill Road, Don Mills,
Ontario, Canada M3B 3K9

ISBN 0-373-82271-5

JENNA'S CHOICE

Chapter One

"Male. Caucasian. Mid-twenties. Possible myocardial infarction. BP 90/60. Respiration's depressed, pulse 120 and thready. I think we're losing him." The paramedic's voice was strained, shrill and a note too high to mesh with the swift, controlled movements of his hands as he wheeled the gurney through the automatic doors of Cincinnati's St. Vincent's Hospital Trauma Center. "Move it, will you guys!"

Beyond a glass partition separating the treatment bays from the attending physician's cubbyhole office, two women watched the well-drilled team swing into action. The patient's clothing was cut away. The plastic catheter feeding life-giving oxygen through his nose was discarded and replaced with smooth efficiency by an airway. The taller of the two women watching the procedure checked off the action against a list on her clipboard, her knuckles white on the ballpoint pen. Wire monitors were attached to the young man's chest. A thin, wavering green line staggered across the screen: ventricular fibrillation—his damaged heart was beating wildly and out of control.

"Bag him," the team leader ordered. "Lidocaine push, stat." A valve mask was fitted snugly over the patient's mouth and nose, forcing oxygen to inflate his lungs. A white-coated intern began CPR while a nurse set up an IV solution to help slow and regulate the careening heart. A crash cart was wheeled into place. The team members stepped back from the high, inclined examining table as though controlled by a single mind. A special paste was used to coat the defibrillator's two paddle-shaped electrodes. They were attached to the man's chest with swift accuracy. The team leader checked the machine with a quick glance.

"Clear!" The word was snapped out. Seconds later a controlled electrical charge flowed through the victim's body. He stiffened on the hard bed as the shock jolted through him. Seconds passed. The monitor line continued to skate madly across the scope.

"Come on, people." Hands clenched on her clipboard, the young woman in the long white lab coat urged her protégés onward. "You can do it."

"Clear!" The sharp command was repeated, followed by a second charge, a second endless wait. There was a momentary break in the line on the monitor screen. The team around the table held its collective breath. The two women in white were motionless. Then, as quickly as it had disappeared, the line returned, faltered and then steadied. The damaged heart had begun to beat on its own again.

"BP 96/72." A grinning nurse broke the silence. "Pulse 90 and steadying. He's coming back."

"Praise Blessed Mary," the second watching female figure murmured fervently. She held up a well-worn stopwatch. "Two minutes, thirty seconds from the time he hit the door."

Jenna Macklin, M.D., smiled at her companion and depressed an intercom button on her left. "Great work! Stabilize and get his history and blood workup as quickly as possible. Alert Cardiac Care we've got another customer for them." She smiled again, an enchanting lopsided grin that softened and personalized her strong-featured, high-cheekboned face.

"They did just fine." Sister Mary Gregory, St. Vincent's director of nursing services, was prone to understatement.

"They did marvelously," Jenna said as she turned to glare with mock ferociousness at the short, stocky nun. "They are without doubt the best trauma team I've ever trained."

"You say that about all of them," the middle-aged director

retorted without the slightest fear of Jenna's scowl. She glanced slyly at her lithe, blond companion. "I've read all your evaluations. But we do good work here at St. V's. You're doing better yourself," she said with less conviction.

"Me?" Jenna smiled quizzically, setting honey-gold flecks adrift in her hazel eyes.

"Yes, you," Sister Mary Gregory replied. "I didn't have to haul you back in here by the coattails once during this procedure. Generally you're out there giving orders right and left and running the show." She smiled benignly to take the sting from her words.

"Habit." Jenna shrugged, but she could feel a stain of discomfort rise in her cheeks. "A good emergency physician has to stay removed from the action; you know that as well as I do, Sister." Jenna's lilting voice was slightly rough around the edges. She spoke as much to convince herself as Sister Mary Gregory. "There are generally half a dozen patients for me to see any hour of the day or night. I can't get personally involved with each and every one. It isn't practical. It isn't good medicine." She repeated the phrases as though they were a litany. She glanced back at the curtained alcove where the young heart-attack victim still rested, watched over by mechanical guardians and vigilant personnel. "Five of those six cases are strictly routine: runny noses, sore throats, dog bites. But the sixth..." She let the sentence hang.

"Diagnose. Stabilize. And move on." Sister Mary Gregory quoted the unofficial motto of every hospital emergency room. A blue-uniformed medical clerk bustled up importantly, holding out a clipboard for the director to initial. The nun broke off what she'd been about to say, taking the proffered pen. Glancing over the work order, she scrawled her signature at the bottom. With a pleasant nod and word of greeting to the clerk, the two women moved on. "It's a system that gives you great satisfaction and presents many challenges. But it also generates a good deal of frustration."

Jenna understood the meaning behind the director's words. Emergency medicine stretched her professional capabilities to the limit every hour of the day and night. But emotionally it left her feeling drained, and at times frighteningly lifeless, adrift in a personal limbo. It was as if she were a kind of photographer taking shots of each and every patient. Snap. Click. Move on. Each subject was distinct, an entity having no connection to the next. Mentally she set them in a framework of eight-by-ten rectangles that she would take out during the long, dark hours of the night, looking them over in her mind's eye. She seldom had the opportunity to follow through on her cases, and she often wondered, alone in her bed at night, what had happened to them after they left her care, wondered what their lives had been like before and what they would be like from this point onward.

The signs and symptoms of professional burnout had been sneaking up on Jenna over the past eighteen months. Sister Mary Gregory had noticed the malaise, too, or she wouldn't be down here so often quizzing Jenna gently about her private life and her professional stability.

Jenna was too honest to lie to herself. She wanted to put the older woman at ease, but she couldn't. She knew what was happening to her; she had diagnosed the condition six months previously when she'd ended her long-standing engagement to Roger Thorpe. Until that time, she'd been able to blame the disquietude and strain on stresses within her personal life. Now she had to admit how little satisfaction she found in her work. She couldn't hide the knowledge from herself, but she did her best to ignore it. She had little else at the moment. Medicine was her life.

"How about a cup of coffee," Jenna said firmly, repressively quelling the beginning of an oft-heard lecture by the good sister on her overworked, undernourished appearance. "It's awfully quiet around here for a Wednesday afternoon." Traditionally many private physicians' day off, Wednesdays were chaotic in most emergency rooms. "My treat."

The director didn't look as if she would be put off so easily. Sister Mary Gregory had come up through the ranks. She was no soft touch. "You look like death warmed over," she said to Jenna, not sparing her feelings. Jenna glanced down at her newly slender figure, its lush curves hidden by the shapeless green scrub suit she wore under her lab coat.

"Thanks. I've been subsisting on plain yogurt and green salads with vinegar dressing and no salt for twelve weeks just to hear my good friend say something like that." The humor in her voice was forced and the nun afforded it only a tiny, twisted smile in response.

"I'm not speaking as your friend. I'm speaking as a nurse and as an employee of this institution," she responded sternly. "You need a rest."

"I'll take some time off at Christmas. I'm going to England to visit my parents." Jenna's father and mother were oil-company geologists stationed at Wilmingham on the western tip of the Isle of Wight, where the huge energy conglomerate they worked for was opening up a new field.

"That's not soon enough." Sister Mary Gregory was not to be deterred.

"I'll think about it," Jenna promised, knowing she lied. Solitude was the last thing she wanted in her life at the moment. "Now, how about that coffee?" A siren's wailing entry into the driveway outside counterpointed Jenna's words. "A 'scoop-and-run'?" The phrase meant that the ambulance attendants were too busy trying to keep the patient alive to have radioed ahead to alert the emergency-room staff they were coming.

"We'll talk later," Sister Mary Gregory said, brooking no argument. Jenna gave an expressive wave with a long, tapered hand as she was already halfway down the row of yellow-curtained cubicles.

Two hours later Jenna looked up from her desk in the crowded doctor's room to rest her eyes and rub away the insistent, painful knot of tension between her shoulder blades. She wasn't surprised to see the tenacious nun gliding down the hall between the gurneys and crash carts, wheelchairs and linen carts lining the emergency room corridor. Earlier Jenna had been far too busy to wonder what had summoned the busy administrator away. One moment she was there, hovering on the edge of the action, radiating calm and gentle tranquillity; the next she was gone. Now, just as quickly, she was back, stopping several times along the way to speak to patients and staff, never seeming to hurry or to give anyone less than her full attention.

"You never give up, do you?" Jenna was too tired to continue sidestepping the other woman's probing. "I'll be with you as soon as I finish bringing these charts up to date. Our 'scoop-and-run' accident victim had a fractured larynx. We've got him ventilated and stabilized. I've gotten in touch with Jack Dawson to do the surgery. He's the best ear, nose and throat man we've got."

"Good work, Jenna. Efficient as always."

"Now I'm stuck with the paperwork. In the end it will be the paperwork that finally does me in," she joked wearily. "If I had my own practice, I'd be bankrupt within the year. I hate the business end of practicing medicine. I'm hopeless with insurance forms and tax reports. At least here the hospital does ninety-nine percent of the stuff for me." The nun waited politely for Jenna to run out of delaying tactics.

Jenna braced herself for a lecture.

Sister Mary Gregory's beeper went off. Reprieve? As always, Jenna thought how incongruous the small black box looked tucked into the surplice of the nun's traditional white habit. Sister Mary Gregory's order had never embraced the more lenient dictums of Vatican II. The nun looked placid and otherworldly in her white robe and winglike starched coif. The serenity of soul was genuine but its outward manifestation was deceptive. The middle-aged director was a dynamo of energy and administrative efficiency, and she could play a wicked game of handball, too.

She silenced the mechanical summons imperiously. Jenna sat up straighter in her hard wooden chair. She'd never seen the conscientious administrator do such a thing before. "Do you want to pick up that page on my phone?" Jenna asked, gesturing to the instrument at her side.

"Later. Jenna, I got a call earlier for you," she said, frowning beneath the shadowing headpiece.

"Between the crushed larynx and the little girl with the slashed foot? Or Mrs. Meddlicut's needing her blood workup?" The last patient she mentioned was one of the Trauma Center's regulars—a lonely, friendless old woman who had no doctor of her own and who looked on the Center's staff as her extended medical family. It was one of the many sad occurrences that Jenna had long ago learned she must tune out on in order to survive in her soul-wrenching profession.

"They tried to get through to you down here, but you've been swamped." The nun automatically glanced out at the busy control center of the unit. Her sharp black eyes missed few details of its smooth-running efficiency. When she looked back at Jenna, her expression grew softer on the smooth oval of her face. "The call was from a man called Locke Singer." Jenna felt little prickles of apprehension crawl up and down her spine. "He was calling from someplace in Minnesota."

"Lake of the Woods," Jenna said in a small voice. "My grandmother lives there." A tight knot of pain wrapped around her vocal cords. "What's wrong, Sister?"

"It is about your grandmother. I'm afraid she's missing."

OVERHEAD, MURKY RAIN clouds thickened noticeably as Jenna stepped from her small, dusty yellow hatchback onto the wide concrete pier. Waves broke along its length with unending regularity, sending a heavy, misting spray to cover the dock and anything or anyone foolhardy enough to be out on it.

Jenna shivered, ducking behind a canvas-covered obstruction to tuck strands of silver-blond hair back under her scarf. Her hands were one of her best features, long and strong, with tapered, sensitive fingers. Hunching her shoulders against the fitful lake breeze, she pushed her fists deep into the pockets of her cheery violet Windbreaker. Pivoting on the ball of her foot, Jenna surveyed the straggling array of gaily painted clapboard houses and single-story buildings that comprised the main street of Oakhelm. She inhaled deeply of the pine-scented air,

letting just released bursts of sunlight sparkle against her closed
eyelids.

Jenna was bone-weary, muscle-aching tired. Late last
night—her second on the road—she'd finally driven out of the
persistent rain that had followed her all the way from Cincinnati.

She bent over, picked up her soft-sided maroon weekender,
her shoulder duffle and her traditional black doctor's bag that
had been a gift from her grandmother when she graduated from
medical school. *"Gram, where are you?"* Jenna asked inside
her head for at least the hundredth time. She glanced around,
unconsciously seeking an answer in the familiar surroundings
of her childhood summers.

The long dusty length of Main Street was quiet in the middle
of a late September afternoon. It was a slack time for the small
northern Minnesota tourist town: too early for hunters, too late
for summer campers. One or two pickups and four-wheel drives
were parked randomly along its length. There seemed to be
some activity in front of Hal's Bait Shop and Marina. Several
people were shopping at Le Satz's grocery-hardware-post office, and one or two regulars could be seen stopping off at
Mike's Blue Ox Tavern.

Summer was on its last legs this far north, but it was going
out with a bang. All around Jenna oaks and maples blazed in
a heady mixture of red and gold. The bright primary hues were
interspersed with the lacy gray-green of tamarack and the sober
shades of spruce and jack pine. Autumn haze rose from the
low hills behind town, lending watercolor softness to their
sharp granite angles.

Now the last obstacle between Jenna and her grandmother's
rustic homestead on Buffalo Point was spread out before her.
Lake of the Woods: a formidable body of water stretching north
to Kenora, Ontario, and beyond, where its tributaries rushed
away under the Trans-Canada Highway on a journey that
would lead to Hudson Bay. Sixty miles of open water, studded
with ten thousand rocky, wooded landfalls rising up from the
shallow glacial scoop of tree-fringed shoreline. Ahead of her

lay miles and miles of twisting, boulder-strewn channels, pine-covered, sparsely-populated islands and rocky shoals. It was wild, unpredictable, untamable and breathtakingly beautiful country. Fayette Macklin, Jenna's paternal grandmother, loved it more than any place on earth. Why had she left her home without a word?

Where was she? Jenna felt an all-too-familiar pang as she bent to brush sand from the cuffs of her blue poplin slacks. She hadn't been as close to Fayette as she should have been these past few years. But that was due to a combination of Jenna's brutal schedule and Fayette's isolation. Jenna loved her grandmother deeply. She had spent almost every summer of her childhood with Fayette. It was the urgency of those feelings that had driven Jenna nearly nonstop from Cincinnati to Oakhelm in the last forty-eight hours.

A low wooden vessel, white above the waterline and dark green below, wide and bulky, of indeterminate age and origin negotiated the sharp turn around the concrete breakwater erected twenty years earlier by the Army Corps of Engineers. Jenna watched impatiently as it made its way to a berth alongside the pier. "Right on time, Locke, old friend," Jenna said aloud to no one in particular. She moved out along the pier, surveying the vessel before her with a jaundiced eye. "Rickety." The word popped out. It was the only adjective that came to mind.

"Are you casting aspersions on the pride of the fleet?" Locke Singer stuck his head out of the pilothouse and waved her aboard. Jenna returned his greeting, lifting her bags over the railing for him to take in his large, work-worn hands.

"Not on your life," she denied. "Locke, it's good to see you. It's been a long time." Jenna took his outstretched hand and hopped lightly onto the deck.

"You haven't changed a bit." Locke grabbed her free hand and twirled her around, whistling between his teeth. His warm brown eyes skimmed over Jenna's trim figure. "Look even better than you did the last time I saw you."

"Don't remind me how many years it's been." Jenna

laughed, retrieving her hand from his grasp. She held up a warning finger. "I'm only thin because I've been dieting fanatically all summer." She glossed over her physical changes. She knew she looked as tired as she felt. "You don't look so bad yourself. A little thinner on top, maybe." Jenna grinned impishly as Locke scowled, grabbing for a Twins baseball cap hanging on a peg beside the wheelhouse to cover the thinning blond curls that proclaimed his Norse heritage.

"That's what I get for reminding a woman of her age." He grinned back, slamming the cap on his head. "At least I learned not to tease *you* about the color of your hair a long time ago."

He rubbed his hand ruefully over his jaw, no doubt recalling the left hook Jenna had landed when she was an indignant thirteen-year-old and decided he'd called her "string head" once too often.

She'd made her point that long-ago June day, but she didn't actually come to appreciate the fine texture and unusual silver-gilt color of her hair until a few years later when she discovered that boys were good for more than companions on fishing expeditions and sparring partners.

"How long are you planning to stay?" Locke asked in a more serious vein. "I wasn't sure you could even get away from that fancy emergency room you're so proud of. That first call I tried to get through to you got shuffled all over the damned hospital." Jenna winced inwardly at the pain the casual words caused her. Was that how all her old friends saw her? As a woman striving so hard to make her way in a demanding, male-dominated profession that she couldn't take time away from her work for a reason as important as this?

"I have friends in high places," she replied, thinking of Sister Mary Gregory's imperious phone calls and the spate of schedule rearranging that had followed Locke's news. "Where is my grandmother, Locke?"

"I wish I knew," he returned honestly, pulling at the bill of his cap. He looked uncomfortable for a moment, as though Jenna's authoritative question brought home to him the difference in their life-styles and the length of time since they'd last seen each other. Outwardly Jenna was much the same. But she wasn't a child any longer. She was thirty-two years old. The widely spaced, intelligent hazel eyes above a pert snub nose were the eyes of a woman in authority. A woman who asked questions and got the answers she wanted.

"I'm afraid something terrible has happened to her." Jenna got the words out with difficulty. She couldn't drown the niggling worries that had pestered her all the way from Cincinnati. "That trouble last winter…" She let the words fade away. The old tug pitched and rolled, bucking against the stout hawsers holding her steady. Jenna reached out to balance herself against the rail. Locke didn't need reminding of the brouhaha Fayette had instigated with her column.

Fifteen years ago Fayette's old friend, Walter Ericson, owner and publisher of the *Oakhelm Flag*, talked Jenna's grandmother into writing a weekly newspaper column. Now her wickedly entertaining, environmentally oriented column was syndicated in over seventy newspapers across the Midwest. Fayette's caustic, witty comments had gained her a wide following. Although her writings wandered over a wide variety of subjects—ranging from attacks on the folly of nude sunbathing in a state where mosquitoes had reportedly been observed carrying off newborn lambs, to the joys and rewards of living off the land, far from the pressures and pitfalls of modern urban civilization—it had been the battle Fayette initiated in the state legislature that lay at the root of Jenna's anxiety.

"She's in no danger, I'm sure," Locke inserted hastily, watching the fear darken Jenna's hazel eyes.

"There's no evidence of…foul play?" Her voice faltered a little on the last two words. "What if she's lost or hurt out there?" Jenna sat down with a plop on a damp coil of rope. Her knees refused to hold her any longer. "I've been so worried. You know how she attracts controversy." Last winter, after reading Fayette's editorializing, a sympathetic elected official had introduced a bill she had proposed to ban the hunting of large game animals from low-flying aircraft. Reaction had been swift and vocal, with sportsmen and hunters lined up toe to toe with environmentalists and animal lovers from all parts of the Gopher State. Even though the bill was stalled in committee, flack still ricocheted off the State House walls. Fayette had loved every minute of the uproar she aroused.

"I don't think that's likely. Unless Clay turns her over his knee for dragging his dad along on this wild-goose chase of hers. They took Clay's four-wheel drive, so they could be just about anywhere in the state, or two provinces of Canada. Clay's fit to be tied."

"Clay?"

"Clay Thornton. My partner in this old girl." He patted the gleaming brass work of the tug lovingly. "He got back from flying in a gaggle of pike fishermen from up north of Kenora a couple of days ago and found the two of them gone."

"His father..." Jenna tried to dredge up particulars on the residents of Buffalo Point, but it was rough going. Her brain felt like a stick of dead wood. Buffalo Point was a semi-isolated hook of land jutting out from the lake's western shore, just south of the Canadian border. Fayette had called it home for almost thirty-five years.

"Harmon Thornton is Clay's dad. He owns the Peninsula Store." Locke filled her in when he noticed the blank expression on her face.

"She's off on another crusade, and she talked Mr. Thornton into going along with her." Jenna was positive of her facts. "She's a seventy-four-year-old adolescent, Locke. It's just like her to sneak off and cause a furor. What am I going to do with that woman?" She felt at least twice the age of her irrepressible grandmother. Jenna was the first to admit that she didn't know how to deal with her. "Why didn't she tell someone what she was up to?"

"She knows how busy you are with your life right now, Jenna," Locke replied, interpreting her question to mean why hadn't Fayette told Jenna of her plans. "And she knew we'd try to talk her out of it. Especially Clay. He's the only man I know more stubborn than Faye."

"That bad, is he?" Jenna retorted with dry humor. "He must

be a bear. I think I'll avoid him if at all possible till she gets back with his father, safe and sound. Do you think that will be soon?'' she inquired with a sheepish, enchanting grin that softened and transformed her austere, high-cheekboned face. ''She's so special, Locke. I love her dearly. I've been—'' Jenna stopped abruptly. She couldn't admit to Locke how afraid for Fayette she really was.

''They'll be fine.'' Locke's tone was firm, confident.

Jenna relaxed for the first time in many hours. Her concern for her grandmother receded to a level just below the surface of her consciousness. She took a deep, energizing breath of the clear, pine-scented air. ''Just fine.'' She repeated the talisman.

Locke took the three steps to the pilothouse in one leap. With a roaring grumble the diesel engine sprang noisily to life.

''Locke.'' The voice behind Jenna was soft and creamy, bringing to her mind visions of magnolia blossoms and moonlit, moss-hung oaks, although Jenna had never been south of the Mason-Dixon line in her entire life. She swiveled her head toward the sound. ''Are we leaving so soon, Locke?'' A small, pregnant woman stood near the open cabin door.

''Right away, Leah, honey. We've got our passenger here, ready and waiting.'' Locke came back on deck as he spoke.

''We were going to stay in town long enough to have dinner. If you can call eating at Mike's tavern a night on the town. Maggie Ericson said she'd mind Cassie. I hoped we could spend some time with other people.'' A melting, disappointed glance was aimed at Locke before the petite woman shrugged off her pique. She held out a small white hand to Jenna. ''I'm sorry. I believe I have the advantage of you. I'm Leah Singer and you must be Fayette's granddaughter. Welcome to the Woods.''

''I didn't think Jenna would be here this early, Leah,'' Locke explained quietly. ''She drove most of the past two days to get here. She's probably tired. We should get underway as quickly as possible. And the weather doesn't look good.'' Tension that was almost palpable radiated between the pair. Jenna could feel it in the air all around them. In the medical profession more than any other, you learned early on to read each and every signal a person gave off. The conversation might have been ordinary but the undercurrents were not.

"You promised, Locke. What will Maggie think when we don't show up with Cassie?" The soft voice held resignation, as if Leah Singer had given up expecting things to turn out right in the world. Jenna experienced a flash of compassion. She'd felt the same way for several long, miserable weeks after she decided not to marry Roger.

"They'll understand. I'll make it up to you next trip, sweetheart. I promise." Locke's eyes were shuttered, his expression patient but unyielding. Jenna felt distinctly ill at ease being party to the scene of domestic friction. She tried to recall everything Fayette had written to her about Locke's marriage. Her old childhood friend, playmate and confidant of all the summers she'd spent with Fayette while her parents traveled to remote and inaccessible assignments, had been married less than two years to the daughter of a wealthy Atlanta businessman.

"We don't have to be off in such a hurry on my account," Jenna said. She smiled down at Leah, Madonna-like and beautiful in a simple pale green maternity smock and forest-green slacks that smacked of money. Lots of it. Her night-black hair was caught in a smooth twist at the back of her neck. Her eyes were a deep, dark blue. She looked a lot like a very young Elizabeth Taylor, with a Dresden shepherdess daintiness that even her thickening waistline couldn't obscure.

"I'm sorry to disappoint you, Leah. But the day's going to turn bad. Dad spent a lot of years teaching me to read the weather, and all the signs say we're in for a three-day rain and blow." He reached out to push a loose strand of hair from Leah's cheek. She shrugged away from the caress.

"Oh, I believe you," Leah said with a hint of malice edging her soft Georgia accent. "At least three days of rain and wind. I'm getting used to it." She laughed shrilly, a sound totally out of sync with her speaking voice. Jenna eyed her sharply. Leah was pulled as tightly as a bowstring, great dark shadows purpling the hollows of her beautiful blue eyes. "Please excuse me, Jenna. I must sound like a spoiled child who's been denied a treat."

Jenna murmured something polite and noncommittal.

"It's best we leave now," Locke repeated woodenly.

"In that case, I believe I'll go below. It's chilly up here, don't you think?" Leah shrugged expressively, turning back to Jenna. "I'm not as good a sailor as I used to be." She patted her stomach, her smile softening and gentling, making her appear more Madonna-like than ever. "Will it be all right if Cassie stays up here with you, Locke?" Leah hesitated slightly before voicing the request.

"Of course." Locke smiled, stuffing his hands deep into the pockets of his jeans. "You know I like having Cassie with me."

"Cassie is my...our daughter," Leah said, including Jenna in the conversation once more. "She's five and quite a handful for me these days."

"I can imagine." Jenna felt more ill at ease with each word Leah spoke. Leah had been married previously, a teenage bride, divorced in her early twenties, if Jenna remembered Fayette's information correctly.

The younger woman held out her hand again. "It was nice meeting you. I hope we get to see more of each other while you're on Buffalo Point." Her honey-rich voice and smile were filled with genuine friendliness. Jenna couldn't help smiling in return.

"Thank you. I'd like that very much."

"I'll send Cassie up as soon as we're underway. Okay?" Leah's smile was less assured as she glanced at her husband.

"Soon as we're out beyond the breakwater. You're sure you'll be all right below?" He shot Jenna a beseeching look, but Leah intercepted it, speaking before Jenna could offer to accompany her. "I'll be fine. I just need to sit down and put my feet up. Right, Doctor?"

"Best advice in the world," Jenna concurred.

"See, Locke. I *do* know what's best for me sometimes."

Leah turned and made her way carefully down the steep companionway. Locke watched her go.

"Anything else you need from your car, Jenna?" He sounded preoccupied. His hands balled into a fist around the brass rail. His brow furrowed and the uncertainty and frustration that darkened his face momentarily was sad to see. He didn't seem to notice how tightly he gripped the metal, but Jenna did.

"No, it's all locked up. I'm sure it'll be fine in the parking lot; Oakhelm's hardly a high-crime neighborhood. There's just no way she'll make it out to the point," Jenna said, pointing to her car. The little import was too light to maneuver the rutted, single-lane logging road that served Buffalo Point. It was a road fit only for four-wheel drives and snowmobiles in winter. The state's reluctance to build more roads into such an isolated area made Locke's ferry service nearly indispensable.

Moments later a three-and-a-half-foot tornado with black pigtails and Leah's deep blue eyes swirled through the hatch of the companionway. "Daddy! I don't want to stay down there until we get out in the lake. I'll be good and sit still, I promise." A huge gap-toothed smile accompanied the plea. "Please, Daddy. I want to stay with you." Locke turned from loosening the mooring lines to placate the little girl. The love and pride in his eyes were painful to see.

"If you're good. But no running all over the deck, okay?"

"I promise." She turned her attention to Jenna, now that the important business was completed. "Hi, I'm Cassie Michaels. When I'm twelve, I'm going to be Cassie Singer. Like Mommy and Daddy and our new baby. I can change my name then. My dad already asked the judge about it." She smirked proudly in Locke's direction. "He's real smart."

"I know he is," Jenna laughed, enthralled by the effervescent, fairylike child. She looked so much like Leah that it was uncanny. "Let's go up to the wheelhouse." Jenna glanced at Locke for permission.

"Your wish is my command, ladies." He saluted and swung

up the ladder behind them to back the boat skillfully out into the channel paralleling the breakwater.

For a time Jenna and Cassie, who'd crawled trustingly into her lap, were content to sit on the wide ledge of the pilothouse windows and to watch the churning wake of blue-green water that foamed and crested alongside the sturdy vessel. Cloud shadows sailed above the water, graying its depths when they passed across the sun. It was a breathtaking, varied picture. Jenna drank in the lonely, pristine landscape with eager eyes. It was good to be back.

"It is going to rain again," she ventured some time later, when her ears were adjusted to the steady drone of the diesel engine.

"Yep," Locke answered laconically, threading his way between two buoy markers that indicated submerged rocks in their path.

"I think I'm cursed," Jenna quipped, resting her chin for a moment on the soft thickness of Cassie's hair. The little girl twisted in her lap.

"Cursed?" she whispered, interest sparking in her great blue eyes.

"By the weather gods." Jenna nodded mock-seriously. "It's been raining on me ever since I left Ohio. Now your daddy says it's going to start again. I'm doomed to wander the earth, followed for all eternity by a huge rain cloud." Jenna groaned in a tragic manner, dropping her woebegone face into her hand.

Locke grinned at her bantering tone. Cassie erupted into happy laughter, touching Jenna's shoulder in a sympathetic caress. "It's okay. You won't melt."

"No need to be so melodramatic, Doc," Locke added, using her old nickname automatically. Jenna had wanted to be a doctor as long as she could remember, as Locke well knew. "It won't be that bad."

"You're the expert." Jenna made a face. "How long have you been back in Oakhelm, Locke? Seems to me the last time I saw you, you were going to set the construction world on its ear."

Locke's good-natured face was no longer smiling. "I found out soon enough it wasn't what I wanted. The money was good, but most people with money aren't as happy as you'd think." He glanced over at Cassie resting sleepily against Jenna's shoulder. "I went to work for a big firm all right; Leah's dad's, as a matter of fact. I hated it. Most of the big buildings are going up in the Sunbelt. It's hot, sticky and crowded. Nothing like up here." He trailed off, embarrassed by his show of emotion.

"There's something marvelous about lots of clean, fresh air and water," Jenna murmured to fill the void left by his silence.

"One good thing came out of it." Locke's keen eyes never left the line of channel markers and small wooded islets that dotted Buffalo Bay, marking their path through the treacherous shallow waters. "I found Leah and Cassie to love and care for, and brought them home with me." He fell silent again, the worn wooden wheel under his hands answering to a slight clenching of his fingers. Locke compensated with smooth efficiency. Jenna wondered if he would be able to compensate so easily with a major emotional upheaval in his life. She wasn't a psychiatrist or a marriage counselor, but Locke and Leah looked as if they were headed for big trouble. It was sad.

"There's Buf'lo Point." Cassie sat up with a child's uncanny sixth sense of knowing when home was close by, no matter how soundly she seemed to be sleeping. "See Granny Faye's place?" She pointed, looking through the pilothouse window. "We live on the other side of the point."

Jenna's frown evaporated. She swiveled her head to get a look at the clearing and the house she remembered so well. Like Oakhelm and the Woods, it hadn't changed a bit.

Locke throttled back the powerful, noisy engines as the boat came around to nestle up to the wooden dock jutting out into the choppy ice-gray water, like a strong arm reaching out to gather them in. When the lines were secure, Jenna jumped onto the dock.

It was getting dark. The sun had disappeared completely behind the towering cloud banks some time ago. The house was silent, wrapped in solitude. Its blank windows stared back impassively. Fayette's garden had the straggly, yellowed, end-of-summer sadness about it that spoke of a task well done and a long winter's rest lying ahead. A lone apple tree, heavy with small red fruit, occupied a sun-catching place of honor in the sheltered clearing. Everything was as still and as quiet as a windy forest glade could ever be.

"Thanks for the ride, Locke. Bye, Cassie. Say goodbye to your mother for me." Leah had not come on deck as they tied up. Jenna didn't blame her; the companionway was steep, the water choppy. Whitecaps broke along the pilings, rushing at them from the horizon in dizzying and disorienting profusion. It took Jenna a moment to secure her own footing before setting off down the dock.

"Are you sure you want to stay out here alone tonight?" Locke asked. "There's plenty of room at our place."

"I'll be fine. I want to be here when Gram gets back. No matter when." Jenna made her voice firm. Locke didn't try to dissuade her and merely waved again before returning to the pilothouse to send the tug on around the curve of the point toward his home on the far side of the cove.

With a last wave for Cassie, Jenna lifted up her bags. She turned away from the lake, running up the gently rising slope to the cabin, putting the specter of strain and unhappiness that hovered over her old friend's marriage from her mind with the ruthless efficiency born of years of experience. In emergency medicine, more than any other specialty, you learned to put what you couldn't change out of your thoughts as quickly as possible. Lives depended on your quickness and accuracy in decision making; you couldn't function efficiently when burdened with guilt or remorse. Yet the grim set of Locke's mouth, the haunted depths of Leah's eyes, would be another snapshot added to her nocturnal album.

Jenna paused in her headlong rush to catch her breath, putting the ache of melancholy out of her mind with an effort that was almost physical. She listened to the moaning roar of wind in the birches and the persistent slap of waves against the rocky

shore. Her nose wrinkled at the smell of wet grass and the
threat of rain carried on the wind.

Oakhelm, the town of her childhood summers, had been the
same. The Woods was the same, and Fayette's homestead was
the same. Time and life moved to a different rhythm on the
lake, and she was suddenly very glad it was so. She scanned
the familiar buildings as she stood at the bottom of the three
rough-hewn porch steps. In addition to the cabin there was the
toolshed, the dugout icehouse and what Fayette always delicately referred to as the "necessary." The small steep-roofed
cabin was constructed of darkly oiled boards-and-batten pine
siding above a foundation of native stone that gave the structure
an air of solidity and strength, as if it had been there for many
years and planned to be around for as many more.

Fayette had evidently been at work to ensure her winter comfort by storing up firewood in a windbreak rick beside the front
door. By craning her neck Jenna could see beside the toolshed
another, much larger woodpile, which nearly filled the small
backyard. To Jenna woodpiles meant roaring, warming fires.
She hurried up the steps, anxious to be inside.

The door was locked.

For a moment she just stood there looking and feeling blank.
Jenna rattled the handle, unwilling to believe the obvious; she
was locked out of Fayette's cabin. Giving the handle one last
twist, Jenna turned and slid down against the doorjamb to a
sitting position, with her back to the door. With a frustrated
groan Jenna dropped her head in her hands just as the first fat
drops of rain splattered against the roof.

Chapter Two

Jenna frowned down at the cup of lukewarm chicken soup in her hand as she curled her icy toes farther under the skirt of her high-necked flannel nightgown. She snuggled into the warmth of the heavy woolen throw she'd appropriated from Fayette's bed. She was safe inside the cabin, cold and still hungry, but at least not huddled out in the rain. A steady, persistent shower had begun shortly after dark; now it was coming down harder still, if the increased rattle of raindrops on the roof was any indication. As though seconding her thoughts, an angry mutter of thunder rolled over the spine of the Point. Jenna shivered and swallowed another spoonful of soup.

It hadn't taken her long to recall where Fayette kept her extra keys. With the help of the trusty penlight from her medical bag, Jenna had groped her way into the musty toolshed and plucked the big old-fashioned skeleton key off its nail above the single window. The lock on the front door worked smoothly, and in a few minutes Jenna had completely shaken off the unwelcome case of the jitters that had assailed her on the porch. She hadn't been alone in the wilderness for a long time. It would take some getting used to again.

Inside the cabin everything had been exactly as Jenna remembered. It was comforting but exasperating, too. If Fayette would invest in some modern appliances, she could have heated this soup to an acceptable temperature without having to resort to holding it over the flame of an oil lamp. Now it tasted distinctly of kerosene. Although she felt completely at ease with the myriad complicated mechanisms in the hospital's Trauma Center, Jenna hadn't felt up to tackling her grandmother's huge black wood-burning cookstove. And that also meant there was no hot water, because it only came from a copper reservoir attached to the stove's side.

Still, if Fayette had modernized her home, that curiously comforting feeling of stepping back in time—of coming home—would be lost. A happy smile flitted across Jenna's face, lightening her hazel eyes and setting gold flecks dancing in their depths. Everything was the same here, from the limp calico curtains at the double-hung windows to the faded maroon velvet upholstery on the lumpy depression-modern sofa and chairs. The room was shabby, comfortable and inviting. She'd grown up with these things; they were like old friends.

Her parents had traveled constantly throughout her childhood, and they still did. So Jenna had spent her winters in a succession of boarding schools and her summers with Fayette. For the quiet, studious young Jenna, her grandmother had been the wellspring of enthusiasm and imagination a child needed to stretch out and to grow spiritually as well as emotionally. In her offbeat, haphazard way, Fayette had provided the stability that Jenna's parents hadn't been willing or able to supply.

It was doing her good to get back in touch with her roots, Jenna realized. It had been a long time since she'd thought so much about a life that didn't revolve around her work. The sound of a plane's engine overhead intruded into her reverie. Jenna listened closely, pushing back the strands of silver-blond hair that fell over her shoulder. The sound grew fainter and disappeared altogether. For one crazy moment she'd thought it might be her grandmother returning. Now she realized it couldn't have been.

Jenna shook her head as she ruefully watched her pathetic attempt to start a blazing, warming fire smolder into a slow, agonizing death dance of spiraling acrid smoke and dull red embers. A woodsman she was not.

Rain or shine, tomorrow she'd have to hike over the steep,

rocky crest of the Point and confront Clay Thornton. Surely, if anyone had further news of the missing seniors, it would be Harmon Thornton's son. Jenna wasn't looking forward to the meeting. Locke had made it pretty plain that Clay considered Fayette responsible for his father's absence. Knowing her grandmother's penchant for enlisting others to support her in her latest crusade, Jenna didn't suppose she could blame the man if he was angry.

But that would be tomorrow. Now she just wanted to close her eyes and rest a moment before she turned out the light. Jenna rested her head on her arm as it lay upon the rolled back of the sofa. She continued to watch her nearly comatose fire with half-focused eyes. Surely an otherwise intelligent woman should be able to get a slightly damp piece of wood to catch fire. Other people did it all the time. There must be a trick to it....

Jenna knew she had to be dreaming. It was a lulu of a nightmare. There was a tremendous pounding in her ears. She was choking and being smothered under tons of cotton balls. They were in her mouth and her nose, and they smelled like smoke. *Smoke!* Jenna flew up off the couch, coming fully awake with the lightning speed of much practice. She was coughing and wheezing, her throat dry and burning from the smoke-filled air.

THE FRONT DOOR of Fayette's cabin flew open just as Clay raised his hand to knock again. Pound it down was a more apt description of what he'd been doing, but he wasn't in the mood to quibble over semantics. He was cold, wet, tired and hungry. And he'd talked himself into taking off on another wild-goose chase. Fayette and his father weren't here. At least, his father wasn't. They'd taken off on their quixotic mission in his four-wheel-drive Jeep—and it was nowhere to be seen. Yet the cabin was definitely inhabited, for soft yellow light poured from the window by the door.

If it wasn't Fayette Macklin, then who was it?

A woman wearing a long white nightgown catapulted out of the smoke-filled room, slamming into his chest with enough force to send him staggering back against the porch rail. He got a quick impression of a tall, softly rounded body and a glimpse of big hazel eyes with marigold flecks, of lashes the color of honey and of silver-gilt hair, like moonlight on the lake, swinging loose and free around her shoulders.

"Have you set the place on fire?" he demanded tersely. There was nothing the residents of any isolated spot like Buffalo Point feared more than fire. The woman didn't seem able to answer. Clay gave her a shake, repeating his question more loudly. "Is the cabin on fire?" He propped her against the rail, looking back over his shoulder into the hazy room. "Answer me, damn it."

"No fire," Jenna managed to croak, sensing his dismay. "It's only the fireplace. The damper must have gotten stuck or something." She might as well have saved her breath and her explanation, for he was already inside. Damn! Why did someone have to come by at this time of night and catch her making a tenderfoot fool of herself?

She could hear him moving around in the big front room. He coughed as the acrid smoke assaulted his lungs. Jenna calculated briefly and frantically what action she'd take if the tall stranger was overcome by the smoke. She needn't have worried. He reappeared in the doorway a few seconds later.

"You can come back inside, Dr. Macklin," he ordered gruffly. Jenna caught herself, wondering if the gruffness was the result of smoke he'd swallowed, or if it was caused by a habitual unevenness of temper. "Dr. Macklin," he repeated her name even more sharply.

He knew who she was. The suspicion that had first bloomed inside Jenna's smoke-numbed brain after she careened off his chest now flowered into certainty. This man was Clay Thornton.

Lord, what a way to spoil a first impression. Jenna had no desire to go back inside Fayette's cabin and face the man whose father her grandmother had abducted, so to speak. Jenna leaned over the rail, dragging deep lungfuls of cold, wet air into her chest, cleansing away the stinging residue of smoke and postponing the inevitable.

"Didn't you hear me, Doctor? It's all right to come in now. Or are you trying for pneumonia as well as smoke inhalation?" There was a definite note of exasperation and something bordering on amusement in his voice.

Amusement at her expense. Jenna didn't see quite the same humor in the situation.

Clay knew he hadn't made a very good first impression, hollering at her like that, but he was just too exhausted and too scared to be polite. She could have burned the cabin down and set fire to this whole end of the lake, letting the damper swing shut like that when the wind changed direction. "There's a hook to keep the damper open. Why didn't you use it?" He tried again to catch hold of his patience and keep his voice level and nonthreatening.

"I didn't see it," Jenna responded with some asperity. She turned to face him reluctantly. He was a big man, towering over her own not inconsequential five feet eight inches by several more. He was roughly dressed in blue jeans, a black waterproof poncho and heavy work boots. He moved with a strong man's natural, unconscious grace. And he was quick, too. Jenna wasn't sure how he'd managed to avoid stepping on her bare toes when she caromed off him, but she was grateful nonetheless. "The fire was burning very well when I fell asleep." "Adequately" might have been a better word. "Marginally" would have been more accurate still, she admitted ruefully to herself, then broke off abruptly. "My Lord, what kind of dog is that?"

Clay had been watching the emotions flit swiftly across her delicately boned yet strong-featured face. She wasn't beautiful in the usual sense of the word, but her face was composed of an interesting combination of wistfulness and strength of purpose. He'd liked the fleeting, self-castigating smile she'd bestowed on him. He also liked the timbre of her lilting voice. Now she was staring down at his big gray dog as if Frieda were the Hound of the Baskervilles.

"The dog is a weimaraner. That's a German hunting dog, in case you're not familiar with the breed. You're getting wet out here, Dr. Macklin. You'd better come in off the porch." Clay finished the sentence in a less belligerent tone, ashamed of his brusqueness. She must be as worried about Fayette as he was for his father, or she wouldn't be here. She couldn't help it if she was entirely out of her element in the wilderness. Some people just didn't belong this far from civilization. "Come on," he urged. "I'm perfectly harmless and so is Frieda."

"Frieda? What kind of name is that for a hunting dog?"

She didn't resemble her grandmother physically except for the hair. Fayette's was more white than silver these days, but once it must have been very like—he sifted through bits and pieces of information in his brain, searching for her name— Jenna's. Yes, that was it. How could he have forgotten? She was one of Fayette's favorite topics of conversation. It probably had something to do with the fact that he'd only had about six hours sleep in the past seventy-two. No wonder she was staring at him as if he were some kind of laboratory specimen. He probably looked like a demented lumberjack out on a binge at best, and a backwoods Jack the Ripper at the worst.

Clay held out his hand in a gesture of peace. "I'm sorry we had to meet under such unhappy circumstances. I'm Clay Thornton, as you've most likely already guessed. I usually don't go around manhandling women or biting their heads off because a fireplace damper gets stuck. It could happen to anyone. Please accept my apology."

Jenna returned his handshake tentatively. His fingers closed around hers, his grasp firm and warm. He held her hand for a fraction of a second and then released her. The gesture reassured Jenna in some curious subliminal way. It was direct and honest, like the man himself. "I'm sorry, too," Jenna said with genuine regret. She hesitated several heartbeats before adding, "Please come in." She'd lived in the city too long to allow a stranger into her home calmly, without some qualms. "I'm afraid I won't ever get this old barn of a place warmed up now." Jenna's tone was rueful. She said the first thing that came into her head to cover her lack of poise.

It was colder than ever inside, since the door had stood open to the damp night air for so long. Jenna curled up her bare toes against the chill. She pushed at fluttering strands of hair in irritation, finally anchoring them impatiently behind her ears. She wondered if she could ask this gray-eyed stranger to start another fire for her. It went against the grain to ask for help, but she was not so full of foolish pride that she preferred to perish of exposure rather than admit her ignorance.

Clay Thornton shut the door firmly, closing out the wet, windy night. Jenna cocked her head to study his rough-hewn features in the dim glow of the oil lamp. She was looking for further clues to his personality. No, she concluded reluctantly, perhaps she shouldn't ask for his assistance. He was polite enough; he even smiled now and then, a slashing off-center grin that was really quite attractive. But his eyes weren't smiling. They looked tired and discouraged, hard and a little sad. There were brackets of sharp-edged exhaustion around his mouth and a tenseness in the rugged lines and angles of his body.

"You need a new fire," he said suddenly, pulling off the rain-slicked poncho and revealing a forest-green corduroy shirt open at the throat. He looked like an advertising man's dream of the perfect lumberjack. But for Jenna he brought to mind a long-forgotten vision of an old woodcut she'd seen of the French explorers—voyageurs they were called—who'd first come to this region in the seventeen hundreds. A two-day growth of beard covered the sculpted contours of his face, accenting bold cheekbones and bringing the arrogant slash of his nose into stark relief. His hair was thick, shaggy, and black as a raven's wing. An arrow-straight part ran high on the left side of his head.

"This isn't necessary. I'll manage on my own." Jenna felt she had to make the gesture of independence. He obviously assumed that she was as helpless as any neophyte camper; to Jenna's eye that fact was embarrassingly clear.

"It won't take a minute. Just remember to hook the damper open from now on." He angled his body down and forward crumpling newspapers from a pile on the floor and sticking them under the half-consumed logs. Jenna gave up arguing with him and turned her attention to his dog. The animal's eyes were truly a startling gold-green. Her head was well shaped, her ears long and aristocratic. Her short-cropped tail hit the wooden floor in quick hard strokes. Jenna held out her hand cautiously. "Does she bite?"

"Frieda? You've got to be joking. She's never bitten anyone—or anything—in her life. She won't even hunt rabbits, let alone stags." Clay looked around for a match, spotted a big box of kitchen-size ones, and struck one against the stone fireplace. The raspy sound was loud in the silence of the cabin. The wind and rain and an occasional drumroll of thunder seemed far away and unimportant.

"Stags?" Jenna was intrigued. She'd never owned a pet. That is, if you didn't count the four tropical fish in a tank back in her garden apartment in Cincinnati. Fish, she'd found, were very undemanding housemates.

"Yes, stags. Don't ask me how they were taught to bring them down. You wouldn't want to know. Neither does Frieda, I suspect." He chuckled. Frieda snorted fastidiously, for all the world as if she understood what he'd said. She laid her big head on Jenna's knee and sighed in contentment when Jenna began to scratch behind one long, velvety ear.

Jenna found herself watching Clay again. His hands were big, the wrists strong and supple. His laugh was warm and vibrant and his smile twisted the right corner of his mouth a little higher than the left. Jenna found it just as attractive as she had the first time.

"You make that look so easy. I don't seem to have the hang of it anymore. And as for that monstrosity of a cookstove in the kitchen…" Words appeared to fail her. She returned his smile with one of her own. It was a brilliant, enchanting gesture that softened and lightened the strong angle of her chin, hinting at a wistful fragility borne out by the delicate structure of her bones. But Clay suspected that it masked a will of iron.

"No one can manage that baby but Faye." He shrugged off her attempt at conversation, suddenly so tired that he didn't have the energy to waste on chitchat. "You'll be comfortable enough here the rest of the night if you stay in bed. I've got to be getting back." He didn't relish the return walk to the store along the shore path, but he didn't seem to have much choice in the matter. He'd come over the rocky spine of the Point on the high path, but he wasn't foolish enough to return that way. The long, soggy walk back should cure him of trying any more stunts like this one. He'd been crazy to set off for Faye's cabin in the first place.

"Did you walk?" Jenna looked as if he'd just told her he'd sprouted wings, other than the ones on his Lake Buccaneer, and flown over the Point of his own accord. "You walked three miles along the shore path in the rain?"

Clay Thornton didn't seem the kind of man to expend so much energy on a wild-goose chase. Or was it that he was the kind of man who cared deeply enough about his father's welfare to have made the long, uncomfortable trek only on the hope of finding him here? She wasn't about to admit she'd done the same thing, driving almost nonstop all the way from Cincinnati, although Locke Singer had told her repeatedly there was nothing she could do.

"I came over the top," Clay corrected. He watched curls of yellow flame lick along the edges of the newspaper.

"You took the high path?" Jenna sat down on the couch too quickly for the action to be called graceful. She remembered that path: steep, twisting and treacherous, with loose rocks and fallen trees. Dangerous in daylight; for a man alone at night in the wind and rain, it could be lethal. "You can't be thinking of going back that way again?" Her tone implied that perhaps he should have his head examined.

"I saw your lights from my plane. I thought maybe they'd made it back this far and were in trouble." Clay was infuriated to feel a blush creep up from under his shirt collar. He poked angrily at the fire with the steel toe of his shoe. "They took my Jeep. It's too rough tonight for a boat; there's no place here to beach my plane. My dad's got angina. He should never have taken off on a damn crazy stunt like this. He never would have if that—" He broke off. "I'm sorry. I didn't mean to criticize Faye. That woman could talk the spots off a leopard, and my dad's just as bad. They're some pair," he finished tightly.

"You don't have to explain to me," Jenna said to try to break the tension building between them. "I'm sure they're fine." The platitude sounded trite and unconvincing even to her own ears.

Clay snorted in frustration. "How can we be sure? They're out in the middle of nowhere playing James Bond, and we're getting gray before our time worrying about them."

"I feel so helpless. There's nothing I can do." Her words were low, breaking out of their own accord. Jenna hated the hint of tears that managed to seep through the barrier of calm reserve she always erected against too much caring. The fire caught hold with a vengeance, pushing the chilling shadows back into the corners of the room. Jenna watched it with unseeing eyes.

"Just put another log or so on it before you go to bed. You'll be nice and toasty for the rest of the night." Clay chose to honor her reticence. He wasn't certain why, but he felt she understood the sense of love and responsibility that drove him on. "I'll let you know as soon as I learn anything of their whereabouts."

"Look, couldn't I get you a cup of coffee or something? It's a long way back." Jenna shook her head to clear the fatigue from her brain and her muscles. Her hair swung free, picking up red and gold tints from the crackling fire—the same logs that had smoldered so hatefully for the last three hours.

"Thanks, but I'd better get started back. I want to fly out at first light if the weather cooperates."

Jenna spoke without conscious thought. "In my professional opinion, you're in no shape to make that climb again." She shifted into the cool detached voice she automatically used with patients. Clay caught the alteration in her speech pattern at once. One dark winged brow climbed up to meet a wayward lock of raven hair. He held back a grin. She was as feisty as her grandmother.

"Why don't you spend the rest of the night here?" Jenna went right on talking. "Then we can both leave first thing in the morning. It's close to midnight now and I haven't had a decent night's sleep since I can't remember when. You look even worse," she finished bluntly.

Clay didn't feel like smiling any longer. "I'll make it all right," he said stubbornly. He wasn't about to explain that he'd already decided against the shorter route over the high path. He didn't like having his foolish gesture brought up again. But if there was one thing that was worse than waving a red flag at a bull, it was anyone, anywhere, anytime, telling him he couldn't do whatever it was he meant to do. It was a character trait that neither the discipline of the Marines, nor six years of flying for a major airline had been completely able to subdue.

"I'm perfectly aware you'll probably make it with no trouble at all." Jenna put a long, slim hand on his sleeve. "But I won't *know* that, and I'm just too tired to stay awake the rest of the night wondering if you fell and broke your neck." A pulsing beat of pain was spearing Jenna right behind the eyes. She was so exhausted that she could hardly stand upright anymore. She had too much on her mind to add the burden of this aggravating, stubborn male to her list of worries. "Please, you can bunk down on the couch."

"That makes sense," Clay finally admitted after a long pause. He looked down at the slender hand on his arm. She was completely cut off from the world out here. Fayette refused even to hook into the two-way radio system the other residents of the Point used—not to mention the telephone. He could use the sleep too. He'd be up and off at first light to check out a few likely places the two seniors might have used as campsites. He'd be back by noon to pick up Jenna and take her to Locke and Leah's, or someplace where she'd be safe and better able to function than here on her own.

"I'll try not to wake you when I leave in the morning." He wasn't going to waste any more energy arguing with her.

Jenna smiled and turned to the bedroom to get blankets and a pillow. "Good night, Clay." She smiled again, fleetingly. If he hadn't been so tired he might have been warned by that smile. Clay remembered it later, but at the time it never crossed his mind.

For her part, Jenna had no intention of being left behind and Clay Thornton would find that out soon enough.

"I DIDN'T MEAN to wake you." Clay straightened up from his stooped position before the fireplace. He'd been arranging dry birch logs and crumpled newspaper in an effort to rekindle the blaze. "It's light enough to start back," he explained, angling his head toward the pearl-gray dawn beginning to ease through the windows.

If Jenna had been a fanciful woman, she might have likened that soft, liquid light to the color of his eyes. "I'd like to go with you," she said.

She looked as if she'd slept well but not long enough, Clay observed. Her hazel eyes were bright and clear. There were tense lines around her generous mouth, but he wondered if that was because she always seemed to be trying so hard not to smile. Her hair was tangled around her shoulders and she ran her long fingers through it self-consciously. He watched her closely so he could pinpoint the exact moment that she remembered she was wearing only the long white nightgown.

"It won't take me a minute to get dressed." Jenna looked pointedly at the box of matches in his hand. "You won't have to start a fire if there isn't anyone staying in the cabin."

"I was coming back later for you." Clay defended himself from the trace of accusation in her tone. "Listen, why don't you stay here. Get some rest. I'll come back in the runabout early this afternoon for you and your luggage. We can decide then where you're going to stay."

"I want to go with you now." She was certainly Fayette's

granddaughter. Clay had seen that implacable set of the chin on the older woman too many times to doubt it now.

"It's going to be a long, uncomfortable day," he warned.

"I'm used to long hours," came back the steady reply. "Can't you use another pair of eyes?" Frieda seemed to second the suggestion, whining encouragingly from the braided rug in front of the couch.

Clay thought it over. "Do you get airsick?"

"No." A ghost of her beguiling smile flitted over Jenna's lips.

"Good. Incidentally, I'm taking the high path back home. Feel up to it?" He gave her one more chance to return to her warm bed. Deep down, he surprised himself by hoping she'd accept his challenge. She never flinched, and Clay found that he really hadn't expected anything else.

"I'll make it."

"I'm sure you will, Dr. Macklin." He hid the beginning of a smile by turning to kick the birch logs away from each other.

"I wish you'd call me Jenna, Mr. Thornton." She emphasized the formal title so lightly that Clay couldn't be sure she was mocking him.

"Jenna." He said her name aloud, savoring the simplicity of it. This time he allowed himself to smile. He didn't do it often anymore, and the muscles of his face felt stiff and out of practice. "There's rain gear in the pantry closet, if I remember correctly."

THIRTY MINUTES LATER Jenna was forced to call a halt to their climb. "Clay, please, how about a five-minute rest? I'm pooped. You're looking at a city doctor, you know. My idea of a lot of exercise these days is working on two different patients at either end of the Trauma Center." She didn't look particularly winded; there was a becoming pink flush to her cheeks, but her voice sounded breathless when she raised it to carry over the rush of wind in the trees.

"How about stopping under that big cedar at the top of the ridge," Clay suggested. "Do you remember it? I know you

spent your summers up here as a kid.'' It would shelter them
slightly from the continuous chilly mist that had already soaked
his shoes and pant legs. Jenna's rubberized poncho came to
below her knees, but her blue cords and running shoes were
soaked, too. The black medical bag in her hand gleamed wetly
in the murky gray-green light. She'd refused to leave it behind
at Fayette's cabin, although she hadn't blinked an eye when it
became apparent that her luggage would have to remain.

''Is that old tree still there? It's so big I figured it would
have blown over in a blizzard or been struck by lightning before now. I always sheltered under it on the way back from the
store when I was a kid. That's when old Mr. Hawkins owned
it, of course.'' She put out her hand to pat the gnarled trunk.
''I haven't been along this path in a lot of years. Locke and I
could make this trip in about thirty seconds in those days. Or
at least the downhill side. Even with a bottle of Coke and a
Hershey's bar in each hand.'' Jenna's laugh was a silvery,
merry sound dancing away on the fitful west wind. ''It was the
high point of my summer weekends, that trip to the store. We
spent every Saturday morning watching reruns of *Sky King* and
The Lone Ranger on Mr. Hawkins's old Emerson. He had the
only set on the Point at that time.''

How old was she? Clay wondered, trying to judge her age
from her reminiscences. His guess put her at near thirty-two or
thirty-three, about five years younger than his own thirty-seven
years. ''Dad still has kids from the resorts every weekend, but
they're usually more interested in the video games we had
shipped in last spring.''

''Here, too?'' Jenna sighed exaggeratedly, shaking her head
in resignation. ''I guess I assumed nothing would have changed
out here. I hoped those electronic monstrosities hadn't made it
any farther north than St. Paul.'' Jenna surveyed the soggy,
moss-covered ground below the old tree. ''I treated nearly a
dozen cases of tendinitis last year in kids—and a few adults—
who just can't leave the joysticks alone.'' She dropped down
onto a level stretch of bare rock—bedrock, she supposed idly—

pulling her legs up under her poncho, hooking her hands around her knees.

"Sorry to have to disappoint you. The Woods is being pulled kicking and screaming into the computer age, just like the rest of the world." Clay hunkered down on the balls of his feet, his back resting against the rough bark of the tree trunk.

Jenna watched him out of the corner of her eye while she pretended to make patterns in the pine needles at her feet. He looked more rested this morning, but there were still deep brackets of fatigue etched between nose and mouth. The path they were traveling was even steeper and more treacherous than she remembered. She'd done the right thing by talking him into staying at Fayette's cabin last night, no matter how unconventional the arrangement might have seemed.

"Computers have their advantages," she admitted, "at least in my work." She pushed her hood back a little, the better to study the man beside her. She wasn't used to spending so much time in the company of a man who wasn't a medical colleague. Yet it wasn't hard to talk to him at all. She enjoyed their verbal sparring, and she was enjoying this more serious conversation even more. "I can get a whole blood workup on a critically ill patient in a matter of minutes now. Five years ago it would have taken hours, sometimes days."

"They are amazing machines," he agreed.

Frieda must have been tired of slogging through the mud in the slackening rain. She trotted ahead up the fern-bordered path another ten yards and barked sharply and impatiently. The sound echoed away down the slope, dying off in the misty, tree-covered distance.

"In a minute, old girl. Come on back," Clay called softly. His voice sounded hollow and muffled coming from inside the poncho's hood.

"I used to spend hours daydreaming under this tree," Jenna confessed, affected by the quiet early-morning solitude around them. "I peopled this place with Indian warriors, French explorers and Paul Bunyan—sometimes all of them at once, with a few cowboys and South Seas pirates thrown in for good measure. I had a very eclectic imagination in those days.''

"At that age all I wanted to be was an astronaut. Right from the day we got out of junior high English class to watch John Glenn go up in *Friendship 7*," Clay revealed, stripping a sprig of cedar between his fingers. The sharp, aromatic scent of crushed needles rose around them on the heavy wet air. He gave a low, rough chuckle, tossing the ruined twig into the brown-tipped ferns beside the path. "I was voted the 'Most Likely to Go to the Moon' in my high school year book." He wondered suddenly what he was telling her all this for. Surely she couldn't be interested in recollections of a boyhood fantasy twenty-odd years gone and forgotten? He hardly knew this woman, having spent less than eight hours in her company, and yet they were talking like old friends.

"What made you change your mind?" Jenna's voice was soft and sweet in his ears. He couldn't refuse to answer her now; he'd brought the subject up.

"I learned to fly." He grinned, holding out his hand to help her rise from the rock. "Mom and Dad gave me flying lessons for my seventeenth birthday. All it took was one hour in that old two-seater Piper Cub and I was hooked." Her hand was cold. He'd kept her sitting in the slackening rain too long. "For me that was the ultimate experience. Leave the moon and the stars to the rest of them."

"A natural born stick-and-rudder man," Jenna responded lightly, picking up his excitement. She bent to retrieve her black bag.

"You've read *The Right Stuff*." Clay was surprised.

"I've read everything Tom Wolfe's ever written. I even got away from St. V's long enough to see the movie."

"Is that a fact, Dr. Macklin?"

"It's a fact."

Frieda barked sharply once again, cutting off anything else Jenna might have said. The big dog butted her great head against Clay's thigh, urging him forward. Jenna bent slightly to give Frieda a pat. The dog's coat sparkling with raindrops was a sleek, creamy gray; she smelled like wet wool. Jenna wrinkled her nose.

"Okay, worrywart. Let's get home," Clay scolded affectionately.

Home. Jenna liked the sound of the word the way he spoke it—as if it really was his home and not just a place to live. "Have you had Frieda long?" Jenna asked, curious to learn more about him. She pushed her hood back a little farther to gauge his features more accurately.

"Since she was a pup. She's about the only thing I got out of the divorce settlement."

So he had been married. For how long? To whom? Jenna was surprised at the extent of her curiosity. There was a harsh edge to Clay's voice, an uncompromising set to his beard-shadowed jawline that precluded further probing in that direction. Jenna altered the subject slightly.

"Your father bought the Peninsula Store about four years ago, didn't he? I seem to remember Gram doing a column on it. That's how I keep track of the goings-on up here," Jenna explained. "She's a terrible letter writer and so am I."

"A little over four years. The store was going to be a retirement venture for my parents. They'd always loved it up here." A cool gust of wind swirled around them. The drum of raindrops shaken from leaves and bracken counterpointed the sound of human speech. "My mother was killed in an automobile accident three months before Dad retired. She would never fly with me because she said if God had meant us to leave the ground he would have given us wings. Then she gets blown away by a damned drunk driver on her way to the market."

Jenna remained silent, letting him come to grips with the residue of grief she'd inadvertently stirred up with her questions. Frieda whined softly, calling him back. "It's all right, girl," he crooned in a tone of voice that sent a warm shiver down Jenna's spine. She blamed the frisson on a drop of rain that had found its way past the hood of her poncho and rolled down her neck.

"Let's see if I remember Gram's columns correctly." She hurried to fill the stretching silence. "You've been up here about three years?" She hoped the dark sadness in his gray eyes would disappear as quickly as it came. "Marine fighter pilot. Youngest man ever offered a full captaincy at…" Jenna racked her brain for the name of the airline Clay had worked for.

"Southeast." He filled in the blank in her recollection.

"Southeast Airline," Jenna repeated thoughtfully. "But you left it all behind to come up here."

"Don't make it sound so romantic. It took one hell of a lot of doing." Clay set his jaw. He'd told her too much already. He didn't want to talk about that year: the breakup of his marriage, the reordering of his priorities, the reorganization of his entire life. "I came up to help Dad settle in and to work things out in my own head. I just never went back. I've never regretted it." What in hell had made him even mention those events? His grief and loss at his mother's death he could deal with, but not his failed marriage to Joann. He never talked about his years with her. Why should he? Joann was no longer part of his life. "We'll be able to see the store about a hundred yards after we crest the top."

"Has the store changed much?" The building itself, she recalled, faced south, huddled in the sheltering arm of a glacial ridge that protected it from the worst of the winter gales. In the next small bay, one or two rustic summer vacation lodges and six or seven cabins, a lot like Fayette's, comprised the homes of about eighty percent of the area's permanent residents. The rest were scattered over the peninsula.

"Not that you'd notice." Clay held out his hand to take her bag and help her over the last fall of scree. Scrambling with him over the top of the rise, Jenna followed his pointing hand. Now she could see it through the trees. It hadn't changed. The single-story white frame building, with its false front, looked more than anything else like a feed-and-grain store picked up from some midwestern town and plopped down in the middle of the north woods. The sign over the porch still read Peninsula

Store in bold black roman characters, but the small lettering proclaiming the proprietor's identity had been painted over; M. Hawkins now was H. Thornton.

Clay's old but well-maintained Lake Buccaneer was tied alongside a dilapidated boathouse nearby. The sleek amphibian aircraft was very different from the big, heavy, pontoon planes Jenna remembered from her summers on the lake. The engine was perched high above the cockpit. The body gleamed white and shiny in the fitful sunlight trying valiantly to break through the heavy pall of rain clouds. Sleek blue racing lines accented the body and wings. She knew that special landing gear allowed the plane to be brought down over the water and then taxied ashore.

It was a beautiful craft, and Jenna felt a surge of excitement deep in the pit of her stomach. "This rain won't hold off long. Let's get her in the air."

"Take it easy. Watch this last little bit; it's pretty tricky up here." Clay's tone was gruff.

"I'll be careful." Jenna couldn't keep the disappointment out of her voice. He'd closed her out. It was as simple as that. Whatever it was they'd shared back there under the old cedar tree, it wasn't going to be repeated or continued. Perhaps she'd been guilty of reading more into their conversation than was truly there. Perhaps he'd only fallen to the lure of confidentiality that others sometimes did, speaking to her only as a doctor—a sympathetic, discreet listener remote and uninvolved—not as a woman, feeling and complete in her own right.

Jenna sighed. For some reason that admission hurt when she applied it to Clay's revelations about his personal life. She wanted to think he had told her these things because she was a caring individual, because she was herself, Jenna, not Dr. Macklin. The realization sent a small, stinging dart of pain through her heart.

"Jenna." Almost as if he sensed her disquietude, Clay swung her around by her hand until she faced him head-on. He threw back the hood of his poncho, the watery daylight still managing to pick out highlights in his dark hair. Clay bent his head slightly so that their eyes were almost on the same level. She looked deep into the gray irises and liked the sincerity she saw reflected in his candid gaze.

"We'll find them." The words weren't what she had expected to hear, but she understood Clay's reluctance to continue their conversation along earlier, more personal lines. "I'll find Faye and my dad if I have to cover every mile of lakeshore on my hands and knees. I promise you, Jenna. I won't fail."

"I never thought *we* would." Jenna moved her fingers to squeeze his, underlining the pronoun with the gesture. His hands were warm and slightly rough; the way a man's hands ought to feel against a woman's skin. Jenna shrugged off the curiously sensual stray thought almost as quickly as it skittered through her brain. "And, Clay—" Jenna cocked her head, shaking back her hood until it slipped off the coiled knot of silvery-blond hair on top of her head "—I told you before that I won't be left behind. If it comes to crawling over rocks on your hands and knees, I'll be right there beside you. That's a promise, too."

She set her jaw in a stubborn line that was so like Faye that Clay couldn't keep back the smile that pushed for release around the corners of his mouth.

"I know." He laughed out loud, a quick, sharp bark of sound that echoed away into the hills. Frieda added her two cents' worth to the confusion, whining and butting her big head against the back of Clay's leg. "I've learned my lesson trying to sneak out on you, Dr. Jenna Macklin. If you're anything like your grandmother, by the end of the week I'll probably be sitting on my duff, minding the store while you're out flying my plane over half the state."

Jenna lowered her eyes in an exaggeratedly innocent gesture. "I wouldn't be a bit surprised." She grinned as Clay's eyes widened at the playfulness in her unexpected response. "I've always wanted to learn to fly. This is as good a time as any, wouldn't you agree?"

Chapter Three

"Do you really think those two are safe, wandering around out here alone?" Jenna laid in her lap the heavy field glasses she'd been using to survey the wooded shoreline passing beneath the wings of the plane. Her head ached from the glare of September sunlight glinting off the light chop on the water. "We've been at this for hours." She slipped on the wire-framed aviator's sunglasses Clay had lent her, patting the severe knot of pale blond hair on top of her head back into place.

"Tired?" Clay asked solicitously, putting the responsive Buccaneer into a slight bank to the east. She was tired. He'd seen her hands tremble from fatigue when she poured coffee from the thermos an hour ago, but she wouldn't give in. Maybe he'd underestimated her stamina back there in the cabin. Perhaps she wasn't as fragile, as physically unsuited to the climate and life-style as Leah Singer was. He'd made too big a deal out of the stuck fireplace damper last night, but he hoped the incident was forgotten. "It is pretty routine, flying a search grid like this."

"I'll do whatever it takes to find them." Jenna's tone left no room for argument. "Did they leave you any clue as to where they were going?" She knew she'd repeated herself, but Clay didn't seem to mind answering yet again. Jenna was grateful for his patience.

"I showed you this morning. All they left was that pretty cryptic note scribbled on the back of a bill for an order of paper towels and toilet paper. Faye said they'd made contact with a guy in Warroad who was supposed to put them in touch with one of these renegade pilots who fly hunters in to take big game from planes. My dad added a P.S. that said he'd keep track of the mileage and wear and tear on the Jeep,'' Clay noted with a crooked, exasperated grin. "I wish they had let me handle it." His voice was no longer amused. "Pilots like the kind they're after give us all a bad name."

"You've got to be kidding. You'd bring the culprits to heel and steal my grandmother's thunder." Jenna tried to smile but her facial muscles refused to comply satisfactorily. Her quip came out accompanied by something closer to a grimace. "I just wish I knew that they were safe and well."

"Fayette knows her way around this lake, Jenna. And my dad's no slouch. The kind of guys they're interested in keep a pretty low profile. What those flyers are doing isn't strictly illegal, but it skirts the edge of the law."

"And it's almost impossible to find a campsite if someone doesn't want to be found," Jenna admitted. "We've proved that today."

"You can even hide a plane." Clay made a small adjustment in their course. The Buccaneer compensated smoothly, as smoothly as Locke's tug had responded to his hand on the wheel the day Jenna had arrived. Had it only been yesterday? She felt as if she'd been back on the Woods for ages.

"It's almost two o'clock," Jenna remarked, looking at her wristwatch. "We've been up here almost five hours, and not a sign of a human being or even another plane."

"It can get mighty lonesome up here. Especially in the middle of February when the wind blows for five days straight and piles the snowdrifts so high up under the eaves that we have to keep the lights on day and night."

"Sounds strange and beautiful to me. Winters in the city are the pits. Especially in ones like Cincinnati, where we get more freezing rain and slush than real snow. To me snowstorms mean fender benders, whiplash, heart attacks from shoveling snow, and poor, homeless alcoholics with fingers and toes

frostbitten because they had no place to get in out of the cold."
Clay felt oddly touched by the unconscious pathos of the statement. Even deeper, he sensed Jenna's pain, the frustration of
not being able to do anything about the conditions that brought
those people into her care.

"Is that a campsite down there?" Her voice rose a little with
suppressed excitement. Clay glanced in the direction she was
pointing, holding his course while Jenna focused the field
glasses on the area. "There is something down there. A cabin
or building of some kind."

Clay put the plane into a shallow dive that sent them skimming only a few feet above the treetops. He smiled a little
grimly as Jenna's hands tightened on the binoculars. She'd
never flown in a small plane before, but she was a good sport
about it. Despite her anxiety over Fayette's absence, and the
less-than-perfect initial encounter last night, she seemed to be
enjoying the time they were spending together—and he found
himself liking that, too.

They circled the small clearing twice before Clay began to
climb back up into the blue-gray sky. "Aren't we going to
land and get a better look?" Jenna couldn't keep the disappointment or the consternation out of her voice.

"It isn't necessary," Clay said, cutting off the words
sharply. He continued more softly, "It's only a hunter's cabin,
Jenna. Probably hasn't been used since last winter at a guess."

"How do you know that?" Jenna craned her neck to look
back at the dilapidated lean-to in the wooded clearing. It was
rapidly returning to dollhouse size as they gained altitude.

"There's no road in. That means they probably use snowmobiles to get out here—deer hunters, most likely."

"But with a plane like this one…" Jenna wanted to go back
and land the plane and take a look around, if for no other
reason than to feel as if she were accomplishing something
concrete.

"No place to tie her down. Rocks right up to the shoreline.
The guys Fayette and my dad are after need a place to land a
plane, a creek or inlet where you can't be seen from the water

or the air if you don't want to be. If they've gone over the border into Canada, it's going to be more difficult still. There are miles of shoreline and small islands so far off the beaten track they've never been explored. Some of them probably aren't even on a map.''

''And I'm not supposed to worry about her.'' Jenna shifted restlessly in her padded seat. She fiddled irritably with the snap of her seat belt.

''They'll be okay.'' Clay wished he could shake off his own apprehensions as easily as he said the words.

''I can't help but worry,'' Jenna repeated with a little gurgle of anxious laughter. ''It's my nature. And Gram has a way of bringing out the worrier in everyone who knows her. I'll never forget the time a bear wandered out of the woods and into the garden. When it started rooting up her strawberry plants, she took after it with a broom! I can see her now if I close my eyes—her braid swinging over her shoulder, her Indian paisley housecoat flapping around her ankles, broom waving in the air.'' Jenna relaxed back into her seat. ''That poor bear never had a chance. I remember I was fourteen that summer. And at the time I didn't think it was one bit funny. I was scared to death.''

''Faye's one brave lady, all right.'' Clay joined her in reminiscent laughter. ''My dad's a lot like her in some respects, although I don't think even he'd tackle a bear armed solely with a broomstick.''

''I'm looking forward to meeting him,'' Jenna said, closing her eyes a moment to rest them. Fatigue made her head ache and her eyes sting hotly.

''He's a great guy. Everyone says we're a lot alike,'' Clay pointed out mock-seriously. ''When we were kids, my two brothers and I thought there wasn't anything he couldn't do.''

''Gram's always been that way, too. So fearless and self-assured. Do you know, she never married my grandfather?'' Jenna glanced over at Clay to gauge his reaction. He was wearing a pair of reflective sunglasses, so she couldn't see the expression in his warm gray eyes.

"Fifty-odd years ago that must have been almost unheard of."

"It was, but she stuck by her guns. She knew they couldn't be happy together. And she was probably right; she almost always is. Anyway, her parents went along with the decision, although they were very upset. They helped her take care of my father when he was small so that she could go to college. She became a buyer for one of Chicago's biggest department stores. Then, when my father had grown up and gone off to college, she came up here on vacation and more or less never left to go back to the city. Or so she tells it. I envy people like my grandmother, who have the courage to take their destiny into their own hands and mold life to meet their dreams."

"Aren't you doing what you want with your life, Jenna?" Clay's voice was quiet, soothing. Jenna found herself succumbing to the hypnotic drone of the engine and the warmth of the afternoon sun shining through her window. They combined with her own tired physical state to give everything a dreamlike quality. She felt she could say what weighed so heavily on her heart and Clay would understand.

"No, not entirely. There's something missing from my life and from my work." Jenna felt sleep hovering beyond the edges of reality, like the pale sunlight dancing off the wingtip. "Why did you give up flying to come up here?" She hadn't worded that quite as well as she'd like. She turned her head slightly to watch his strong brown hands move with unhesitating accuracy among the myriad switches and gauges on the control panel.

"Why did I give up flying for an airline?...I don't know how to explain it." Clay didn't take the time to analyze why he was telling Jenna this; she was so easy to talk to. Perhaps it was because of her training. People were supposed to be able to tell ministers and doctors anything, but he didn't think that was the cause of his sudden loquaciousness. It was because she was Jenna, a caring, sympathetic woman in her own right. "It's mostly point A to point B to point C and back again. Do you understand what I'm trying to say? It's flying strictly by the book, which is the way it ought to be with so many lives at stake. But after the Marines…''

"You missed a little seat-of-the-pants flying?" Jenna mused with a sympathetic nod. She sat up straighter, pushing exhaustion away with the sheer force of her will.

"Well…'' Clay gave a shrug of his shoulders, easing the Buccaneer into a neat little roll, dropping down to skim along at water level for a heart-stopping few seconds before climbing back up to cruising altitude. "See what I mean? You can't do that with a DC-10 loaded with scores of bored businessmen and housewives with small children, headed to Milwaukee.''

"No, I imagine you can't,'' Jenna answered, her lilting voice faintly breathless. She swallowed to settle the lump that had risen to her throat, but the feeling was more of excitement than apprehension. "Up here you're the boss. Was it only boredom that caused you to leave the airline?'' She held her breath, fully expecting him not to answer. Or to tell her it was none of her business. He did neither.

"No, there was a lot more to it than that." He was silent a moment. Jenna found her thoughts drifting like the fat rain clouds crowding back into the sky around them. Clay was a very private man; she had recognized that about him already. He was also an enigma—an intelligent, educated man who'd given up a successful career with a major airline to live the life of an island-hopping bush pilot. Why? Had the pressure been too much for him? It hardly seemed likely. Had he lost all the joy in his work? The way it was happening to her?

"My marriage had failed. My mother was dead, all within a year. Then one day I took off from Atlanta in a DC-10 with two hundred and twenty-seven passengers and crew. We were headed for St. Louis. It was twilight, not quite dark. Some poor overworked S.O.B. in the control tower gave me and a Piper Navajo clearance on the same runway. I'll never forget watching that plane taxi out in front of me. We were almost up to speed, thank God, so I kicked her hard and pushed the throttle to the wall. We sheared off his left wing with our forward landing gear, but made it off the ground. I was able to bring the Ten around and land her without anyone being seriously injured. The poor schmuck in the Navajo barely made it out alive. After all the formalities were cleared up, I took a leave of absence. I guess, to sum it up, I was tired of being responsible for all those souls and all that machinery—responsible, but not in control.''

''So you came up here.''

''And never looked back.''

''Just like that,'' Jenna said softly, sensing intuitively how hard it had been for him to tell her this. Could it be he'd truly found the peace and satisfaction that everyone searched for here on Lake of the Woods and not in the fast-paced, high-tech world that seemed so far away in time as well as distance? Jenna hadn't yet coalesced her own feelings enough on the crisis she felt growing in her career to put them into speech. ''You'll never go back?'' she couldn't keep from asking, although she was so tired again that she could barely keep her eyes open.

''I don't want to go back.'' Clay headed the plane westward toward the sun. Heavy, dark rain clouds threatened on the far horizon.

''It's going to rain again.'' Jenna felt the need to return the conversation to more prosaic matters. She couldn't cope with all the conflicting sensations Clay's revelations had brought her.

''Off and on, I'd say, for the next four or five days—at least, according to the National Weather Service. It's unusual weather for this time of year. Indian summer doesn't last this long into September most years.'' Clay made his tone as soothingly monotonous as he could. The steady drone of the overhead engine wove a soporific undertone to their words.

''I'm not complaining—except about the rain.'' Jenna rested her head against the back of the seat.

''Me, either,'' Clay responded. ''Winter's long enough without wishing it here early. It'll take us nearly an hour to get back home. Why don't you try and get some sleep?''

"Mmm. I think I will." Home. Once again the word went straight to Jenna's lonely heart and lodged there. Home.

"THAT SMELLS HEAVENLY. What is it?" Jenna kicked out a foot, wiggling her toes in the warmth of a pair of Clay's heavy wool socks. She pushed automatically at the listing knot of hair on her head, then gave up the attempt to tame it into its usual severe roll. Somehow, here, in this place, alone with Clay after the long day of worry and searching, it didn't seem nearly as important that she convey her professional image as strongly. And as she was also wearing a pair of Clay's pajamas—forest-green and brand-new, he'd assured her, a gift from an aunt who'd never been to Minnesota and assumed her nephew would need their heavy flannel protection on long, cold winter nights—her dignity was pretty well compromised, anyway.

"This little delicacy is called a pasty, Dr. Macklin. Pronounced past-y—as in long-gone," Clay lectured as he swung around to open the oven door and check on his creation.

"Past-y," Jenna repeated dutifully. "Are you sure there's nothing I can do to help you? I'm not much of a cook, it's true, but I can punch up a microwave as well as any woman alive."

"Patience, Doc. You're not going to reduce my pasty to shoe leather by putting it in the microwave." Clay sounded genuinely horrified as he pulled the traditional crescent-shaped Cornish meat pie out of the oven with a flourish. He held it out for Jenna's inspection. The crust was indeed a deep, flaky brown. The mouth-watering aromas of potatoes, carrots, onions and steak wafted over her in a tantalizing rush.

"I'm starved," Jenna confessed, licking her lips. She twirled around on the tall, leather-seated bar stool, making herself comfortable, curling her toes around the bottom rung in anticipation of the feast. She ought to be miserably uncomfortable sitting here in Clay's kitchen, watching him cook, wearing his pajamas and a threadbare old terry robe. Unbidden came the fleeting question as to what he did wear to bed, if not these things, but Jenna ignored the quick rush of pleasantly stinging heat it brought to her veins. It was enough to acknowledge the comfort and companionship they shared without complicating matters unnecessarily by dragging sensual undercurrents into play.

She did feel wonderfully secure, warm and cozy in his clothes and in his too-big socks, while her own blue cords, yellow T-shirt and long-sleeved blue shirt whirled merrily in the electric dryer hidden behind folding louvered doors at the far end of the kitchen. The rhythmic, continuous clatter of zipper and snaps hitting the metal sides of the appliance punctuated their conversation and added even more to her sense of ease and homeyness.

"I'm pretty hungry myself. Those peanut butter sandwiches we had in the plane were a long time ago." Clay pulled plates from an overhead cupboard as he spoke.

"And a day old." Jenna cocked her head and grinned, waiting for Clay's reaction to her sally. She propped her elbows on the counter to watch his sure hands chop apples for a salad.

"At least." Clay smiled, too, and Jenna liked the way it tilted up his lips and echoed in his eyes. He had such nice eyes, cool and clear, but changeable—sometimes like smoke on the wind and sometimes nearly as dark as storm clouds in a troubled sky. He'd shaved and had changed into a red-and-black-plaid wool shirt and dark pants. His lean, coiled grace, coupled with the traditional look of the clothes, again gave Jenna the whimsical notion that she was sitting in a very modern kitchen with an eighteenth-century voyageur.

Silence grew and lengthened between them, but Jenna didn't feel compelled to break it. She let her gaze wander over the big low-ceilinged room. Clay and his father had worked hard to make the pine-paneled combination living-room-and-kitchen into a comfortable, casual home. Big double-hung windows flanked a native stone fireplace fitted with a high-efficiency, wood-burning insert. The wide plank floors had been lacquered a deep yellow-brown that blended with the walls. Chintz throws softened the lines of a cushioned couch and chairs. Narrow-slatted decorator blinds covered the windows, adding a surprisingly sophisticated note to the setting. A stereo tape deck and video recorder shared a row of built-in bookshelves, set at right angles to the fireplace wall, with paperback thrillers, hardback tomes on aeronautics and magazines of various style and description. Jenna liked what she saw. The kitchen was equally inviting and well-designed.

"I hope you aren't a purist." Clay interrupted her meandering appraisal of his home. "I always have mine with gravy."

"Oh, Lord, gravy? There goes my diet," Jenna mourned. "The mere mention of the word gravy makes me salivate like one of Pavlov's dogs. But only a spoonful, please." She held out her portion of the steaming meat pie. "Who taught you to cook like this, your mother?"

Clay was jolted out of his pleasant preoccupation with watching the play of expressions cross Jenna's face and the way she tried, unthinkingly he was sure, to keep all that emotion tucked away somewhere behind her hard-won mask of professionalism. "Not my mother. Between my dad and my brothers she had to limit her cooking pretty much to hamburgers, steaks and apple pie. It was my ex-wife, Joann." This time it was slightly easier to insert her name into the conversation, Clay found.

"Your ex-wife's hobby was gourmet cooking?" Jenna inquired interestedly. She spooned the crisp apple-and-raisin salad he'd concocted onto her plate while Clay placed coffee and glasses of cold springwater on the butcher-block dining bar. He shot her a quick glance from beneath dark brows drawn together in a near frown. Jenna returned his scrutiny with calm serenity. Clay decided to go on.

"Not her hobby, her career. Joann's a very talented chef. Her restaurant is one of the best in New Orleans." He tried not to sound bitter. He didn't want Jenna to think he begrudged Joann her achievement. He wondered if he'd succeeded very well from the wary, quizzical look that passed briefly across her face.

"A French restaurant, I suppose," she inserted around a mouthful of pastry. "Haute cuisine, with tons of rich sauces and sinfully elegant desserts tempting hard-working doctors to break their diets?''

"Bavarian, actually," Clay corrected with a twist of his mouth that just missed being a grin as he watched her eat. "Do you have to diet? You look just fine to me."

"I'll take that as a compliment." Jenna returned the quip with a rueful glance down at what she was wearing. There wasn't an inch of her figure that wasn't covered by something big and baggy. "And I do have to watch my weight, off and on," she added honestly. "It's a hereditary affliction, you see." She made a face and spoke in a dramatically confidential tone, lowering her voice as if the walls might have ears. "My hips. The family curse, my grandmother calls it." She scooped up another bite of savory meat pie and studied it closely, avoiding his eyes as they searched her face. A delicate tint of color washed across her cheeks. He must think her foolish to be indulging in such useless banter.

"Family curse?" Clay would have liked to tell her that most men preferred a softly rounded derriere like hers, as opposed to the sharp angles of a less womanly body, but he didn't think their relationship had progressed quite that far, so he held his peace.

"Wide pelvis." Jenna held up a hand to ward off his reply. "I know, I know. Good for childbearing, but hell when you're trying to find a pair of designer jeans." Good Lord, what had ever possessed her to say such a thing? She never, never talked this way to men. Especially to a man who intrigued her as much as Clay Thornton was beginning to do. Jenna was astounded at her lack of discretion and at the unusually sensual overtones she felt had crept into her voice. She changed the subject back to his ex-wife, willy-nilly. "I'd be out of control in a really good French restaurant."

"Bavarian," Clay corrected, and something cold and sharp that he'd been carrying around inside him for so long eased a little. It was good, sitting here trading quips with Jenna, becoming familiar with how swiftly her mind worked, how hard she tried to keep her smile from changing to laughter at something he said. He could even talk about Joann without the angry pain he'd always felt in the past. Perhaps it was because his mind wasn't dwelling on the old hurts? He was by far more interested in considering how quickly Jenna's mood might change again to passion if he took her in his arms and kissed her.

"Bavarian?" Jenna repeated, and Clay realized he'd let his wandering thoughts cause a lull in the conversation. This time it was his high, angled cheekbones that darkened slightly.

"Her family came over after World War II, but Joann was born and raised in New Orleans. We used to work out recipes together when we were first married. You should taste my filled noodles, by the way," he added with a definite spark of mischief in his smoky-gray eyes as he watched Jenna surreptitiously sneak a walnut out of the salad when she thought he wasn't looking. "They aren't so bad, if I do say so myself."

"Filled noodles. With lots of shredded cabbage and three kinds of sausage?" Jenna looked up with real longing in her hazel eyes. She pushed absently at the too-long sleeves of his pajama top, a small wistful smile tugging at the corners of her mouth. "I don't think I can stand much more of this kind of talk."

"And a little added variation of my own—lemon pepper," Clay went on, deliberately ignoring her plea.

"Don't! It's cruel taunting someone who practically exists on green salad and melba toast." Jenna came from a long line of hearty-eating Pennsylvania Dutch ancestors. Her hectic lifestyle that required too many vending-machine sandwiches, hospital-cafeteria lunches and frozen-entrées-for-one made her long for the time and expertise to create healthful and delicious food in a kitchen of her own.

"You don't have to exist on green salad and melba toast." Clay was serious now and Jenna answered in the same manner.

"I know, I'm not going to." She'd been punishing herself in a way for breaking off her relationship with Roger, but she was through with regretting and mourning what was past. "It must have been nice to have an interest that you shared with

Joann that involved her work.'' Jenna hesitated slightly over
the name to make sure she had it right. Clay nodded curtly.
Would it have made a difference with Roger if she could have
been even remotely interested in his corporate-law practice and
the behind-the-scenes wheeling and dealing that accompanied
it? Or if he had cared at all about her commitment to emergency medicine?

''We didn't have time to do much of anything else together.'' This time Clay didn't even try to hide the darkness in
his voice. What had come over him, mentioning his marriage
twice in the same day to the same woman?

She was easy to confide in. She seemed to appreciate how
hard it was to talk about a love that had failed. She listened,
she understood, and she didn't press beyond where he wanted
to go. Jenna looked so much at home in his dad's threadbare
old robe and his socks. Her silvery hair was coming loose,
curling around her shoulders. It was a deeper blond than usual,
still damp from the shower he insisted she take when they got
back to the store and he found she'd been wearing wet shoes
and clammy corduroy jeans all day long without complaint.

''I'm sorry. I know something about ending relationships,''
Jenna said quietly. She longed for a moment to reach out and
touch his strong brown fingers where they clenched on the
table. She didn't, folding her own hands firmly together in her
lap to quell the urge to comfort him. The need to convey her
understanding physically surprised her. She wasn't a touching
kind of person, preferring to show her caring and empathy in
less intimate ways. She didn't know how to explain the sudden
impulse to soothe and caress. ''No matter how civilized the
separation is, no matter how relieved you might be that an
intolerable situation has ended, it hurts.'' The last words were
barely above a whisper.

''Were you married?'' Clay's start of curiosity held a grating
note. He felt guilty. He wasn't one to dig into other people's
lives. He valued his privacy too much to intrude lightly into
another's pain. But with Jenna it *was* different. She understood.
She wouldn't make judgments on his failure or pass sentence

on his past actions. He wanted to help her in the same way. He wasn't certain, yet, why he felt that way, but he was sure he did.

"I was engaged to be married," Jenna explained. She looked down at her hands folded too tightly in her lap. She uncurled her fingers, aligning her silverware with surgical precision. "He's a lawyer. Very successful. We would have been the perfect, upwardly mobile couple, Roger and I, if I'd only co-operated and taken a job with an HMO. Health maintenance organization," Jenna elaborated as Clay's forehead creased in puzzlement. She slid off the bar stool, picking up her plate and cup as she did so. "I'll help tidy up while my clothes finish drying."

Clay stopped her forward movement with a light grip circling her wrist. Jenna looked down at their hands touching and became still. Clay released her almost immediately and began to trace patterns on the counter top with the tip of his spoon. "I gather you didn't take the job?"

"No." Jenna's tone was adamant. She moved toward the sink, now that his touch no longer held her back. "Strictly nine-to-five medicine. An insurance mill. Not the way I saw myself practicing the healing arts." Her tone held a vestige of sadness. "When I told Roger I wanted to stay with the Trauma Program he was…annoyed."

"Annoyed?" Clay didn't try to filter the surprise out of his words. He could see himself irritated with a woman as complex as Jenna, infuriated, perhaps, if she pushed him too far, intrigued and enthralled, surely, if she touched his heart. But merely annoyed? Never.

"Not a very flattering description of a lover, or the way you end a love affair, is it?" Jenna smiled a little bitterly as if the admission of missing out on a grand passion hurt her more than she could admit.

"Go on, Jenna." Clay's directive was low and quiet, soothing but nonetheless still an order.

"That's all, really. Roger was willing to have a wife with a career but a convenient one." Funny how easy it was to talk about the broken engagement now. Almost as if it had happened to another woman, not herself. Even at the time, she'd recognized her heart wasn't broken, but it was pretty badly cracked; so was her self-esteem for a short time. But she was getting over it. It hadn't been that simple for Clay, she surmised. Had breaking up his marriage to Joann been the first failure of his life? To lose a love was hard enough. But for a man who'd known only success in whatever endeavors he'd undertaken, it must have been harder still to admit defeat.

"Big of him." Clay didn't like the idea that this faceless character from Jenna's past could make his blood simmer with the need to make him pay for hurting her.

She made a little face and poured her cold coffee down the drain while he watched with hooded eyes. Shadows thrown by the overhead light hid the expression on his face, so Jenna didn't notice his reaction and Clay was glad. "When my career began to interfere with his…well, a wife who might be on call the night he was supposed to wine and dine the senior partner in his firm…and a fiancée who walked out in the middle of an intimate, catered dinner party with his parents to answer her beeper not once, mind you, but three times—do you get the picture?"

"I get the picture." Clay felt a cold, squeezing pain in his gut. He'd never considered that Joann might have felt that way about her restaurant. Had he made those kinds of demands on her during their marriage? He didn't want to think he had. "So you let this Roger…" he fumbled mentally for a noncommittal, nonabrasive ending to the sentence and a reprieve from his own unsettling cogitations.

"Off the hook," Jenna supplied with an airy wave of her hand. The effect was spoiled by the slight tremor that accompanied the gesture. She tipped her head to see better Clay's reaction to her revelation. Would he think her a weakling for not fighting for her love and her career? For not being able to have it all and make it work?

"He wasn't worth it." Clay regretted the words as soon as he said them. He didn't know how badly she'd been hurt by the breakup of her affair with this Roger creep. There was real pain in her eyes, old but lingering. He wondered if it matched his own. Perhaps she'd loved this guy to distraction, the way he'd first felt about Joann. It was none of his business, after all. He hadn't done a sterling job of keeping his own marriage viable, so he couldn't make judgments on others.

"I can see that now," Jenna replied with false brightness. She obviously wanted to change the subject but didn't know how. "We couldn't reconcile two lives going in opposite directions." The gold flecks in her hazel eyes had vanished in the wake of that old pain. "It was best for both of us, as I suspect your divorce was for the two of you, if you stop to think it through." She closed the discussion firmly. "Now point me toward the dish soap and I'll get these dishes out of the way in no time. I warn you, I'd rather wash than dry."

"This isn't your grandmother's cabin, with her quaint but anachronistic kitchen and sanitary facilities." Clay rose from his seat with a flourish. She was right about one thing. You couldn't go back. Regrets got you nowhere. His life with Joann had been a dead-end street; neither of them had wanted to give up anything to keep their love alive. It was sad, but it was the way it had been. "The dishwasher is behind that cupboard to your left. Just stick in the plates. I'll run a full load before I fire up the backup generator for the night. We don't have too much trouble with the electricity up here anymore, but I can't take a chance, with all that frozen food and produce in the store."

"A dishwasher? Gram still has to pump water into the kitchen with a hand pump. And that's a lot of work for ice-cold water, let me tell you. This is my idea of wilderness living," Jenna gurgled, scraping her leftovers into Frieda's bowl while the big dog watched with worshipful eyes. "All the conveniences of the real world and none of the hassle." Her voice was gently self-mocking but less strained, as if his insistence on getting things back on a more ordinary basis was helping her to regain her equilibrium.

"Conveniences courtesy of the J.C. Penney catalog," Clay

joked, following her actions, lightening the mood still further. "And there are fewer hassles, I admit. I told you I've never regretted leaving the rat race. But neither is this Walden Pond." Their hands met for a second time as they both reached out to pick up the salad bowl at the same instant. Clay felt all the way to the soles of his feet the surge of electricity that the touch of his fingers on her skin produced. He'd touched her before, several times. But this was different, very different.

"I know it isn't Walden Pond." Jenna's voice was husky. She cleared her throat. Had he felt that peculiar jolt of sensation, too? She took the bowl as if nothing had happened, but her mind was flying off on other tangents. His touch was warm and strong, comforting and strangely exciting. How would it feel to be held in his arms, surrounded by his strength, filled with his love and virility? Jenna slammed the refrigerator door on that thought. She didn't allow herself any sexual imaginings where her male colleagues were concerned. It shouldn't be any different with Clay. But it was.

Thunder rolled and echoed over the ridge behind the store. She was grateful for the diversion. "Drat! It's going to start raining again. I hate walking in a storm." She stared out of the big windows that faced the ridge. Mist hung like tattered cobwebs above the serrated tops of the pine trees marching up the slope.

"There's no need for you to go back to Faye's, Jenna. Stay here. There's plenty of room." Clay spoke from his heart, without thinking. He didn't want her to go and take all the warmth and light that was left in the dark, wet day with her.

"What will your neighbors think?" Jenna retorted, still as lightly as she could manage. She whirled to face him. More tendrils of silver-blond hair escaped their confinement. She tried not to betray how nervous the suggestion made her. For the first time she felt at a disadvantage in his too-large pajamas and the soft old terry robe. The pajama legs were too long; she had to hike them up high on her waist to keep from tripping over the hems. The sleeves were even worse. They needed about three turns to get them above her wrist. She began tug-

ging at the right one. None of this had bothered her until he
touched her, until their hands met on the salad bowl. Now she
couldn't shake the realization from her mind that he was a man,
a fascinating, dangerous creature. And she—she was a woman.

"I'll get the rest of your things as soon as possible. But what
good will it do you to go back to the cabin tonight? I can't
even get word to you if those two should turn up—and if they
should need your help."

"I hadn't thought of that." He hadn't moved any closer, but
Jenna had felt constrained to take a step backward. Now she
momentarily forgot her disquietude at his nearness. Two seniors alone, perhaps lost in the wilderness, invited too many
other scenarios, terrifying ones.

"That they're hurt or ill is a possibility we have to consider.
My father's health is questionable and Fayette is in her sev-
enties." Jenna couldn't argue with his reasoning, as much as
she wanted to. She was having trouble concentrating on much
of anything at all. "Do I have to repeat all the arguments you
used on me last night?" Clay quizzed her with a slightly self-
conscious grin. "I remember all of them." He remembered
more than that—the feel of her body in his arms as she flew
across the porch to escape the smoke-filled room, the determination in her eyes and the set of her jaw when she insisted
he stay the night and get the rest he had so desperately needed.
"They were good, strong reasons. They still apply."

"It's not the same." Jenna made a last attempt to deny the
strength of his argument, the appeal of his lean, hard body so
close to hers.

Clay reached out to capture her hand in his. "You're worn
out. I'd lie awake all night worrying about you, or end up
escorting you back and catch my death of cold." He watched
her face closely. The last remark brought a smile to her gold-
flecked eyes, although her mouth remained a straight line. Clay
took a chance on teasing the smile to full brilliance. "But it
might not be so bad if I could count on your exclusive atten-
dance on my poor fever-racked body."

Jenna caught her breath at the remark. She watched Clay

closely, but the daylight was nearly gone and his face was a shadowy blur in the twilight gloom. "My grandmother doesn't even know I'm in Minnesota." Jenna purposefully ignored his suggestive gambit because she didn't know how to deal with it or with the sudden rush of desire it stirred to life. "She'd come here first. I want to be here when that happens. I'll stay as long as you need me, Clay. As long as I can be of help."

"You're a very special lady, Dr. Macklin." Clay suddenly remembered that he still held her hand in his. He didn't release it, although Jenna tugged slightly to be set free when she saw him looking down at their intertwined fingers.

"I'm not special at all, Clay. I work too hard. I worry too much. I'm not too good at anything but being a doctor."

"Don't sell yourself short, Jenna." He moved a step closer, sealing off her escape. Rain splattered against the windowpane at her back. Jenna didn't hear it. "You care passionately about everyone you love. I don't have to know you well to see that. It's why you're here; it sets you apart. It will keep you special all your life." Clay's voice was a soft, deep growl that set her nerve ends tingling. The words should have embarrassed her, but the sincerity in his voice allowed her to accept the compliment without discomfort.

"Thank you." She inclined her head with touching dignity. Jenna didn't know what would happen next. Would he take her in his arms as she almost hoped he would? They'd compressed a great deal of learning about each other, of mutual exploration, into a mere twenty-four hours. A physical closeness seemed the next most natural step in a wonderful continuation of that learning process. Clay reached out, tracing the line of her jaw with a gentle callused fingertip.

"That buzzing in my ears—do you hear it, too?" He wasn't quite smiling, but silver lights danced in his gray eyes. Jenna leaned forward without thinking, to better catch the play of fading light across his chiseled features.

"I hear it, too. What is it?"

"I don't know. I think it's my brain overloading. May I kiss you Jen?"

The request struck her like a bolt of pure bright light. She closed her eyes for a second to shut out the dazzling display. "I couldn't hear it if your brain were overloading," Jenna pointed out, but let him pull her close into the circle of his arms. She saw him lean closer, then shut her eyes again, waiting with her breath stuck somewhere in her throat for the touch of his mouth on hers.

Her lips were firm and cool beneath his touch. Clay smoothed his fingertips along the corners of her mouth, feathering them upward into a smile as he threaded his fingers into her hair, loosening the silver-gilt curls even more. He let the tip of his tongue explore the honeyed sweetness of her lips until her mouth flowered open in acceptance of his quest. Clay drew her closer, sliding his hands down over the soft roundness of her hips, fitting their bodies together with a low groan of satisfaction.

Jenna sighed, the sound sifting past her lips almost inaudibly. He felt so good, so right, as if their bodies were made for each other. Her breasts pushed against the hard planes of his chest; her arms moved naturally to glide over the lean muscles of his back and waist. His passion pushed hard and urgently against her thigh; his virility defined and complemented the yearning softness of her own body. The kiss seemed endless as they sought eagerly to learn more of each other, but, even so, it was over much too quickly.

"Did that eliminate your disturbing symptoms, Mr. Thornton?" Jenna asked, still breathless from their embrace but unwilling to display just how shaken she'd been by the wonder of his kiss.

"It's caused a whole new series of complications." Clay pressed her closer to demonstrate. Jenna flushed and then laughed, able to accept the gentle teasing.

"I think I can safely diagnose your problem."

"Already? I'd hoped you might need a second consultation." Clay felt the same need to lighten the situation that Jenna did. He hadn't expected the depth of feeling she stirred in him by acquiescing to one kiss. He wanted to go on kissing her for the rest of the night, possibly for the rest of his life. It was a sobering thought, one that could and did lead to a host of bewildering conclusions.

"It's not a serious physical condition. And that buzzing— it's just the dryer going off. My clothes are dry." She pulled away from him and turned back to the window; the rain had begun to come down in earnest.

There was tension in the way she held her head, in the stiffness of her shoulders. Clay sensed her distress as well as her desire for him and the anxiety those conflicting feelings had produced. "Come on, Doc. If that's all it is, then help me fold this stuff and we'll call it a night. Tomorrow's another long, long day." Having her with him would give them both a chance to explore these new and unexpected emotions surfacing between them. For the first time in longer than he cared to remember, Clay was more than anxious for a new day to begin.

"I'll be a lot more comfortable on your couch tonight than I bet you were on Fayette's," Jenna said to let him know she would stay with him. Clay turned her to face him again. His hands were warm and hard on her shoulders but the pressure he applied to turn her around was tender.

"I could have slept on a bed of nails last night." Clay's tone and the look in his pewter-gray eyes thanked her without words for insisting he get that much needed rest. "You take my bed." He halted Jenna's instinctively polite refusal with a wave of his hand. "The sheets are clean. I haven't been home for a week," he reminded her, finishing up with a rueful, slanting grin and a disbelieving shake of his head. "I'll bunk in Dad's room."

"Thanks, Clay. I..." Jenna didn't really know what she wanted to say. Remarks that might have come easily a few moments before—before he'd kissed her and made everything change—couldn't make it past the lump in her throat. Clay put a finger to her lips, stilling her halting attempt to explain herself.

"The circumstances of making your acquaintance could

have been a hell of a lot better. But do you know something, Dr. Jenna Macklin?''

''No, what?'' She let her eyes be snagged and held by his compelling gaze. Clay's words were low and slightly ragged around the edges. He reached out and touched her lips with a fleeting, half-disbelieving gesture.

''I think I'm going to be very, very happy I met you.''

Chapter Four

The sun was shining. Jenna took a bite of her apple as she watched dust motes slip through the watery golden light pouring in the big windows at the front of the store. It had turned out to be a glorious day, her third on the Woods. Her gaze wandered over the modern glass refrigerated cases, marching side by side with rows of durable goods on shelves that had been old and worn at the turn of the century. They were in turn flanked by three very colorful, high-tech video games, partially hidden by an alcove in the rear. On the front counter beside the ornate heavy brass cash register, a wicker basket piled high with red and gold apples, purple grapes and bananas, added color and heady aroma to the atmosphere. She was completely alone in the building, but for once she didn't mind the solitude.

Immediately after breakfast Clay had taken off in his sleek Buccaneer to continue the search for his father and Fayette. Jenna had volunteered to mind the store. The inactivity of the past two rainy days had made Clay short-tempered and edgy. Jenna had played cribbage with him for hours; they'd watched old movies on the VCR until she thought she could recite most of the dialogue in every John Wayne movie from *Stagecoach* to *McClintock*. They both knew that he was looking for a needle in a haystack, but at least he was doing something, not waiting passively for events to develop.

It was funny how easily she could read him now. Clay was

a doer, a leader, never content to wait for others to take the initiative. It was unusual for Jenna to feel the urge to delve deeply into another human being's character. She preferred to live and let live, for the most part. Perhaps if she'd been more discerning with Roger, their relationship wouldn't have progressed to the point it had before their differences became insupportable. Understanding what made a person the way he was meant getting to know that person better, getting to care about him. She'd never made that effort with Roger. It was a luxury her job and her life-style didn't allow.

Most surprising of all was how often in the hours since Clay had left she'd found herself standing at the wide windows listening for the sound of his return. And not just because he might be bringing Fayette home.

It bothered her that she'd allowed Clay to become so important to her in the short time they'd spent together. She wasn't sure she liked the speed with which her feelings for him had grown. She had known Roger for months before their relationship became at all personal. Already, she liked Clay far too much ever to pigeonhole him in an out-of-the-way corner of her thoughts as she always had done with Roger.

"Hey! You the lady doctor they've been talking about all over the Point?" A wizened old man with wisps of gray-white hair stood in the doorway staring at her. His face was as ruddy and wrinkled as her apple would be if she allowed it to sit out on the counter for a couple of weeks. The top of his head came to about her shoulder. His stooped, shuffling gait and shabby ticking coveralls made him look even smaller and older than he was. "Name's Horatio Alger Gibbs. My dish is busted."

"I'm sorry to hear that," Jenna answered politely, hiding a grin of puzzled amusement behind another bite of apple. His dish was broken? Couldn't the poor man afford more than one plate to eat from?

"Need to use the phone," he rattled on. "Got to get some help."

"Perhaps we have something here you can use. There's plenty of paper ware over on that shelf." Jenna pointed helpfully with the core of her apple to the high-stacked assortment of staple goods that ran back to the far wall. "I'll help you look."

"Dagnab it, woman. What good will paper plates do me? My Darkstar 1000 satellite receiver dish is on the fritz, I tell you. I can't watch the National League play-offs if I don't get it fixed pronto." He shook his head as if she were even more dense than he'd expected a female to be. "I need to use the phone to call the repairman."

"It's over there," Jenna managed to say. His satellite receiver? The computer age had indeed made it as far as Lake of the Woods.

"Know where the phone is, missy. Been in the same spot these twenty-five years past." Horatio cocked his bullet-shaped head, his beady black eyes taking in her jeans-and-gray-sweatshirt-clad figure. "My oldest boy. He bought the gadget for me for Father's Day," he elaborated with a grin. "Must say it was one of his better ideas. 'Course when the electric goes off, my little one-horse generator can't pull it. But that ain't too often anymore since they buried the cable. Didn't mean to snap at you, missy. But I've been a Cubbies fan for thirty years. They almost made it all the way last season. This is gonna be our year, you know. You like baseball?" He hooked his thumbs around the straps of his venerable Oshkosh overalls.

"I'm a Reds fan myself," Jenna acknowledged.

"Cincy? Too bad," the old man muttered, digging in the pockets of his overalls for a coin. "Ain't never been the same since Johnny Bench's knees gave out."

"But we've got Pete Rose back," Jenna called down the aisle as he headed to the phone. She was enjoying the acerbic old gent, now that she was over her initial bewilderment at his unexpected appearance in the quiet store.

"Too late," the words floated back down the row. "Too late."

Jenna was afraid he might be right. Her Reds were having another so-so year.

"KNHW 515 Amber Base to KYZX 777 Store Base, come in, please." Jenna glanced in dismay at the complicated-looking two-way radio receiver on the walnut desk in the corner behind the counter. "Store Base, do you read me? Come in, please."

"That's Myrtle Langley." Leah Singer's melodious Georgia accent filled the room. "Just pick up the receiver, Jenna, and answer her by pressing the button. There." She pointed to a switch on the machine. "She'll do all the talking."

Jenna smiled in gratitude and welcome. She waved at Cassie as the little girl danced into the store behind her mother, letting the old-fashioned wooden screened door slam shut with a bang. "I'll give it a try," Jenna said, thumbing the mike. "This is Store Base, Mrs. Langley. What can I do for you?"

"Who's this?" The metallic intonation in the woman's voice gave Jenna's unseen caller a distinctly menacing sound.

She introduced herself. "I'm Fayette Macklin's granddaughter. I believe we met some years ago when I visited." Jenna vaguely recalled a short, dumpy woman with improbably red hair and orthopedic shoes.

"Oh, yes. The woman doctor." She made the title sound faintly distasteful. Or perhaps it was merely the distortion of the radio. "I need to talk to Clay Thornton. Where is he? Out looking for that gadabout grandmother of yours, I'll reckon. That woman should learn to act her age."

"Clay is away from the store at the moment," Jenna revealed, choosing not to reply to the barbed comments on her grandmother's behavior. "He's been gone for several hours."

"I didn't get my pension check in the mail today. I didn't get my mail, period! I want to know where it is! That Hiram Walker is a disgrace to the U.S. mail. It's high time he retired." Jenna glanced helplessly toward Leah.

"Tell her you'll call Oakhelm and see what's holding up the mail boat. She's lonely, poor old thing, since her husband died and her children moved downstate." Leah's lovely deep blue eyes smiled into Jenna's bewildered gaze.

"Uh...Mrs. Langley, the mail boat must be held up. We

haven't received any mail here at the store today, either. I'm sure your check will be here before too much longer. Just be a little patient." She'd almost forgotten that the residents of Buffalo Point received their mail by a water carrier, the same as the Thayers had in *On Golden Pond*. Jenna switched into her working voice pattern unconsciously. She caught herself and smiled. She wasn't sure the practiced reassurances would even carry over the airwaves.

"Well, if you say so," Mrs. Langley said, but she didn't sound convinced. "But be sure and tell Clay when he gets back," the querulous voice admonished. "I can't be going without my pension."

"Of course not, Mrs. Langley. I won't forget, I promise."

"Amber Base, out." The machine clicked off.

"Store Base, clear," Leah prompted.

Jenna depressed the button a final time, signing off. "Whew, what a day!"

"Most likely she was more interested in her soap-opera magazines than her pension check. Jacob Langley left her pretty well off, croaking when he did and gittin' double indemnity on his life insurance." Horatio Gibbs must have reached his repairman. He looked in much better spirits despite his caustic observations about his neighbor. "Good afternoon, Mrs. Singer. Howdy, little Cassie." He touched a grimy finger to his forehead in salute.

"Hi, Horatio," Cassie warbled, her nose pressed against an antique glass case filled with candy bars and bubble gum. "I didn't have to go to kindergarten today because the boat's got engine trouble."

"She does? Pity. Well, maybe you can tell your dad to speed up his repairs. My dish is on the fritz and the fix-it man will be coming out tomorrow. Don't want him to have to swim, do we?"

"No. It's way too far," Cassie replied with a five-year-old's literal interpretation of the remark. "Except if he was Jesus and walked on the water like it says in my Sunday school book."

"Now that would be a sight to see," Horatio cackled. "I could use a little miracle of my own about now. It'll cost me an arm and a leg to git this dadblamed thing fixed. But it'll be worth it to see my Cubbies win the pennant. I'd best be gittin' along. Nice to meet you, Doc. Welcome to Buffalo Point. Hope that gallivantin' grandmother of yours gits back in one piece. And brings Harm Thornton along with her." He laughed again, shuffling through the door to disappear down the steps leading to the shore path.

"Good grief!" Jenna burst out laughing. Leah joined in after a moment, but her merriment was only surface-deep. Her blue eyes remained shadowed with a private sorrow.

"How about a walk and some fresh air? We're all coming out of hibernation around here after the rain." Leah spread her hands in a gesture that encompassed the store, the radio receiver and a tail-end glimpse of Horatio Gibbs. "We can walk out along the Point. You'll never be out of sight of the front door if anyone should come along and want something."

"Sounds marvelous. I'm getting cabin fever, being shut up in here. How did you learn I was staying with Clay?" That had been one of the nice things about the continuing bad weather—there had been few distractions for Jenna to cope with. She'd slept most of the time when she wasn't with Clay.

"He called up and asked us to keep an eye on you today."

"He must be worried that a city girl like me won't be able to cope with all the solitude." A trill of laughter bubbled up and spilled out of her throat. It felt good to laugh about it. Up until a few days ago, the thought of too much solitude would have sent her running in fear.

"Exactly. Locke and Clay think alike a lot of the time. We've been here nearly a year, and Locke still honestly can't believe I'm not pining away for the bright lights and nightlife of Atlanta. Men—they're mighty hard to deal with sometimes."

"It's not easy for them, I suppose," Jenna answered thoughtfully. "Just think about it. They've been conditioned by thousands of years of hunter's instinct to be provider and protector. Now, boom! They're faced with 'women of the eighties,' as all the magazine articles and pop psychologists insist on describing us.''

"I never considered it from that point of view. It makes sense, in a way," Leah responded.

Jenna frowned down at the door handle. "Shall I lock up?" she asked, undecided as to procedure.

"No need. I'm not much for climbing over rocks anymore, anyway. But I thought you might like to go a short way out on the Point, though, and take in the sun. It'll be headin' south for the winter soon enough."

"Autumn is just around the corner." Already, here and there trees were starting to shed their red and gold leaves. Fortunately, the weather was still unseasonably warm. Leah commented on the fact and Jenna nodded in agreement. "Did you find winter hard up here after having spent most of your life in the South?"

"It was long," Leah admitted with a wry twist of her full carmine mouth. "But beautiful, too. Pristine, quiet and so peaceful. One night we even heard wolves calling out over the ice. Do you know how rare timber wolves are, even up here? And we found plenty of ways to keep busy." She blushed enchantingly and patted the smooth bulge of her stomach.

"Something to do when the wind blows five days straight and the snow is up to the eaves?" Jenna remarked absently.

"I beg your pardon?"

"Nothing, just something Clay said about the weather."

"It was nice having Locke to myself. We never had much time together to be alone when we lived in Atlanta. My family is very active socially, very protective and set in their ways. I'm afraid that made it hard for Locke to feel accepted. My momma just about had a fit when we decided to move up here. I was pretty much a puny, sickly little thing when I was a girl...Northern Minnesota seems as far away as the North Pole to her. I guess she just can't believe this is where I really want to be." She paused as if uncertain how much to confide in

Jenna. "Locke works so hard to prove to them that I made the right choice."

Jenna remained quiet, looking out over the water, saddened by the revelation of problems crowding in on Leah and Locke that dated back to the very beginning of their time together.

Evidently Leah found the opportunity to talk to another woman, as a friend, too tempting to pass up. She took a deep breath, overcoming with an effort the natural reticence that was so much a part of her character. She smiled shyly, enchantingly, and as she continued to speak, Jenna felt a small, warming glow creep over her heart at this sign of Leah's confidence in her, because she knew instinctively that Leah was talking to Jenna, the woman, not the doctor.

"Living here isn't easy, Jenna. Locke works even harder than he did back in Atlanta. He drives himself to provide the best living he can for Cassie and me. Now that the baby's coming, he worries about me even more, and he shouldn't. I'm healthy as a horse. But if Hiram Walker does retire soon, we'll be in a very good position to pick up the mail contract. That will help; it will take the pressure off." She stopped speaking for a moment, and her gaze seemed focused on nothing in particular.

Jenna wondered if Leah even recognized the telltale, wistful emphasis she'd placed on her last utterance. Leah wanted very much that Locke consider her a partner in his life; it didn't take a great deal of special insight to discern that.

Abruptly Leah shook off the reverie and began to speak again. "You knew Locke as a boy. What was he like? Was he always so serious, so protective?"

They scrambled over one or two more huge boulders worn smooth by the ceaseless action of wind and waves, while Jenna considered her answer. She watched Leah's daughter scamper on ahead, jumping over water-filled crevasses and clambering over every obstacle in her path.

"Not that serious, but it comes to all of us with age and responsibility. He was fun—my summer brother, taking the place of the one I never had. He taught me to belly flop and to bait my own hook, telling me I'd have to get used to touching uglier things than a worm if I wanted to be a doctor. And, of course, he was right. He usually was," Jenna said with a laugh, remembering. "Yes, I guess you'd call him the typical big brother: half bully, half superhero." She smiled again, shivering at the hazy memory of more than once following Locke helter-skelter into the icy water of the lake far too early in the season, only because he'd called her a chicken. "He taught me to skip stones on the water and to spit with great accuracy. That I can assure you is not part of the curriculum at Mrs. Arthur Pettry's School for Girls! I was a lonely kid and he was good for me," Jenna concluded.

"He's good for me, too. But sometimes I wish…" Leah didn't finish the sentence. "Go on, Jenna. He's the fifth child of eight, you know, so my mother-in-law declares she could never single him out of the pack."

Jenna sifted through times past for a moment in her mind's eye. "He was an adventuresome boy but he took all his responsibilities seriously. I only spent my summers here, so I don't know what he was like in school."

"He wasn't a very good student; he's the first to admit that," Leah revealed. "But he reads voraciously. He's interested in everything that goes on in the world. I think Cassie's already catching the bug from him. She makes me read *Babar the Elephant* at least twice a day." She shook her head. "I've spent years of my life studying this subject or that, and I feel I don't know half the things he does." Pride shone from her deep blue eyes. "Except for keeping business records, I'm pretty helpless, actually. That's one place I do shine." Her soft Georgia accent had taken on a soulful quality. "It's one area of our life where I feel I contribute my share. I do all the bookkeeping for Locke's business and for Clay and his father, too."

"Believe me, if you were as inept as I am with finances, you'd realize it's a great accomplishment." Jenna grinned, but her tone was serious as she offered a hand to help her less agile companion over a rocky crater. "I'd make a shambles of my own practice if I had to worry about the paperwork as well as the patients.''

"We'd make a good team. I take after my daddy's family, businessmen born and bred. If only Locke could see that side of me,'' Leah burst out with sudden ferocity. "Between him and Momma, you'd think I was some kind of porcelain doll that might fall off the shelf and break into a thousand pieces. But I'm not. Where is that child of mine?'' Leah changed the subject too quickly to bring off the casual tone she affected.

"Imitating a mountain goat,'' Jenna observed, shielding her eyes with her hand to watch the little girl at play. Sunlight sparkled off whitecaps at the base of the rocks, fragmenting into prisms of rainbow-tinted spray so bright that it hurt the eyes. She could understand, now, at least part of the problem weighing on Locke and Leah. A pampered and protected childhood hadn't lessened Leah's need to search for an identity of her own, to want to be an equal partner in sharing all the good and not-so-good aspects of a relationship. Jenna hoped that Locke would recognize that important fact before it was too late for them, or that Leah would be able to overcome her natural shyness and her retiring personality enough to make her wishes known to him more clearly.

"She and Locke are two of a kind, barely still a moment. Cassie!'' Leah raised her voice to carry over the splash and gurgle of the waves. "Don't go any farther, honey. Stay here, close by.''

"This is marvelous.'' Jenna sat down and leaned her back against a sheltering rock. She wondered vaguely what Leah's first marriage had been like, but put the thought from her mind. It was none of her business. Leah had gone on to make a new life for herself and her daughter. All it did point out, perhaps, was that even the greatest material advantages didn't guarantee happiness.

Leah gingerly lowered herself onto a higher ledge more slowly than Jenna had. Above them gulls circled and called out in the blue September sky. Jenna took a deep breath of the pine-and-lake-water-scented air. She watched several fat white clouds with dark edges sail by, for all the world like old ladies with soiled petticoats.

"I'd forgotten how addictive this place can be," Jenna said. "I've only been here for short visits since college. It's no wonder that my grandmother never went back to her life in Chicago."

"The view from every window in our house almost makes up for all the other inconveniences of living so far from everything." Leah's musical voice was low and less strained now, as though the reminiscences of Locke's boyhood had brought her momentary peace. Jenna hoped she'd gauged the other woman's mood correctly, for she cared for Locke and always had. She was coming to value Leah as a new friend and she didn't want to see either of them in pain.

"Sort of like Walden Pond," Jenna said, recalling Clay's comment.

"In some ways it is," Leah responded seriously. "And in some ways it's much harder than life back in Atlanta. There isn't all the posturing, the outward emphasis on material success and on being successful. But the stress is here also. It's just channeled in different directions, less apparent directions. Little things—political disagreements, personal opinions—they assume more importance than they actually deserve. But when you need someone, you aren't surrounded by a bunch of strangers walled up in separate concrete cells, like a hive of urban bees. People are here for you. I believe it's much easier to sort out what is truly important, and what is only important today, when you're as close to God and the elements as we are here."

Leah laughed, giving a stilted little shrug of her shoulders, lifting the wide, gathered sleeves of her silky white knit top. She wore it with deep red linen slacks that managed to give her a look of classic elegance despite her advanced state of pregnancy.

Suddenly Jenna felt underdressed in her jeans and gray sweatshirt. She tugged at her sleeve, laughing privately at her momentary spurt of feminine overreaction.

Leah caught the tag end of Jenna's smile from the corner of

her eye. "I'm sorry to have bored you with my half-baked philosophies," she apologized quickly, with a diffidence Jenna recognized as characteristic. "Locke's reading is rubbing off on me, I suppose. It's another consequence of living up here: too much time to think and too much of a temptation to talk your head off when you have an audience." There was a brittle quality to the last words that sent a shiver down Jenna's spine. There was steel beneath Leah's Southern belle facade. Perhaps even she didn't recognize its existence in herself as yet, but someday she would.

"It does take a special kind of individualism to make a success of living on the lake," Jenna agreed, although she didn't quite know how to answer Leah's remark, or if the other woman even expected an answer to her musings.

"Locke's always belonged to the wilderness by birth and temperament," Leah continued, studying her fingernails. The nails were bitten short, out of keeping with the rest of her sophisticated, salon-styled appearance. "Clay and Harmon, even your grandmother, are all transplants but they are all the same breed. They work hard; they're independent and successful. They've found what all the rest of us would give a fortune to possess." She lifted her hands helplessly, as if putting her feelings into words wasn't something that came easily. Jenna nodded in encouragement. Leah watched her companion closely for a reaction as she struggled to express herself.

"I understand to a certain extent," Jenna answered with equal candor. "It's hard for them to accept that others can make the same choices, can come to love this place, find contentment and lifelong challenges as surely as they did. It's a very private thing. I don't know how to explain it more plainly." She'd been having thoughts of her own along those lines. Perhaps that was why she could put them into spoken language so readily. For the first time in years she'd had the leisure and the opportunity to analyze her own desires for the future. She hadn't wanted to entertain such thoughts at first, but they'd come unbidden and refused to be displaced. The answers she was coming up with were embryonic still—and unexpected, to say the least. One word kept repeating itself in her mind with the regularity of waves breaking at her feet. *Stay. Stay.*

Suddenly the drone of a plane's engine cut across the soughing rush of wind among the birches. "It's Clay!" Cassie's shrill, high-pitched squeal carried clearly across the water. "I'm waving Mommy, do you see? Do you think he'll wave back?" To the child's delight the wings of the streamlined craft dipped in response. Cassie clapped her hands excitedly but then clamped them over her ears to shut out the roar of the plane's push-prop engine.

Jenna laced her fingers around her upraised knee, watching with interest as Clay brought his plane in for a smooth landing about three hundred yards out on the lake and taxied slowly toward the pier. Outwardly composed, Jenna strained to catch a glimpse of faces at the windows. Only Frieda's floppy-eared silhouette was discernible. Jenna was disappointed. There was no sign of her grandmother or Clay's father. The always present worry for Fayette's safety wiggled out of the tightly sealed corner of her brain where she kept it shut away as much as possible. Where were they? Were they safe and well? When would they return?

Jenna jumped up from the rock to cut off the refrain inside her head. Reaching out a hand, she helped Leah struggle to her feet. "That gets to be more of an engineering feat every time I try it. Thanks for the help, Jenna," she said shyly. Her smile this time was rich and full; the shadows of worry and strain had retreated farther behind her arresting blue eyes, leaving them clear and bright.

"What are friends for?" Jenna quipped, surprised at the genuine rush of pleasure she gained from thinking of Leah as her friend. Women friends were a luxury she did not have time for in the male-dominated world she moved in.

"Friends," Leah repeated simply. She turned to hold her hand out to Cassie. "Come on, honey. We'll say hello to Clay and then we'll have to be getting on home. It's turning late. Daddy will worry."

The words were no sooner out of her mouth than a well-preserved Chris Craft speedboat raced around the far point and headed into the pier. Locke threw the lines over the wooden uprights and strode over to speak to Clay as he checked the tie-downs on his plane. Jenna could see Clay shake his dark head and surmised, with a dart of pain, that Locke had asked about his father and Fayette and received a negative answer. Again the frisson of unease skittered across her skin, but she pushed it ruthlessly back into the shadows where it belonged.

"Daddy! We're over here," Cassie called, obviously tired of being unnoticed by her stepfather. "We're visiting Jenna for the afternoon," she lisped with charming old-South formality. "We've had a lovely time." She bent to throw her arms around Frieda who'd ambled unconcernedly up from the plane after inspecting Clay's procedures with a critical eye. She licked Cassie's face in friendly but restrained greeting.

"I'm glad, pumpkin." Locke swung the child up over his head. Jenna laughed in sympathetic recognition of the heady little-girl thrill of being swung high in the air and safely brought to earth again by someone tall and strong, loved and trusted.

"Do it again!" Cassie begged. Locke obliged and then set his stepdaughter firmly on the ground. "You do it, too, Clay, please," she wheedled but Clay shook his head.

"Only daddies are allowed to swing little girls so high in the sky. It's the law. But I'll give you a piggyback ride up to the house. How's that?" Cassie nodded enthusiastically and Clay hoisted her effortlessly up onto his broad shoulders. Her slight weight pulled the poplin fabric of his rust-colored jacket tightly across the muscled expanse of his back. Jenna swallowed against a sudden tightness in her throat. She'd missed him.

"No sign of them?" she asked quietly.

"None." His eyes mirrored her own disappointment.

"Leah." Locke's voice cut across the silence that had fallen on the group. He covered the few steps that separated him from his wife in the space of a heartbeat. He reached out to cup her face in his hands and study her features worriedly. "I thought we agreed you wouldn't exert yourself like this so close to the baby's coming. You should have stayed at home, gotten your rest." He turned his head toward Jenna, running his blunt fingers agitatedly through his thinning blond curls, his tone slightly distracted. "Leah lost a baby—" he hesitated, glancing in her direction once more "—near the end of her first marriage. We don't want that to happen again."

"Locke." Leah's slender hands clenched at her side. "We've been over this and over this. I'm fine. That was a long time ago. The doctors told you that just last week when we went to the county clinic for my checkup." She lifted her hand as if to reassure Locke with her touch, then thought better of the idea. "Our baby," she placed the emphasis on the pronoun so quietly that Jenna wondered if the others even heard, "isn't due for another four weeks. You can't expect me to behave like an invalid. I have far too many things to do." There was a tightness around her mouth that made her look spoiled and petulant, but Jenna guessed that she was only miserably unhappy.

"And if you overexert yourself—" Locke's attitude toward Leah's pronouncement wasn't much different from the way he treated Cassie "—I'll have Jason and Maria to answer to." His light, teasing tone didn't mesh well with the hurt, unhappy look in his eyes.

This is where I came in, Jenna thought resignedly. The Singers were locked into parallel courses; they talked, they listened, but they didn't understand each other. Leah was a grown woman, capable of contributing a great deal to her relationship with Locke, but she lacked the confidence to assert herself. And Locke seemed caught up in a pattern of overprotective behavior that was just as destructive to them both.

She glanced across the few yards that separated her from Clay. His warm gaze snagged with hers. He felt the same way, as they felt the same way about so many things. There was compassion and resignation in that look. Clay didn't expect his friends' marriage to survive.

Jenna felt it, too, the anxiety, the sadness in the air between Locke and Leah. Clay could sense her instinctive reading of the situation. She was aware that the marriage was in trouble. Yet not because of the same reasons that he was, surely? There wasn't any cause for her to transpose the incredible stress such divergent backgrounds had placed on the Singers' relationship into the context of any developing involvement between them.

Clay had been hurt so badly by the breakup of his marriage that he could only see Locke and Leah's troubles in the light of his own experience. He'd tried to build a life with Joann, to merge two careers, two differing life-styles and to hold it all together with love. It hadn't worked for them. It wasn't working for his friends. He couldn't believe, didn't dare believe that it might be different if he tried again with Jenna. He was beginning to care a great deal for this remarkable woman.

But he couldn't let himself forget that loving sometimes wasn't enough.

Chapter Five

"Why don't you three stay for supper," Clay invited hurriedly, to turn the course of his thoughts. He wasn't sure how his resolve to remain aloof from his feelings would stand up to another night alone in Jenna's company. He didn't want to do something he'd regret, something that would rush both of them down a path where they might not want to go. She was so easy to talk to, so easy to be silent with, so bright, inquisitive, sensitive. All the things he wanted in a woman, a friend, a lover. "I've got all the makings for curried-lamb-and-snow-peas in the freezer."

"Ugh," Cassie grumbled, leaning her small pointed chin on both hands while resting them on top of Clay's dark head. "Sounds yucky."

"How about a hamburger and fries for you, squirt?"

"Big Mac, Big Mac," Cassie hollered in delight, bouncing on Clay's shoulders. It didn't matter that the nearest fast-food restaurant, like the clinic, was an hour's flying time away.

"One Big Mac coming up," Clay promised. The tension in the group diminished.

Leah smiled at Cassie and turned her head to look over at her husband. She put a small delicate hand on Locke's teak-dark arm. "I'd like to spend the evening with Jenna and Clay very much." Locke hesitated a long moment, searching her features. Leah dropped her blue-velvet eyes to watch the stony ground.

"You're not too tired?" It was apparent Locke didn't see how constraining his solicitude was for Leah. How much longer could he continue treating her like a child before she rebelled?

"I'm fine." There was a hint of asperity quickly masked by Leah's melting smile. "Really I am, Locke."

"I'd like to stay myself." He smiled in return, reaching out to help her along the path. The confused emotion in his brown eyes was stark and almost painful to see. Jenna turned her head away, her eyes catching Clay's gaze for a long moment.

"We might even get in a game of Scrabble." Leah hadn't seen Locke's conciliatory gesture. She had turned her back on her husband to follow Jenna along the path.

IT WAS THE MOST pleasant evening Jenna had spent in ages. Clay's dinner was excellent. Locke and Leah were quiet but seemingly content. After the meal Jenna and Leah laughingly agreed to put aside their feminist principles and do the dishes while the two men saw to evening chores around the compound. Outside the kitchen window a happy Cassie tumbled around on the lawn with Frieda. Jenna and Leah continued to work steadily as they loaded the dishwasher and cleared off the countertops. Jenna even picked up a broom and swept the brick-patterned vinyl floor. They didn't talk a great deal. When they did, it wasn't of any earth-shattering subject, but only of things that have been close to women's hearts for countless ages past.

It wasn't until much later that Jenna would look back and decide that the conversation had sown the seeds of her future dreams. They discussed fashion trends, in which Jenna wasn't interested and Leah was. They spoke of favorite recipes, books and movies, babies and the logistics involved in getting Leah to her obstetric visits at the county clinic seventy-five miles away. After the men returned, they added sports and the weather to the agenda, but nothing more complex.

Over dessert and coffee Jenna was coaxed into telling a little about her work at the Trauma Center. She tailored her anecdotes to her audience, shying away from anything maudlin or tragic, ignoring the aching frustration and guilt she always felt when they had all worked so hard to save a patient, yet had to watch helplessly as a life slipped away. She concentrated instead on the foibles and eccentricities encountered in supervising a large and divergent medical team and the people they served.

During a hotly contested Scrabble match, Locke and Clay inserted several funny and risqué anecdotes about the inhabitants of Buffalo Point in an unsuccessful attempt to throw Leah and Jenna off their game. It didn't work. Leah won the contest, with Jenna only a few points behind.

"I'd have beaten you all if I could have gotten rid of that *Q*," Locke insisted, wrapping a sleepy Cassie in the soft Popsicle-green jacket she'd worn that afternoon. "So don't get too cocky." The last of a blue-and-mauve sunset was fading away over the western basin of the glacial lake when the Singers made their way home.

The intruding roar of the Chris Craft's engine died away. Silence returned to Lake of the Woods. Even the breeze was a mere whisper in the twilight. Far out on the bay a loon called. The haunting, melancholy cry twisted something deeply primitive within Clay's soul. He reached out unthinkingly, letting his arms settle on Jenna's shoulders as she stood one riser below him on the porch steps. Her skin was warm beneath the soft raspberry-pink velour of the man-styled shirt she'd changed into for dinner. "Hear that?" he asked softly.

"No. What is it? I was watching the lights come on across the water." The rest of the world seemed very far away. Her voice was low and quiet, matching his mood of wistful fancy, echoing the silence all around them.

The loon's mate answered the waveringly haunting cry. "There, do you hear it now? They sound like a pair of lost souls in search of each other."

"I used to hate that sound when I was a little girl visiting Gram. I couldn't believe they were only birds. I was sure they were Indian ghosts or demons, laughing in torment. But now

it's different, beautiful and eerie. They sound as if they belong." *And I'm beginning to want to belong here, too,* Jenna
surprised herself by concluding.

"Would you like to sit out here on the porch, or is it too
chilly?" Clay's voice was dark and low above her head. Jenna
shivered, too, but not from the cool night air.

"Myrtle Langley didn't get her mail this afternoon," Jenna
said, searching for the most commonplace subject she could
find to help alleviate the sensual undercurrent his touch stirred
within her.

"Locke told me Hiram Walker had engine trouble again,"
Clay replied. "It's about time for him to retire. Locke's going
to bid on the mail contract when it comes up again in the new
year. He'll get it with any luck, and then the freighting end of
the business will be in pretty good shape."

"I'm pleased for both of you." She moved restlessly beside
him.

"There's going to be a moon." Stick to the mundane, Clay
told himself.

"And the mosquitoes seem to have called it a night." Jenna
reached up, resting her hand on Clay's where it dangled over
the curve of her breasts. He pulled away.

Jenna turned quickly enough to see Clay blink in surprise,
as if he hadn't been aware that he was touching her so intimately. "I'll share the hammock with you. Come on, there's
room for two." Perhaps it was the flash of uncertainty in Clay's
eyes that gave Jenna the courage to take the initiative. All she
knew was that she would very much like to feel Clay's arms
around her. She held out her hand, and he folded his big rough
palm around it, leading the way along the weathered veranda
to a large rope hammock at the end.

"Wait. Me first," Clay ordered. What the hell? He wasn't
going to fight what he felt any longer. It was a fantasy of his—
a quiet night like this, good food, good friends and a beautiful,
loving woman to share the end of a busy day. He sat down,
swinging his long, denim-covered legs up into the hammock's

folds. "Come here. Getting two people into one of these things requires a master's touch."

Jenna hesitated a fraction of a second. Suddenly she wanted very much to be close to his lean, strong body, to feel comforted, safe and protected, with the world held at bay by the cherishing circle of his arms. She wanted to be able to share the little things that made life so good. She settled gingerly at his side. The hammock dipped and swayed, then steadied into an even, slow swing. Clay's arms came out to gather her closer still. Her head rested just below his chin. Jenna put a hand on his chest to steady herself. Beneath the light beige wool of his crew-neck sweater she could feel the springy roughness of dark curling hair and, deeper still, his heartbeat, slow and strong.

"You did that very well. Do you bring a lot of ladies out here to swing?" she teased in a voice that should have been a shade less tremulous to hit just the right light note.

"One or two. There isn't a surplus up here, you know. Few and far between," Clay grunted, matching her facetiousness and missing by the same slim margin. "Are you fishing for details of my love life, Doctor?" He hadn't had much of a love life, or a sex life for that matter, the past few years. Until Jenna came into the picture, he hadn't really cared, but now he did. All at once he wanted her to know how much this moment meant to him. Longings and stirrings in his blood that had been dormant since his divorce were coming back painfully to life.

"I'd never subject you to that personal an interrogation," Jenna protested righteously. "It's been a good day," she said a bit dreamily. "I met a couple of your neighbors. I already told you about Myrtle Langley, remember? Then Leah and I had a long woman-to-woman talk. I can't recall the last time I expended so many words on non-medical subjects. There is life beyond the Trauma Center. Now all we have to do is get those two wandering senior citizens back home safely."

"Would you like to come up with Frieda and me again tomorrow?"

"But what about the store?" Idly she traced a pattern with the tip of her finger on his chest.

"We'll close it up for a few hours; business is slow this time of year, anyway." Clay shifted his position abruptly, covering her wandering hand with his own much larger one. His voice was husky with suppressed emotion.

"Well, it would make me feel as if I'm doing something constructive to find them." She fell silent as his lips brushed the hair above her ear so slightly she couldn't be sure it was meant as a caress at all.

"That's important to you, isn't it, Jenna?" Clay murmured against her hair. "Being needed."

She nodded, shivering slightly with the sensual shock of his light caress. They fell silent again as the loons called a last good-night. "They've found each other," Jenna murmured under her breath. Frieda snored in her sleep beneath the hammock, where she'd flopped down seconds after they had settled into its woven-cotton folds. Perhaps she was chasing rabbits in her dreams. Perhaps she was being chased by an energetic five-year-old. "I think I could get used to this domesticity very easily," Jenna said in a sleepy whisper a few minutes later.

"I know, it's addictive." Clay tried not to let his thoughts seep into words. Her observation meshed so closely with what he felt. He found himself speaking of his marriage again despite the inner warnings of his intellect, working through some of his own unresolved feelings in the quiet intimacy they shared.

"Joann and I never had this kind of evening when we were married—and that was nearly five years. Our schedules didn't allow it. I'd take a commercial flight to Kennedy and pick up my plane, a DC-10 usually. Then it was on to Miami, back to Atlanta, then St. Louis, Dallas, and Miami again. Last leg was back to Kennedy and then catch a flight home to New Orleans. If I did make it in for the weekend, she was always involved in some big party or another that her restaurant was catering. During the week…"

Jenna wasn't sleepy anymore. She felt the shrug of his broad shoulders beneath her cheek. He was telling her something she instinctively understood that he'd never spoken of to anyone before. She listened quietly, realizing this was how her life with Roger would have turned out. Separate lives joined only by habit and convenience.

"Well, if I did make it home, she was usually busy with problems at the restaurant. At the end we were just two strangers sharing a house."

"Sometimes no matter how hard you try, it doesn't work." Jenna's tone was soothing, gentle and tempered by her own recollections of her time with Roger.

Clay grunted a noncommittal reply. Conflicting schedules, a lack of communication and differing goals were real problems in his marriage. And Joann had hated his flying. He'd learned early on not to tell her anything about his work. That had sown the seeds of silence. Whenever there had been a hijacking, a near miss caused by an overworked air traffic controller, or, worst of all, a plane crash anywhere in the world, it only drove Joann farther from him. He couldn't talk her out of the phobia, and after a while, he quit trying.

Would Jenna understand that it had been those accumulating tensions, that diversity of thought and feeling, as well as a lack of time together, that had driven a wedge so deep into his marriage that it had finally split in two?

"Perhaps if she'd come up here with you?" Jenna lifted her eyes to watch his face in the fading light. A dull amber glow from the western sky cast his sharply angled features into silhouette. He turned his head to look down at her, effectively hiding his expression in his own shadow. "There was no way I could have brought a woman like Joann to live here." His voice was harsh and uncompromising. Was it from pain or anger? Jenna didn't know. "She would never have left her restaurant, her career. She would have been as miserable and out of her element as Leah—" He broke off abruptly, leaving her own name unspoken at the end of the sentence.

Jenna stiffened beside him. Clay wasn't sorry he'd said what he did. Always in the back of his mind there'd been the gnawing, unanswerable question. If he'd left commercial flying before he did, could he have done something to save his marriage? From the standpoint of time and hindsight, he'd decided it wouldn't have been the answer. But it didn't change how he felt now. "I've been watching my friends' marriage disintegrate before my very eyes. It's hell; I've been there. And there isn't a thing I can do to help them."

"It could make a difference when the baby is born." Jenna paused. "Not that I mean a baby will be able to save their relationship if it's truly on the rocks. But it could ease some of the strain. Locke spoke of a former miscarriage...."

"He's worried sick about Leah," Clay agreed. His fingers traced over the pattern of blue veins on the inside of her wrist. The touch of his hand was warming, sending little shock waves of sensation streaking along her veins. "Her parents don't help the situation. They're at him constantly to get her back to Atlanta, where they can bring in the best specialists, the most expensive doctors."

"Is Leah's condition that serious?" Jenna was puzzled, her lethargy dissolved by the onslaught of professional curiosity. She forgot for a moment the exciting caress of Clay's fingers against her skin. Leah was under a great deal of strain, it was true, but she looked healthy enough and seemed to be carrying the child well. Of course, Jenna hadn't examined her, but she was confident of her expertise and judgment in medical matters.

"No, she's fine. Jason and Maria Purchase just don't want her to live here. They can't seem to let her go." Clay's voice was thoughtful, as though he hadn't seen the problem in quite that light before.

"Or forgive Locke for taking their little girl away from them," Jenna added perceptively. "And he's afraid to believe she's truly happy with the choice she's made."

"Something like that. And her parents do have a point. Leah would be better off back in Atlanta where she belongs, with her charity teas and horse shows."

"That's ridiculous," Jenna flared up in defense of her new friend. "Leah loves it here. She deserves a chance to make a success of her life. You all treat her as if she's too delicate even to be left out of doors alone." She needed to make Clay, at least, understand that too much protectiveness was strangling Leah's marriage. Jenna sat up in such a huff that the hammock rocked dangerously. She clutched frantically at Clay's sweater to keep from being pitched over the side. "Sorry." Her expression was sheepish. "I tend to get carried away sometimes."

Clay pulled her close but his arms were rock hard with tension. "Hold still, Doc. I wouldn't have you any other way."

Jenna's anger evaporated like fog in sunshine. She nestled against him, not wanting to mar further the fragile new intimacy growing between them. "It's not easy watching others suffer," she admitted in a statement that was all the more expressive for its simple matter-of-factness.

"I know." Clay groaned in the darkness as he cuddled her to him. Damn it, she felt good. He just couldn't stay mad at her. And she did have a point. Maybe it was Locke's fear that Leah couldn't make it up here that was putting undue stress on their marriage. He wrapped her in cotton wool, making it impossible for her to adjust successfully in her new life. It was something he needed to think about, but not now. Not with Jenna so close, nestled in his arms, her breast pushed against his chest, her thigh lying soft and warm along the length of his. "I'm not going to ruin my perfect, tranquil domestic evening by arguing with you." His words were low and level, but there was a hint of granite beneath his teasing. Jenna gave up her one-sided mental struggle, snuggling against him, her body betraying her intellect with its sybaritic longings.

"You can't keep treating Leah like a difficult child. She's going to break out. Or break down." Jenna wasn't sure how she'd come to that conclusion. Some diagnoses were made as much on gut instinct as medical expertise; nonetheless she felt it was a valid conclusion. Would the same thing happen to her if she tried to stay in this world—Clay's world, where she didn't as yet belong?

"I don't want to talk about Locke and Leah's problems anymore tonight. We'll do our best to help them, but not now," Clay said with sudden ferocity. His hands moved up the curve of her spine to cradle her face between his palms. His fingers tangled in her silky, silver-blond hair, sending pins flying off to land with small explosions of sound on the wooden floor of the porch. "I don't want to argue with you about anything: politics, sports, or the state of the world," he stated recklessly. "I want to kiss you. I've wanted to do that for hours. Will you let me?" His mouth was inches from hers.

Jenna watched his expression closely for several long seconds, searching for reassurance in the stormy gray of his eyes. He had known pain, as she had. She was filled with a great longing to ease his torment, to smooth away the sorrow of his past, to bury her own former demons in his arms. Closing her eyes against a thrill of longing and desire that was completely foreign to her sober, controlled image of herself, Jenna curled her arms around Clay's neck and pulled his head down to hers.

"I don't want to argue at all. I've never felt less like arguing with anyone in my entire life, Clay Thornton. I want us to be friends, not adversaries," she whispered pleadingly. "It's been a lovely evening, a lovely day. If only Gram…"

"Hush." His voice was gentle, but his hands were urgent on her skin. "We can't change that situation now. In the morning we'll do our damndest to find them again. I'll keep trying as long as necessary. You do believe me, don't you?" His lips were almost touching her temple. His breath stirred the soft hair, sending goose bumps prickling along her flesh. "I won't fail you, Jenna. But now, what's between us is more important than anything else."

He was crazy to make love to her like this, but it didn't seem to matter much at the moment. He needed to learn the touch and taste of her, to memorize the scent of her hair, the curve of her mouth and throat, the ripe fullness of her breasts. It was most important to become familiar with the erotic touch points of her body so that he could make her happy, to fulfill Jenna so that he in turn could reach fulfillment. The problems he'd foreseen for them just moments before were real and true; there was no denying them. They wouldn't dissolve like fairy smoke on the wind, just because he wanted to kiss this woman. But with her nearness working magic on his senses, anything was possible—even a long and happy future of loving and sharing, a wish and a dream that just a few short days ago he'd thought beyond his reach forever.

"I have no doubt you'll find my grandmother. And, Clay, I have no objections whatsoever to being kissed," Jenna prompted without hesitation.

"Jenna." Her name welled up from deep within him. His lips brushed over hers tentatively at first, then more boldly as she opened to his gentle, testing thrusts. After the first fleeting touch of their mouths, the last of Clay's questions died a quick, unlamented death. Her body was warm and compliant in his arms. Jenna's hands covered his as they slid beneath the cotton velour of her shirt, urging him on in his sensual exploration of her soft curves. For a moment she stiffened against the sudden boldness of his touch, then relaxed against him, trusting, desirous, a breathy little sigh escaping from low in her throat. He lifted the garment over her head and dropped it to the floor. The hammock swayed with the movement.

"You do this very well, seducing ladies in your hammock." Clay listened closely for any intonation of censure in her words and could detect none.

"Not so very many," he answered with equal candor, smoothing back loosened tendrils of stardust-colored hair from Jenna's forehead. "But it seems as if I've been waiting half my life for just this night, for just this kiss." Clay couldn't stop the flow of words. His tone held as much resignation as triumph. She was so right for him. Her breasts filled his hands perfectly, as he'd known they would. Her nipples tightened against the filmy wisp of lace bra that was all that separated his palm from their opulence. Her hips pushed against him in a pattern of desire that exactly matched the rhythm of his heart. Clay felt himself tighten with a physical need so intense that it was almost as if another man had taken control of his body, someone bolder and more aggressive, less scared in heart and soul, who would sweep every barrier from his path in order to possess the woman he loved.

Love? Was he falling in love with Jenna? For a long, sweet

moment he looked deep into the swirling gold of her hazel eyes. He let his whole being concentrate on that assumption; on the pleasure she could give him, on the passion that they could explore together.

Flashes of a future with Jenna, of having her with him, of her giving herself to him alone, made him dizzy with need. He wanted to make love to her, and with her. His fingers slid over the smooth expanse of her rib cage. He felt her shiver slightly under his touch—whether from the caress of the cool night air or from some stronger emotion he wasn't sure.

"Jenna, don't be afraid." His hands were light and gentle on her skin, but the words came out rough along the edges. He was giving her a chance to back away from their escalating intimacy, and Jenna was grateful, but it wasn't what she wanted. Yet how could she tell him that? She wasn't sure she liked the idea of her body ruling her actions so absolutely. Yet, to admit that her heart was ruling her behavior was almost as upsetting.

"I could never be afraid of you, Clay," Jenna replied with total honesty. She began to work his sweater loose from the waistband of his jeans. Her hands wandered over the lightly muscled expanse of his chest, around to the long slope of his shoulders and down to his waist. He settled his weight more firmly atop her as her bra followed her top and his sweater to the porch floor. This time their activity set the rope hammock swinging more forcefully, but Clay was kissing her again, his tongue moving inside her mouth in long sweeps, and Jenna couldn't be sure it wasn't her own heightened senses that accounted for the dizzying motion around her. She didn't care.

"Jenna." Clay rested his cheek along hers. His hand fondled her breast, his palm covering the soft roundness, shutting out the cool touch of night air, but causing a response in the shape of her nipple as quick as a breath of evening breeze. She covered his hand with her own, while the other threaded through the layers of his hair. "Do you know where we're going?" He sounded confused, happy, but still slightly lost.

"There is a logical progression to making love," Jenna answered, more boldly than she'd ever thought she could. She took her hand from over his and trailed her fingers along the hard, corded length of his thigh. "It would be very lovely to make love with you, Clay."

He sucked in his breath and pushed against her touch. It was a heady, powerful feeling to have a strong man so firmly in her control, and Jenna reveled in the sensation. She fitted her hand around him and pressed back.

"Jen! Lord, you feel good." This time there was no gentleness in Clay's kiss. Jenna felt the momentum of power return to him. He reached behind her, dragging her full against him, crushing her breasts against the roughness of his chest. He moved his knee to open her legs, and only the layers of clothing separated them from an intimate joining that Jenna desired more with each passing moment. This time their urgency set the hammock swinging so violently that Clay was forced to reach out a long arm and steady them with a hand on the porch railing. "Damn. The logical progression to making love in this thing will lead to falling out on our fannies." He chuckled, but the sound was full of frustration. Clay laid his chin against the top of Jenna's head, inhaling her light floral fragrance, fighting to steady his breathing and make some kind of coherent words leave his throat. "Jenna, you're trembling."

"So are you," she came back. Fine tremors coursed along beneath the bronze skin of his arms. Jenna smoothed her fingers along the ridges of bone and muscle and tried to get her own ragged breath under control.

"For different reasons, I think," he growled in a husky baritone. His breath was warm and smelled slightly minty. "I don't want to hurry you into an involvement that will spoil everything for us with too much haste."

"I understand." Jenna didn't *sound* as if she understood, and Clay cursed himself for not choosing his words with more care. But with her lying half-naked in his arms, he probably couldn't have found the right ones, anyway. All he really wanted to do was compare her eyes to forest pools, her lips to honeyed wine, her hair to corn silk, and he couldn't do that...not yet, anyway.

God, he was scared, scared of loving again, of failing again, and he couldn't tell her that, either. At least not in those words that would bare his soul.

"You don't have to explain anything to me, Clay. I'm just as confused by this attraction as you are." Jenna shrugged, having difficulty choosing her words also, he suspected. "We'll just blame it on the moonlight and the loon's calls." She mustered a pale imitation of her quirky, enchanting smile. Clay sat up carefully and pulled her out of the hammock with him. Jenna avoided his eyes and started to reach down for her clothes.

"No, Jenna. Please let me look at you like this, all gilded in the moonlight. Out here your skin is almost the color of your hair, did you know that?" He lowered his head to taste the rose shaded tip of her breast, and Jenna sighed, pulling his dark head closer, forgetting instantly the unhappy dart of pain his words had caused. When he lifted his head, his eyes reflected a stray beam of moonlight silvering the gray depths. "There's no blame to place. Will you believe me if I tell you I'm just not ready for this?" He shrugged and Jenna watched with fascination the play of muscles under his skin. She knew in detail how they were attached, muscle and tendon, how each and every one worked in harmony with the others to produce the movement, but never had she been so caught up by their beauty.

Clay traced a finger across her parted lips, and Jenna couldn't stop herself from kissing it. Clay took the small gesture as a sign to continue speaking. The whine of a mosquito came out of the darkness, and he drew Jenna back into his embrace, covering her with his arms, fitting her into the curve of his body. "I hadn't bargained for how strongly I've come to feel for you in just a few short days. I always thought you had to take your time falling in love. I've screwed up so badly in the past, Jenna; I just don't want to hurt you as well as myself this time." Jenna felt his hand ball into a fist against the skin of her back. "I'm not making a bit of sense, am I?"

His hesitancy, his uncertainty and his concern for her was

almost Jenna's undoing. She reached up on tiptoe and fitted her hands along the planes of his cheeks, forcing his eyes to meet hers. For once in her life she wanted to throw caution to the winds and act solely on her instincts. Her body still sang with frustration, and she felt a great longing to gather Clay into her embrace and to pull him down atop her, allowing nature to take its course, and to answer all their questions with their bodies' coming together. But she couldn't do that to him.

"I understand everything you're trying to tell me, Clay." She touched her lips lightly to his. "Thank you. I don't think anyone has ever cared so much about doing what was best for me. When you're ready, I'll be ready. There will be a time for us, I'm sure of it. And it will be good, very good." There were problems to be worked out, differences that mere physical attraction wouldn't overcome. Neither of them was the kind of person to indulge in a casual relationship.

It would be wonderful to find love with a man like Clay. He was complicated, intelligent, loving and passionate, so many of the qualities she'd instinctively searched for and knew with the same intuition that she could have never found with Roger—or any other man, perhaps, until now. Clay's love would be worth waiting for.

"You must think I'm some kind of a throwback." Clay's tone was rueful.

"I think you're a marvelous, old-fashioned kind of guy." Jenna reached up on tiptoe once again to place a quick kiss on his cheek. The scratch of day-old beard made her lips tingle pleasurably. Clay grazed his hands along her cheek, then reached down and gathered up her clothes. He helped pull her sweater back over her head, and he kissed her once more, a kiss soft and quick as a butterfly's touch. Jenna began to regain a little of her equilibrium when his eyes could no longer send across her breasts tingling caresses that were every bit as potent as the actual touch of his hands.

"It will be good for us, Jenna. I know it." Clay's words were a low, husky growl. They were a promise of joy.

"I know." She twined her fingers through his. "It's late,

Clay. I think we should call it a night.'' Her voice was wistful in the darkness.

''Sunrise is about seven.'' Clay tucked her hand under his arm to lead the way back inside the store. ''How about a flying lesson tomorrow?'' Jenna could feel the tension slacken between them, lowering the flame of desire to a pleasant simmer.

''I'll set my alarm.'' She was proud of how normal her voice sounded, for inside she was still flying along on billowy clouds of excitement and passion. It was a big step, this process of falling in love...and now, secure and desired in the strong circle of Clay's arms, she was sure she was doing just that—falling in love.

Chapter Six

The sky was blue overhead, the pale washed-out blue of too many rainy days in a row. Jenna stared up at it with narrowed eyes, her expression thoughtful and calm. "It's good to see the sun out," she said, lifting her face to its gentle warmth. She spoke idly and didn't particularly expect a response from her companion, but Leah chose to answer anyway.

"It is nice, though I don't think the rain will hold off long; it never does at this time of year. But I intend to enjoy it while I can." She held up an apple-green baby blanket she was knitting on oversize plastic needles, shielding her eyes from the sun as she scanned the lawn for a sign of Cassie's moppet form. As the child appeared around the corner of the store, shrill giggles and commands to a patiently suffering Frieda spilled from her lips. She skipped merrily into view, dragging the dog behind her, attached by a string tied around its collar.

Jenna giggled, too, at the sight of Frieda's sorely tried dignity. Leah smiled indulgently at the animal's lively captor. "I think we'll have to get her a puppy, or she'll be trying that stunt with the baby when it starts to crawl."

"Good idea. And you were right, it does feel stormy." Jenna changed the subject amicably. The air was heavy and sticky with heat and humidity. The blustery west wind mischievously picked away at Leah's needlework, but was welcome as it tugged at Jenna's hair and the tail of her mint-green shirt.

"This warm front's moving very fast, Locke says, and

there's a big cold front behind it. That means bad weather, or I haven't learned anything at all about the climate up here.''

"Do you think so?" Jenna swiveled around on the granite ledge where she was sitting. It jutted out like a ship's prow over the clear blue-green waters of the lake. The view was windswept and peaceful. She stretched full length above Leah, watching her friend's skilled fingers at work on the baby blanket. Jenna leaned her chin on her forearms, her hands curled around the simple piece of red garter stitch that might—or might not—someday be a scarf, depending on whether or not she ever learned to knit successfully. She couldn't remember the last time she'd had the leisure to pursue any type of craft or needlework. It was interesting and relaxing, but at the moment her attention was on the weather. Low on the horizon she could see a mass of dark clouds that seemed to grow larger by the moment.

"Damn! I told Cassie the weather gods had cursed me. Now I'm beginning to believe it myself." She gave the skein of red yarn a jerk. "I wish my grandmother would come home."

"This weather has held up her plans, too, I'm sure. You and Clay only managed two afternoons of searching. She's probably holed up in some camp somewhere, also. Give her some credit, Jenna. She just didn't walk off into the bush half-cocked." Leah's tone was firm and edged with something close to impatience. Jenna twisted her head to be sure she'd gauged her companion's intonation correctly. Leah's head was bent stiffly over her work, her hands tense on the pastel-colored yarn. She refused to meet Jenna's inquisitive gaze.

"I don't mean to imply that my grandmother's incapable."

"Didn't you?" Leah questioned softly. "You and Clay both act as if Faye and Harmon were suffering from advanced senility and had wandered away from their keepers."

"She's seventy-four years old," Jenna responded with a flush of mortification. She *had* implied as much. It made her uncomfortable to recall her own patronizing tone. She attempted to put her unease into words. "She's probably on foot in the wilderness—"

"In country that has been her home for over thirty years,"
Leah came back firmly. "I don't mean to criticize or belittle
your concern, Jenna," Leah continued with a return of her
usual diffidence. She held out a graceful hand in a gesture of
apology. Again Jenna noted the bitten-off nails that attested to
inner stress not altogether subdued. "But Fayette is perfectly
capable of taking care of herself. So is Clay's father, despite
his medical problem, which I understand is slight. And they're
accomplishing something of value to us all while they're out
there."

"I haven't looked at it in just that way before," Jenna responded thoughtfully. She jabbed at a fault in the rock with
the tip of her knitting needle. "I've only been able to see my
grandmother's actions in terms of my own worry over her
safety. Clay and I have told ourselves time and again to stop
worrying, but it doesn't help." She gave up her prodding with
the knitting needle when Leah pulled the instrument out of her
hand with a gentle tug. There was a wry smile on Jenna's lips
as she focused her gaze on where Clay and Locke worked over
a sticky aileron on the plane's right wing. Wind, rain and mechanical problems had kept them grounded for most of the past
two days.

"I have trouble taking the broader view. I don't think Clay
has considered his father's absence in those terms, either. I
know that whatever Fayette and Harmon find out will go a
long way to resolving the issue of hunting animals from the
air. But I'm still scared to death they'll come to harm, and I've
been reacting accordingly."

"I wouldn't credit you with any other motive than acting
out of love. But loving also means giving others space to grow
and achieve in their own right." Leah folded her knitting into
the plastic bag she'd brought along on their short walk. She
surveyed Jenna's handiwork critically and then put it with her
own, giving a doubtful little shake of her head at its ragtag
appearance. "You wouldn't be the caring, sustaining woman
you are if the feelings of your heart didn't come first." That
wasn't the way Jenna saw herself, as soft and nurturing. She'd

always felt—regretfully—that her compassion was tempered and held in check by a too-generous dose of common sense. It was the armor she assumed to protect herself from too much involvement in other people's lives. But in the past few days that armor had been little protection.

Leah didn't seem to notice her preoccupation and continued talking. "Do try and remember what I've just said when Harmon and Faye return. I know the very straightforward and upright Dr. Macklin will be there to meet them. And be ready to light into them for causing us all so much worry." She smiled fleetingly, more Madonna-like than ever in a pale blue smock top, matching chambray skirt and Italian leather sandals. "They have a lot to contribute because of their years and their experience, not despite it. Let the Jenna you are today, the real Jenna, be there in her stead."

"I'll try to take your advice," Jenna returned sheepishly. She did feel like two different people sometimes and it bothered her. She wondered what it would be like to be more spontaneous, more open and vulnerable to what life had to offer. Leah's words made sense.

Jenna and Clay had tried hard to view the adventure from Fayette's point of view, but their attitude had been indulgent and almost patronizing, she was ashamed to admit. Fayette wasn't a child, nor even approaching her second childhood. She knew her limitations, both physical and practical. She wouldn't act foolishly, and, Jenna hoped, not too impulsively.

Leah felt stifled and tended to let that frustration color her judgment of other people's actions. Jenna was more than willing to rethink her own opinions. But she couldn't, on the strength of one conversation, suddenly endow her grandmother with all the logical virtues. That was asking too much of her intellect and intuition. Fayette simply wasn't always logical.

Still, from now on she would try very hard to look at Fayette as the competent, knowledgeable woman Leah saw her as and not merely as her irrepressible grandmother. It did her good to have time to consider others' opinions as well as her own, Jenna realized. She didn't have that prerogative back in Cincinnati. Her judgment was the final word, her actions and their results always on the firing line. In a matter of a few days she'd come to value Leah's friendship and counsel a great deal.

The younger woman stood up a little stiffly, one hand supporting the small of her back. "Where has that child of mine gone?" she asked, clicking her tongue against her teeth. "Is she out on the dock or with Clay and Locke?"

Jenna glanced in the direction indicated, her perch on the ledge giving her a better overall view of the store and its watery environs. "Not a weimaraner or a child in sight."

"She can't have gotten that far away in just a few seconds." Leah didn't sound as if she was convinced of the fact.

The words were barely spoken before an earsplitting squeal tore through the heavy air. Jenna looked up to see Cassie sprawled in the sandy grass below the porch railing. For a long moment there was only silence and the painful rush of Leah's indrawn breath. "Dear God, what happened, Jenna? You can see better than I."

"I'm afraid Cassie must have climbed up on the porch rail and tumbled off." Just then, Cassie began to cry and call out for her mother. It was the wailing sob of a terrified child, but not of one hurt so badly that she couldn't make a sound.

"I'm coming, sweetie," Leah called out as she pulled herself to her feet. She moved quickly despite her bulk, but she failed to watch her footing on the rough granite boulders. With a little gasp of pain she stepped down off one rock and slid to her knee. Jenna was there instantly, one eye on Cassie, one eye on Leah as she struggled to regain her footing. "I'm fine," Leah said, shrugging off Jenna's hand. The bag of knitting lay forgotten where it fell.

Cassie's cries had brought Locke and Clay on the run from the plane. Locke seemed to cover the distance in the blink of an eye. He was there before Jenna and Leah, kneeling in the grass raising Cassie to a sitting position, his face as ashen as the child's.

"My leg. Daddy, my leg hurts so bad." The words were

scarcely intelligible. Locke rocked Cassie comfortingly against his broad chest, cutting off Jenna's view of the child.

"Let me see," Jenna ordered, brushing past Leah to kneel beside Cassie and Locke. With practiced efficiency she removed Cassie's red sneaker and rolled her white anklet down over the already swollen foot. "Is this where it hurts, honey?" The child's sobs were so violent that it took almost a full minute to understand her garbled speech.

"My ankle. It hurts," Cassie finally managed to get out. "It hurts a lot," she wailed. Twigs and dead leaves were tangled in her black pigtails. Dirt and tears smudged her pixie face. Blood from several deep scratches oozed down her cheek. Fortunately, a long-sleeved, sunny-yellow T-shirt and heavy jeans had saved her from further scrapes and cuts.

"Is it broken, Jenna?" Leah moved to peer over Jenna's shoulder. Her hand was clenched in the folds of her pale blue smock, the knuckles white with strain. Jenna didn't reply; instead, she ran gently questing hands over Cassie's arms and legs, conducting a quick but thorough check.

"I can't tell about the ankle without an X ray, but I don't think she's seriously injured elsewhere. Children most generally aren't when they can still bellow like that." Jenna caught and held Locke's anguished gaze, attempting to defuse the highly charged atmosphere with her quip. She almost succeeded. "Let's get her somewhere more comfortable. I'll support her leg, Locke. We'll lift her on the count of three. Clay, will you get my bag? It's in my...in your bedroom." Jenna didn't have time to wonder if she was blushing or not. Since that night on the porch, Clay had been the perfect gentleman. He spent a great deal of time working on his plane or on his business accounts, when they weren't busy searching, leaving Jenna to her own devices. Jenna wasn't sure if she was grateful or peeved. She missed him when he was away; she looked forward to his return.

Two long minutes later they placed Cassie's shaking, sobbing form down on the counter in the store. Clay had fetched Jenna's bag and spread a thick old blanket on the cool wood surface for Cassie's comfort. Jenna smiled in gratitude, and he rewarded her with a quick, slashing grin that went straight to her heart and settled there with a fierce, warming glow.

Aside from an array of scratches and bruises, there didn't seem to be any other injuries, except for the possible broken ankle. "Children's bones are much softer than ours," Jenna explained after Cassie had been soothed and cuddled into quiet, punctuated with an occasional hiccuping sob. "We can't rule out a greenstick fracture at this point. That's a break like a tree branch—" she went on to explain when three pairs of adult eyes were turned on her questioningly "—partially broken, partially bent. It isn't serious if it's dealt with properly. And we may only have a severe sprain. As I said, we'll be able to tell when I see the pictures." Jenna snapped the lid on the bottle of mild antiseptic she'd used to clean the scratches on Cassie's face and hands, and dropped it back into her bag.

"We have a splint in the first-aid kit in the back room," Clay offered. "I forgot about it for a moment, since you used your own supplies to treat Cassie. It's one of those inflatable ones, made for an adult, but I think we can adjust it to fit her."

"Yes, I need it," Jenna said in approval. Her mouth was set in a firm line, but her eyes were gentle as she looked up into his.

"What's that?" Cassie lifted her tear-streaked face from Locke's shoulder long enough to stare suspiciously at the blue-colored inflatable splint that Jenna was affixing to her ankle. She uncurled her fingers from Leah's hand, reaching out to touch it curiously.

"It will keep your ankle from getting bumped or twisted till we can get you to the clinic, honey," Jenna explained, tightening the Velcro straps to keep it snugly in place; pulling the straps as tight as possible made the splint acceptably snug around Cassie's sticklike lower leg. "At the clinic they'll take X rays and decide what to do about your ankle."

"No shots!" Cassie wailed, deciding to cry again. She rubbed a fist in her eye and managed to look pathetic and mulish at the same time.

"Maybe just a little one," Jenna said, sidestepping the issue, "if you haven't had your tetanus booster—to keep you from getting very sick because of all your cuts and scratches."

"They are pretty awful," Cassie said with a proud sniff, surveying the back of her hand closely. "Really awesome." A quivering smile tugged at the corners of her mouth as she checked Locke's expression for confirmation.

"Her inoculations are current," Leah said, stroking Cassie's black hair back from her hot forehead.

"No shots, then." Jenna smiled conspiratorially for her patient's benefit. "I can promise. But you have to be a very brave girl for me. Okay?"

"I'll try," Cassie promised. "But it wasn't my fault," she added hastily. "I think Frieda pushed me."

"Cassie! Don't tell fibs. Frieda wasn't even up on the porch with you. You shouldn't have climbed on the railing at all. You scared us half to death."

"I wanted to be a tightrope walker, like in the circus, but I guess I don't know how. When I pulled on Frieda's rope so she could climb up, too, it broke and I fell off." Tears threatened again. "But she didn't push me. I'm sorry I said that, Clay," Cassie admitted with a bewitching, teary grin, taking advantage of the opportunity to recant her previous testimony.

"Everything's okay now, honey," Locke said soothingly. "I hate to ask, but will you fly us to the clinic, Clay?"

"I'll be ready to go in fifteen minutes. I just want to get the current weather report and run one last check on the Buccaneer. We don't want any surprises up there." He turned toward the radio as Jenna prepared to pack up her bag and grab a jacket. This late in the year, a front moving through would lower the temperature dramatically. It was bound to be chillier by the time they returned from the clinic.

"I'll be ready when you are, Clay," she said, watching Locke and Leah comfort Cassie. The child was more comfortable now that Jenna had given her two children's aspirin and all the T.L.C. she could absorb.

"You can't come with us, Jenna." Clay whirled away from

the radio, receiver in hand. His expression was carefully non-committal, his high brow creased with worry. He stared over her head directly at Locke, and some unspoken communication passed between the two men on a level Jenna couldn't comprehend or decipher.

"What?" She was stunned and at a loss for words for several moments. "I don't understand. Of course I'm coming along. Cassie is my patient."

"The weather is deteriorating too fast to risk having us all go," Locke broke in. He glanced at his wife, reaching out to touch her cheek, as he held Cassie cradled in his arms. For once, the ever-present tension, the wall of reserve between them seemed to have evaporated in the stress of events. Their shared anguish for Cassie's plight had brought them close again. "Leah understands." Leah nodded, covering his hand with her own. "Jenna, you have to stay here with Leah while Clay flies Cassie and me to the clinic for treatment."

"But I won't leave my patient," Jenna answered obdurately. She hadn't taken the time to sort through the myriad feelings swirling around in her brain while she'd been so busy caring for Cassie. But now she did. She was helping, healing, using all her expertise and hard-won knowledge to eliminate suffering and restore health. It was the way she'd always wanted to feel when practicing medicine. It was an emotional involvement too often lacking in the high-tech, frantic pace of trauma medicine. Couldn't Clay see how much it meant to her to follow through on Cassie's treatment, to work with her one-on-one?

"They won't let you proceed with Cassie's treatment at the clinic, anyway, Jenna," Clay said bluntly. He took her firmly by the shoulders, giving her a tiny shake. "You have no authority there. Maybe you can't even practice medicine legally in this state. I'm not an expert on the law."

"I'm a doctor. Cassie is my patient," Jenna answered flatly. "Now isn't the time to argue protocol." She didn't have staff privileges at the clinic; what Clay said was true. It might only create more problems if she insisted on accompanying Cassie.

"Jenna, the flight wouldn't be good for Leah. She needs you even more than Cassie does. It's going to be a rough trip." Clay's tone was flatly adamant.

"All right," Jenna agreed reluctantly. She felt like a balloon with the air leaking out. Moments before, she'd been exhilarated. She'd handled the emergency like the professional she was. She loved the feeling of bonding she'd initiated with her small patient. It had been too long since she'd experienced that joy. She couldn't help wondering what it would be like to live and work among these people, to have a practice where she knew all her patients by name and followed their lives from cradle to grave. A private practice, a life with friends, not just acquaintances and colleagues, a husband and in time possibly a family of her own—all the things she'd denied herself these past hectic years.

"You do understand why you have to stay here, don't you, Jen?" Clay gentled his tone, trying once more to make her see reason. Jenna wasn't really listening to anything he said. She seemed lost in her own thoughts. Her gold-flecked hazel eyes, brilliant and dynamic, had suddenly dulled with inner misery. "Jenna, I'm sorry you can't be with Cassie."

"It's all right. It would just complicate matters to have me along. I'll give you a note for the doctors at the clinic, with my diagnosis and the medication I've given her. That's all I can do right now." She spoke woodenly, defeat and disappointment etched in twin lines between her brows. Clay felt like a heel. He'd seen how well she worked with the hysterical child, how she had kept Locke and Leah from coming apart at the seams. She was good at her job: competent, self-assured, a born leader, a born healer. But he was doing this for her own good.

And for himself, too, Clay had to admit. He'd been a part of her work, felt that he was sharing something strange and wonderful with Jenna, although he knew his contribution to Cassie's treatment had been small. He wasn't ready to acknowledge, even to himself, how good that made him feel, to be truly sharing life with another human being on a level beyond the merely physical. But maybe it was only illusion, something his lonely heart had concocted to make him start feeling deeply again. He had to keep reminding himself that there could be no lasting love without sharing. He'd learned that lesson the hard way with Joann. Sharing hearts and minds and bodies took time—the one thing they didn't have.

Chapter Seven

"You're going to wear a groove in the floor if you don't stop pacing back and forth like that." Leah's voice was clipped and slightly breathless, but Jenna failed to notice. She continued prowling around the room. The stormy weather made her nervous and on edge. Clay and Locke had taken off almost four hours before with the injured Cassie. In her mind's eye she'd followed the little girl's treatment and knew they should be starting back soon on their trip home.

"Jenna."

"Sorry." She grinned down at the mother-to-be as she reclined in a big vinyl chair in the comfortable living room. "It's storming hard south of here. Right over Oakhelm, I'd imagine."

"I hear the thunder. Sit down," Leah directed firmly. "That storm's past us."

"Do you think Clay will try to make it back in this weather?" There was no use trying to hide her tension from Leah. The long afternoon had passed slowly in easy conversation and comfortable convivial silences. They were beginning to know each other well. "I'm afraid Cassie will be frightened to fly through a storm," she finished lamely. Jenna put her hand on the cool glass coffeepot on the counter that divided the kitchen from the living area. "Shall I make more coffee?"

"Not for me, thanks," Leah answered. "I hope they don't even try to get back. Cassie gets airsick," Leah explained with a wry smile. "Locke will know what's best for her, and Clay won't do anything foolhardy, I'm sure. If they have to stay overnight near the clinic, they'll let us know by phone. If the storm hasn't knocked down the lines." She added the rider with a frown etching parallel lines in her smooth forehead.

"I'm glad you're taking being separated from Cassie so well," Jenna said with a smile, perching on the edge of the couch. She reached down to fondle Frieda's ears as the big dog slept stretched out alongside the sofa. A white-hot streak of lightning arced past the window behind Leah. Jenna shivered involuntarily. Dark shadows pushed out of the corners of the room, intensifying after the bright flash. Disliking the gloomy atmosphere, Jenna stood up and moved to turn on the lights.

"Cassie's in good hands. Locke loves her as dearly as if she were his own. He's been much more of a father to her than my first husband ever was. I'd give anything to be with them, but it isn't possible. And now, I'm afraid I'm going to have to impose on your medical expertise even further."

Jenna whirled from the totem-carved lamp where she'd been fiddling with the base. The room sprang into sharp focus as her fingers found the switch. Leah's face was pale and strained, her classic beauty sharpened by pain and emotion. Jenna felt a prickle of apprehension crawl down her spine. "Leah, what are you trying to tell me? Are you ill?"

"I feel terrible," Leah admitted smilingly. "I'm in labor. I have been—" she glanced at the clock on the wall above the kitchen sink, visible from her chair "—for at least an hour and a half. The last contraction was about eight minutes ago." She shifted a little in her chair. "And here's another one." Her voice was reedy with excitement. "It's stronger than the last."

"That's impossible! You aren't due for another month yet," Jenna sputtered. Then a picture of Leah stumbling on the rocks after Cassie's fall popped into her dazed brain. Could it have been a severe enough jolt to bring on premature labor? "Are you sure?" she asked unnecessarily. The intent look of inner focus on Leah's face was confirmation enough.

"I'm afraid so. We aren't positive about my due date, you

understand. The doctor meant to take one of those sound pictures on my next visit.'' She leaned back in the chair, taking
a series of deep breaths, trying not to fight the tightening across
her distended abdomen. ''After I miscarried, my doctors in Atlanta thought there couldn't be any more babies. We'd been
married over a year without anything happening—'' tension
drained out of her voice as the contraction eased ''—so Locke
and I just quit thinking about a pregnancy. We might have
miscounted.'' Leah grinned at Jenna's discomfiture. ''Come on,
Jenna. You're an expert. I'm the one who should be hysterical,
delivering out here in the back of beyond, not you.''

''I'm not hysterical,'' Jenna answered in a huff. ''Just...
surprised, that's all. Maybe if you lie back, put your feet up...''
Jenna ran over possible complications in her mind as she spoke.

''Too late.'' Leah reaffirmed her condition. ''I think my water just broke.''

''Good Lord, no!'' Jenna's denial was heartfelt.

''Jenna, how many babies have you delivered?'' Leah whispered as a ripple of true fear crossed her face. Her skin looked
waxy in the yellow lamplight. Jenna avoided her searching look
as she helped Leah rise from the chair and led the way down
the hall to her room. Actually, it was Clay's room, although
the poor man hadn't set foot in it for days.

''Seven,'' Jenna answered, doing some quick mental addition.

Leah stopped dead in her tracks. ''When was the last one?''
Her deep blue eyes caught and held Jenna's gaze unflinchingly,
demanding an honest response.

''The last one—all of them, in fact—were while I was in
medical school,'' Jenna reluctantly revealed. ''Five years ago.''

''Oh, Jenna.'' Leah grabbed the bedpost for support. Now
she looked as scared as Jenna felt already. ''What will we do?''
Leah's frightened reaction was exactly what Jenna needed to
calm her own nerves and bring her professional training back
into dominance. She was the strong one. The one in control.
She motioned for Leah to start undressing.

"We'll do whatever we have to do, of course. Get out of those wet things, and I'll change the bed in Harmon's room. After I examine you, we'll radio the clinic and the airport, anywhere they might be able to find Clay and send him back to get us." Jenna pulled a nightgown out of the bureau drawer she'd appropriated for the few things she'd brought with her from home and carted over from Faye's cabin. Leah took it gratefully, but didn't move toward the bathroom. The long contraction passed, and with the end of her discomfort some of her spirit seemed to return.

"We've already been through that, Jenna. Can't you hear the wind rising? And the thunder's getting close again. I won't risk my husband and child, or Clay's life. We're in this together." The steel Jenna had glimpsed underlying Leah's spun-sugar prettiness was coming through with a great show of strength. "I know the drill." She laughed with a shaky attempt at bravado. "Don't you have babies at your Trauma Center, for heaven's sake?"

"Carryouts only," Jenna bantered. "We don't deliver." Habit took over. Her smile was confident, serene. But she was scared to death. "Trauma centers aren't maternity wards." If and when a pregnant woman was brought through the unit, her stay was brief. Jenna's crew stabilized her condition, monitored the fetus and sent her on her way as quickly as humanly possible.

She'd done well on her rotations in Obstetrics and Pediatrics, but that had been several years ago. She hadn't kept up with advances in those fields. And she was hundreds of miles from the facilities she'd come to consider essential to her practice of the healing arts.

Yet, this afternoon she'd treated Cassie with what could surely be considered primitive methods and she'd fared very well. It wasn't the way she wanted it to be for Leah, but women had been having healthy babies for thousands of years without benefit of space-age technology. Tonight would be no exception.

"We're in this together," Leah whispered, holding the gown

across her swollen stomach. She might have been reading Jenna's mind. And if she had, she needed her doubts put to rest.

"All three of us are going to be just fine." Jenna smiled her most practiced smile. "I'll help you into bed; then I have to get my bag."

"JENNA DO YOU HEAR the plane? It's Locke and Clay coming back. I'm sure of it this time." Leah roused herself from the lethargy that had overtaken her between contractions that were becoming increasingly hard. It was pitch dark beyond the bedroom window that faced the ridge sheltering the building from the north. Only above the tops of the highest pines could Jenna see the fading light of the evening sky. Out on the water the last pale gray of daylight would be fading away over the lake.

She soothed a wayward strand of Leah's ink-black hair from her forehead and straightened the thin sheet covering her while she rested. "Honey, you say that every time a branch scrapes the roof or thunder rumbles over the hills. I didn't hear anything."

"I want Locke with me," Leah sobbed, twisting on her side as another contraction tightened across her middle. "He wanted to be with me when our baby's born. I need him."

And I need Clay, his strength of purpose, his warmth and tenderness, Jenna thought. She wasn't sure when she'd come to that earthshaking conclusion, but she had. She needed Clay Thornton as she'd never allowed herself to need another human being in her life. She'd make it through this ordeal for Leah's sake and the baby's, but she didn't want to be alone. Not ever again.

"I'm sorry I'm so much trouble," Leah moaned, cutting short Jenna's musing. "I'm scared. It wasn't like this with Cassie." She moved restlessly against the pillows Jenna had propped against her back, in the arrangement most comfortable for the laboring woman.

"I wish Locke were here for you, too, Leah. But it isn't

possible, remember? We're in this thing together. We'll have to see it through by ourselves.''

Ten more minutes passed with two more long, tiring contractions that did at last seem to move the baby into a better position. There was no way Jenna could be certain. She'd never realized how much she depended on the instruments, the mechanical devices, monitors and other apparatus she took for granted in the unit. "One or two more pains like that, Leah," Jenna encouraged, "and you'll be ready to push. It won't be much longer now.

Jenna was still wishing for one good long look at her medical textbooks, piled on a closet shelf back in her apartment in Cincinnati when Frieda began whining restlessly outside the closed bedroom door. It was chilly and damp at the end of the dark, stormy day, so Jenna had shut the door to keep the heat from a small electric heater concentrated in the room. Since the animal's restlessness was affecting Leah, she'd have to be exiled to the enclosed rear porch. Frieda gave one short, happy bark as Jenna twisted the knob to open the door and quiet the animal.

Clay Thornton stood framed in the doorway, one hand on the molding, one hand raised to knock on the panel. His raven-black hair was ruffled by the wind; his red mackinaw was dark with rain. He looked tall and commanding and, oh, so good.

"Clay! I told you I heard the plane," Leah cried with a happy relieved sob. "Oh, Clay, where's Locke? I want him to be with me."

His experience with pregnant women was pretty much limited to what he'd observed with Leah these past few months, but Clay didn't need any special coaching to figure out what was going on in the confines of his father's spartanly furnished bedroom. A shaft of purely male, purely primitive fear coursed through his veins like cold fire. Leah was having her baby. Now. A month too early, and hours away from proper medical facilities.

"He couldn't come back with me, Leah." Clay glanced at Jenna. Her face was composed, but almost completely expressionless. She'd pulled her silver-blond hair into a knot on top of her head and rolled up the sleeves of her mint-green oxford cloth shirt high on her arms. Her stethoscope was draped casually around her neck. She looked every inch the professional, except for her eyes. His own disquietude stared back at him from the depths of her eyes when she turned her head to meet his gaze.

"It stormed like the very devil over at the county seat, knocked out power all the way back to Oakhelm." Clay sent Frieda off down the hall with a low-voiced command as he moved into the room with a slow, purposeful step. He wasn't about to let either woman know he was weak in the knees, that his stomach was churning so hard that the bile rose in his throat. "They got X rays of Cassie's ankle, decided it was cracked, not broken. Set it. And then the lights went out. Boy, did that kid howl!" He barked a short laugh and was pleased that it sounded so normal. "They need another picture of her ankle to make sure everything's lined up okay, I guess, but there's only a small backup generator, and there are a lot of people coming in with injuries from the storm. Locke and Cassie decided to stay the night. They'll come out with the mail boat in the morning." He leaned one hand on the bedpost and bent closer to Leah.

"I came back. I was afraid the power was out here, too." He hadn't wanted Jenna or Leah to be alone. "I was worried you two might not be able to start our generator. It's pretty finicky. Dad's got a lot of money tied up in the stuff in those coolers out there." He gestured with his head toward the store. "I sure didn't expect to find this. What happened?"

Jenna glided back to the foot of the bed to check Leah's pulse. Her movement had the grace of a long-familiar action. "I'll explain what's going on, Leah," Jenna advised. "You save your breath for the contractions. Clay will show me where to find the things we'll need for your delivery." She was all business now. No more relating to Leah as one lonely woman to another. She was a physician and a healer. Too much emotion didn't help; it was something she'd fought against for years. Leah needed touch points, direction to complement and enhance her own inner focus, not sympathetic vibrations of fear and worry. From now on Leah would be able to rely on Jenna's strength because Jenna would draw strength from Clay's presence.

"Cassie and Locke are truly safe?" Leah reached out, gripping Clay's hand with the force of a man twice her size.

"They're fine. Cassie's getting everyone she sees to autograph her cast. And when I left, they were going to send out to McDonald's for Big Macs and fries." Clay smiled down at Leah, so pale and fragile against the stark-white pillowcase. His thoughts chased around in his head like a pack of demented squirrels. Was that deathly pallor normal? Should she look so uncomfortable, so obviously in pain? He wished he knew something, anything at all, about bringing babies into the world.

"She is fine, then," Leah sighed, dropping back against the pillow with a wan smile. "Cassie adores Big Macs."

"Are the phone lines down, Jenna? Why didn't you try and contact us earlier? Or call the county sheriff?" Clay glanced over at Jenna again, surprised to see her smiling, too, but no longer surprised at what her smile did to his heart.

"No." Leah's voice was strong again, brooking no argument. "It's too dangerous. You shouldn't have come back yourself."

"I know what I'm doing," Clay stated with quiet conviction. "The risk was acceptable for me alone. But you're right. I'd hate to try and get that plane back up and out of the water anymore tonight."

"We've known that all along," Jenna pointed out. "And we also knew you'd try and come back for us, whether it was safe or not."

Clay couldn't deny the allegation, didn't want to try, so he let it pass. "Is there time to get her to the clinic by car?"

"Car?" Jenna looked mystified. She felt stupid for saying the word in such a disbelieving voice. She hadn't seen a car since leaving hers in Oakhelm.

"Yes, a vehicle with four wheels and a motor." Clay grinned, taking his cue and doing his best to keep up his end of the conversation in an ordinary tone. "Dad and Faye took my four-wheel-drive, but we could borrow one from Horatio Gibbs. We aren't completely dependent on air travel out here. It's just a hell of a lot quicker and more convenient, given the general state of the roads."

"How long to Oakhelm?" Jenna began weighing her options.

Clay did some quick mental calculations. "An hour to Oakhelm, another hour to the clinic in this weather."

After a pause it was Leah who finally replied. "No. It won't be that long." Her fingers crushed Clay's in a grip that made him wince. "Jenna," she gasped, trying not to fight the contraction. "How many minutes has it been?"

Jenna checked the bedside clock, grateful for its digital readout of minutes and seconds. "Three minutes and a half. We're committed, Leah."

"Yes. I won't risk my baby's life in the back of Horatio Gibbs's Jeep, or all our lives by flying at night," Leah went on before Clay could object. "We are committed, as Jenna says, and we'll all be fine." She closed her eyes, concentrating her resources inwardly, breathing with the contraction, not fighting against it as she had minutes before. Jenna breathed a sigh of relief. Leah was determined to show the world that she could survive in this environment even if it meant having her baby alone in the wilderness. Jenna was coming to believe that under Leah's passive exterior beat a heart of solid chromium steel. She'd do fine—with a little help from her friends. Jenna intended that she should have that help.

"I'll only be gone a minute or two, Leah. Holler out if you need me. Or just holler, if that will make it better." She grinned down at Leah. She couldn't pinpoint the cause, and didn't want to, if the truth be told, but the moment she'd seen Clay's lean, rangy figure filling the open doorway, her fears had diminished.

Clay disengaged his fingers from Leah's, making a conscious effort not to rub his aching knuckles. Jenna preceded him down

he hall. In the darkened living room she turned and came into
is arms so naturally that he didn't have time to react in any
ashion but the way he'd longed to for days. He gathered her
nto his arms, resting his chin on the top of her head. Her hair
melled good, soft and heathery, or maybe more like ferns in
he woods.

"I'm so glad you're back," she whispered against his chest.
o him the words were more arousing than any love potion.
Ier breath sifted through the cotton fabric of his shirt, warm
nd exciting against his skin. His arms tightened reflexively
round her, his hands soothing the tense muscles of Jenna's
houlders and back, in the way he had discovered she liked.

"What happened, Jenna, love?" His voice was so quiet
enna couldn't be sure she'd heard him correctly. Had he really
alled her his love? She couldn't take the time to dwell on the
vonder of that now, so she stored up the feeling in her heart,
s though she were putting a stopper in a bottle of the most
recious scent in the universe, setting it aside to savor later
vhen she was alone.

"I'm scared." She'd never said that aloud to another human
eing in her life. She hadn't been able to reveal that much of
er vulnerability to anyone before, not self-reliant Jenna: not
nce through all the long, lonely years at boarding school and
nedical school, not to Roger, although once upon a time she
nought she could love him, not even to Fayette, who always
eemed so self-reliant herself. And certainly not in the past few
ears when she held the power of life and death and the re-
ponsibility for making all the right decisions squarely in her
vo hands. But Clay would understand. He'd support her, not
ensure her insecurity. She stumbled over her words in her
aste to bring her unstable emotions back under control. "I'm
cared to death, Clay. Thank God you're back. This afternoon
eah tripped and fell on the rocks while she was trying to get
 Cassie. The jolt precipitated her labor. An eight-months baby
hould make it okay in a home birth. But I can't be certain."

She could see Clay's perplexity in the glow of a lamp on a
orner table. "Do we have any other option?" he asked in a

low, gruff voice that betrayed his agitation far more than the gentle soothing pressure of his hands on the back of her neck would indicate.

"I'm afraid not. We'll have to take our chances that Leah will be strong enough to accomplish the birth safely on her own."

"Jen, I'm out of my league," Clay confessed. "I haven't been around any babies but my nieces and nephews. And that's strictly in an advisory capacity. I can change a diaper if I have to. And I'm not bad at spooning strained spinach down their throats, but not this. Butterfly McQueen didn't have anything over on me in *Gone With the Wind*: 'I don' know nothin' about birthin' babies.'" There was no humor in his face or voice.

"Well, Leah and I do," Jenna stated firmly, fortifying herself with the touch of his lean, strong fingers and the rock hardness of his chest under her flushed cheek. "We're going to come out of this just fine. All three of us. Only I'm so glad you're here," she couldn't help repeating. "I don't feel so trapped anymore. You'll get them out safely if I'm in over my head, won't you?"

"Even if I have to carry Leah and the baby out on foot to do it. You can count on me to do whatever I can, Jenna. Always." It was more than just reassurance. It was a pledge to her and to himself. He wouldn't rush her with feelings that there was no time to explain. Jenna had confided in him; she trusted him. Clay wanted more than anything in his life to sweep Jenna up into his arms and carry her off to a haven of peace and quiet, to make love with her so passionately and so completely that it would erase each and every tiny worry line from between her brows. Instead, he made a fist and battered gently at the stubborn tilt of her chin. "Aren't you an old hand at this, Doc?"

There was a husky timbre to his deep voice that shook Jenna to the core. The brush of his fingers against her skin was so light she barely felt it. But the jolt of intense sensation it caused might have been from a true blow. She caught his hand and held the palm against her cheek.

"I don't have time to explain my limited experience in obstetrics again tonight. Let's just say there are other things I'm more comfortable doing." She looked up at him with a glint of tears in her eyes. It was the last straw for Clay. His head came down to nestle against her forehead. He shifted his stance. His hands rode low on the curve of her waist, fitting their lower bodies together as he leaned back against the wall.

"You can do anything you set your mind to, Doc. What old movie line do you want me to quote next? Not the Duke tonight. Maybe something old Judge Hardy used on young Mickey Rooney? Better yet, I have a suggestion of my own." His lips found hers in a kiss that was gentle and sweet, but tasting rich and full of passion held on a tight leash. Jenna opened to the probing caress of his tongue, glorying in the depth of feelings that swelled into her heart and her head.

She was falling in love with Clay Thornton. The knowledge came unbidden and undeniable. It didn't seem possible. Perhaps for the first time in her life, her questioning intellect was silenced by her heart. It didn't matter. She only knew that in his arms she was complete. The kiss might have gone on forever, but a low, stifled moan from Leah brought both of them back to reality with a guilty jerk.

"This isn't the time or the place, Clay," Jenna began to apologize breathlessly.

"You don't have to tell me that." Clay grinned down at her so tenderly, his gray eyes silvered with desire, that Jenna swallowed hard against the pain of longing in her chest. "What can I do, Doc? Boil water?" he questioned half jokingly.

"As a matter of fact, you can. And lots of it."

Chapter Eight

"All right, Leah. This is it." Jenna made her voice matter-of-fact, firm and emotionless. "When the next contraction starts— push. And I mean *push*!" She made the command sound as unyielding as she could. Leah needed her encouragement, but she also needed direction. The next few minutes would be vital to the baby's survival and perhaps to Leah's own.

Leah grasped the iron rail at the top of Harmon Thornton's bed and did as she was told. A low groan edged past her lips, but for the most part she was silent, conserving her resources for the job at hand. "Good girl, Leah, good girl," Jenna encouraged as she readied the makeshift equipment she'd considered necessary for the delivery. There had been disposable surgical gloves in her bag, and several small hemostats to use in clamping off the cord. She'd devised a suction for the baby's nose and mouth from a plastic syringe. She was as ready as she could be. Now it was up to Leah. "Shall I call Clay in to help support you against the pillows?"

"I'm fine," Leah insisted, panting with exertion. Her hands and knuckles were as white as the painted iron bed frame above her head. "Clay would faint.... He doesn't seem the type...to take well to being a labor coach." The sentence seemed to exhaust her. She fell silent with the beginning of another contraction.

"You're right there. We're making a shambles of his routine and a wreck of his nervous system today." Jenna laughed dryly. "Okay. One more push," Jenna urged as Leah panted her way through the last of a long pushing contraction. "Try to remember, we won't have any more free time in just about forty-five seconds. This is a team effort, but you're going to be doing the hard part." Leah gave a tiny breathless chuckle at Jenna's pedantic tone of voice. "We want to get him born as quickly as possible to minimize any involvement of the umbilical cord that could interfere with his oxygen supply. Understand?"

Leah grunted in reply, already beginning to bear down with another contraction. "I'll do my part.... I'm not going to fail.... I want to show...I'm strong...belong here, too."

"You're doing fine. You both are." This was no time for self-pity on either of their parts, Jenna thought, then said briskly aloud, "Ready. Here we go! That's it, one more push.... Leah, it's a boy!"

Leah's head dropped back onto the pillows, exhaustion claiming her, after the monumental effort of bringing her baby safely into the world. Jenna didn't see any reason to alarm her, but the baby's color was poor, his movements sluggish.

She worked quickly to suction mucus from his nose and mouth, noting automatically the five basic criteria for judging a newborn's condition. A perfect score of ten was what every doctor wished for, but Leah's new son was going to score much lower.

"Jenna." The razor edge of hysteria was in Leah's voice. She sat up among the pillows. "He isn't crying. What's wrong?"

"Just a little slow waking up to the world, Leah. He'll be fine." Jenna caught up a soft white terry towel and wrapped the baby in its warm folds. She flicked her middle finger sharply against the soles of his feet. He stirred but still didn't take the first big life-sustaining breath he needed.

"Jenna." Leah's voice rose to a wail.

Clay couldn't stand his inactivity any longer. The muted, almost animal sounds of Leah's labor had nearly driven him up a wall. He hated knowing there was nothing he could do that would be of any value. He wasn't cut out to be a passive bystander. Now Leah was crying, almost hysterical. He couldn't remain uninvolved any longer. He strode into the room, taking in Jenna's rapt attention to her tiny patient and Leah's distracted figure on the bed.

He couldn't help Jenna or the baby. God, the little creature looked so tiny and so blue; but he could comfort Leah. He gathered her shaking and sobbing figure into his arms, keeping her face averted, catching Jenna's swift but graceful and rhythmic movements as she worked to coax life into the tiny body.

Jenna looked up for a fraction of a second, sensing his involvement with her, smiling slightly as, almost imperceptibly, the baby moved under her ministering hands. She looked down at her charge, closed her eyes briefly in silent thanksgiving, then smiled her enchanting smile, full and unrestrained. Clay grinned automatically in response to its brilliance.

Jenna picked up the baby, gave him a shake, turned him over and slapped him between the shoulder blades with the edge of her hand. With an angry squall that was the most beautiful sound Clay had ever heard, Leah's son at last accepted his entrance into a cold and rainy world.

"Clay!" Leah's head came up, her strength again far beyond her size. She pushed him away, staring at the baby whose color was rapidly turning a healthy newborn-pink. "Jenna, is he all right?"

"He is," Jenna confirmed. She broke off, swallowing a lump of tears. It would never be routine to her, this age-old ritual of bringing life into the world, but she'd end up crying if she said anything more—and that would be the last straw. A doctor never cries, even if she's suddenly the happiest woman on earth. "Lie back, Leah," she said brusquely to cover her lapse. "I'm tying off the cord, and then you can hold your son."

Clay stayed where he was, on the edge of the rumpled bed. He was fascinated by the tiny, mewling creature Jenna placed against Leah's breast a few minutes later. "He's awfully small," he ventured, reaching out to touch one flailing pink finger.

"Not too small, thank goodness," Jenna interrupted from where she was doing what was necessary for Leah. "I'm not sure how we can weigh him, but my guess is that he's about four and a half pounds." It was a low but acceptable birth weight for a four-weeks-premature newborn. What was even more encouraging was that Jenna's evaluation of her patient at the critical five-minute stage of his new life was very good. She was going to give him a strong eight on the judging scale.

"He's got awfully big hands. And feet," Clay observed looking the infant over closely. "Must be going to take after his old man. And bald as a billiard ball. He's Locke's kid, for sure. Too bad, Leah."

"Clay Thornton! I'm going to have to ask you to leave the room if you can't find something nice to say about the most gorgeous baby I've ever delivered," Jenna ordered with patently false offense. Leah giggled at the banter, tears still shining in her midnight-blue eyes and on her pale cheeks.

"I'll take that compliment in the spirit I'm sure you offered it, Jenna. After all, he's only number eight. Clay's right, too, I'm afraid. He is bald," she admitted, maternal pride giving little importance to his lack of hair. "And he is beautiful. Thank you both."

"I've already told you, you did all the hard work. Would you like me to weigh him—" All at once Jenna's throat clogged with emotion. When it had been most important, most imperative, her special skills had been all she needed to see her through. But Clay's presence, his caring, had given her the serenity to take every advantage of that skill in difficult and unfamiliar circumstances. She wanted him to know that. She wanted to tell him as soon as they could find a moment alone together.

"How about weighing this miniature lady-killer on the produce scale?" Clay suggested with a twinkle in his silver-gray eyes. He was only half-serious. "He's about as big as a bunch of bananas. He ought to just fit." He made a great show of sizing up the infant. Relief and reaction made him light-headed. He'd never been so scared in his life as he was when he'd walked into the room and seen Jenna working over that tiny, seemingly lifeless form. He'd flown combat missions in Vietnam, set down his damaged DC-10 that long-ago day and never felt one-tenth as terrified as he'd been during the past hour.

"Oh, yes, could you weigh him and measure his head and how long he is? Just like they would do in the hospital." It was hard to resist the pleading note in Leah's soft voice. "And footprints and a birth certificate?"

"There's plenty of time for all that later," Jenna said with a laugh. "But I would like to know his birth weight so we can monitor his progress." Newborns were handled routinely by a number of doctors and nurses in most delivery rooms. She didn't have the heart to deny Leah's request. "If we keep him bundled up and get him back to you as quickly as possible for a long, warm nap I don't see a problem."

"I could use a nap myself," Leah admitted as she curled a finger around the tight fist poking out of the soft terry wrapping. "I didn't notice the time he was born." She looked up with a frown of disappointment between her great blue eyes.

"Eight-seventeen P.M.," Clay answered promptly. "I looked at the clock."

"Good." Leah's frown changed to a happy smile. "All the details for his baby book." She handed the infant into Jenna's waiting arms.

"Be back in a jiffy." Jenna looked down at the baby, then across the bed at Clay with such a glorious light shining in her hazel eyes that he was stunned. For a moment he was privileged to feel, through some chemistry growing between them, the private marvel of helping a new life to come safely into the world.

Clay wanted to grin like an idiot at the revelation. It had been hard waiting, doing nothing, to be constrained to sit on the sidelines, for all intents and purposes a passive bystander. But Jenna was good at her work. Very good. And she'd handled the emergency as if she'd been delivering babies in the wilderness all her life.

As if she belonged here with him beside her.

Clay longed to gather Jenna into his arms and tell her, but something stopped him—some small, stinging doubt deep in his brain, some residual pain from loving unwisely in the past. He pushed it aside in irritation, but it refused to be completely subdued. He followed Jenna and the baby from the room in silence as Leah sank back among the pillows with a sigh of contentment.

Clay switched on a dim wall light to keep from startling the baby with the bright fluorescent lamps overhead. The low-wattage bulb illuminated a very modern, digital-read Toledo scale on the dark-varnished hardwood counter. Jenna laid the infant, towel and all, on the scale. "Four pounds, fifteen ounces, with the towel."

"Is he a keeper?" Clay asked, coming up close behind her to peer down at the blinking LED readout.

"Of course he's a keeper. I'll weigh the towel later. It can't be more than five or six ounces," Jenna said, picking up the baby to cuddle him against her shoulder. She kissed the top of his fuzzy head, stroking his back, unaware, Clay surmised, of the ageless, soothing sounds she made in a cooing, singsong voice of great sweetness. He'd never seen a gesture so beautiful in his life.

"Four and a half pounds? That's awful small, isn't it?" He couldn't stop himself from reaching out a finger to trace the tiny shell-like curve of the baby's ear. The heel of his hand brushed the rise of Jenna's breast. "He'd make a nice size walleye." Clay swallowed to clear the hollow scratchiness from his voice.

"Don't be silly, Clay," Jenna said, holding on a little desperately to the euphoria of a successful delivery. She didn't want anyone to be around when the lightness drained away, leaving her empty and alone. It was a moment of vulnerability she never allowed anyone to share. Doctors didn't cry, and Jenna was very much afraid that she was going to cry now. "He's adorable, but I do wish he were a pound heavier. Still, he'll catch up soon enough if we get him back to his mother for his first meal."

"I still say he's as wiggly as any fish I ever saw." Clay's smile lifted the corners of his mouth for a moment and echoed in his eyes. Jenna smiled back, blessing him for holding back the darkness a little longer. She looked down at the baby in her arms. He *was* as bald as a billiard ball; only the palest of blond fuzz covered his skull. His hands and feet were big. A basketball player for Locke and Leah? She wondered if she'd be around to see him at that age, or see him take his first step—or even learn to smile.

The baby nuzzled at her shoulder, turning his head to seek his mother's breast. The sensation sent a shaft of longing through Jenna that she'd never experienced before. Tears pricked behind her eyes more insistently. "I've got to get him back to Leah."

"Jenna, what's wrong?" Clay was quick to sense her change in mood.

"Nothing." She tried not to sniff. "He's hungry, that's all. It's a good sign."

Clay chose to honor her reticence for the moment. "We're all hungry. Did you miss dinner, too?" Jenna nodded. "I'll heat up some of my famous beef-noodle soup while you get this little guy settled with his mom."

Leah was watching the door with sleepy anticipation when Jenna brought the baby back into the bedroom. She laid the child in Leah's arms and watched her open the buttons of the pale pink nightgown to allow her son to nuzzle hungrily at her breast. Jenna felt another even sharper pang than before. Would she ever have a child of her own to nourish at her breast? She'd have found time in her busy life to have Roger's child, if they'd married. But she had the terrible suspicion that it would have been more in the nature of an obligation for both of them—not the most wonderful, challenging, learning experience a couple could know together.

The way it would be if Clay were the father of her child.

"He's going to be fine." Leah nestled her cheek against the top of her son's head. He suckled noisily at her breast, tugging strongly—a good sign, Jenna noted. "Locke will be so proud.

It's going to make all the difference. I did it myself. Me. Leah Purchase Singer.'' She laughed aloud.

"You're one fantastic lady," Jenna agreed with a teary smile.

"Jenna, what's wrong?"

"Absolutely nothing." Jenna made her tone as bracing as she could manage.

"Good." Leah covered a yawn with her free hand. "I want everyone to be as happy as I am tonight. From now on I'm not going to let anything stand in my way. I'm going to have it all. My husband, my children, my own home. It's going to be good, very good."

"It's time to rest. Tomorrow will be a busy day," Jenna urged in a quiet monotone, calculated to bring Leah closer to the edges of sleep.

"I can't imagine what Locke's going to say when you get through to him." Leah allowed Jenna to settle the baby comfortably at her side. "Tell him to decide on a name, will you please? We had it narrowed down to three. And that I'm fine, the baby's fine and that I love him very much. Oh, and tell Cassie I love her, too...." Leah's words trailed off. Her eyes drifted closed. "I'm tired, Jenna."

"You have every right to be." Jenna smoothed the covers over her friend. "I'll be back later to check on both of you. Pleasant dreams."

"Mmm, very pleasant," came the sleepy reply.

JENNA STOPPED in the shadows of the living room and rested her hand wearily on the wall. She could see Clay moving around in the kitchen. Its light and its beckoning warmth, the aroma of rich beef broth and hot rolls reached out to enfold her, yet she held back. He looked like a domesticated voyageur again tonight, in a gray shirt and dark cords—sexy and exciting, yet gentle and caring, too, the kind of man she'd always hoped she'd find to love.

Love.

She was falling in love with Clay Thornton, she was afraid.

Hopelessly in love, and she wasn't sure if she should laugh or cry.

She'd come close to love with Roger, but that experience only made her realize how much more binding her feelings for this man would be. He was everything that she'd found lacking in her ex-fiancé. Jenna was far too honest a person to try to fool herself very long when the facts were laid out in front of her. Yet, was this relationship destined to go nowhere? Unless…

Deep in her heart, in the most secret corner of her being, was the germinating seed of a dream long suppressed—a dream of practicing medicine the way she'd always wanted to practice it. The way she'd done today with Cassie and Leah. One-on-one—a partner, a friend to all her patients, not just a face behind a name tag.

If the feelings she sensed growing between Clay and herself were real and true, if Clay was learning to care for her, was that dream of a practice of her own here, on Lake of the Woods, also a possibility? She couldn't be sure. At the moment she couldn't be sure of anything. A single tear, one that she'd been trying so hard to hold back, escaped and rolled down her cheek. She reached up to brush it away just as Clay stepped through the doorway.

"Jenna? What are you doing standing here in the dark? Come and eat. You haven't had time to touch a bite since lunch." He held out his hand.

The simple, endearing gesture was too much. Everything that had happened to Jenna today was too emotional, too heart-wrenching; her equilibrium was completely disrupted. And now she was going to start crying in earnest. She couldn't let Clay see her that way. Her flight from the room was punctuated by a thunderclap that shook the building and heralded the onset of another storm. Lightning forked across the low, black sky, adding its exclamation point to the slam of the old-fashioned wooden screened door and the metallic patter of rain on the roof. Clay was right on her heels. His hand brushed hers as she ran down the steps.

"Jenna, slow down. Wait for me."

"No, go away." She stumbled over a tree root and Clay caught her by the shoulders, saving her from a wet, undignified tumble.

"I won't go away until you tell me what's wrong," he ordered, then softened his tone. "Surely that's not too much to ask?"

"I don't—" Jenna stared fixedly at the top button of his shirt, which was made of gray oxford cloth and matched his eyes exactly. Already raindrops peppered his back and shoulders with dark spots. Clay turned her slightly to shelter her from the downpour.

"Jenna." He gave her a little shake. "Answer me." His tone was composed of nearly equal parts of exasperation and concern.

"I don't want you to see me cry."

"Cry?" Clay lifted her chin with the tip of his finger. Jenna resisted for a moment then lifted her eyes to meet his. "Why are you crying, Jen?"

"Because I'm happy." The words came out in a defiant rush. "Because Leah has a wonderful baby that *I* brought into the world, and everything is going to be fine for her and Locke. Because I did my job and did it well under trying circumstances." *Because you knew I needed help, somehow, and came back to give me your strength.* But she didn't say that aloud. "Please Clay, just leave me alone for a few minutes and I'll be fine." Rain drummed on the top of her head and filled her eyes and lashes. "I don't want you to see me cry," she repeated with pathetic dignity.

"Why not, Jenna sweet?" Clay drew her close, tracing the crystal tears that mixed freely with raindrops on her cheeks.

"No one wants to see a doctor cry," Jenna answered with a brave attempt at a smile. "Not for any reason, good or bad." Her tone was adamant.

"You have a point," Clay conceded.

Jenna nodded. "Crying women doctors are even worse. They make patients nervous. They think we're too emotional.

I make it a point never to cry." She was getting some of her runaway feelings back under control.

Clay still held her tear-washed gaze captive. "That's for the rest of the world, Jenna. You don't have to hide *anything* from me. Never. And for the record, I think you're the bravest woman I've ever met. I've been scared witless since the moment I set foot in that bedroom. But you handled it as if delivering babies alone out here is something you do every day and twice on Sunday."

"Because you were there," Jenna found herself saying. She felt much like the weather—confused and unsettled. She was warm and balmy one minute; then hints of arctic cold blew over her skin with the next buffet of night wind. Now the tautness of pulled nerves drained out of her as the rain beat down on her head and spangled her lashes, mixing with tears of fatigue. She wanted to be held close to Clay's heart so that she could hear its strong, even beat and be comforted. "You're so good for me, Clay. You give me strength."

His mouth came down to cover hers, making the world go away with the power of his kiss. Jenna's lips flowered open; she welcomed the probing warmth of his tongue as he searched out the dark sweetness of her mouth. Lightning dashed across the sky in fiery splendor. It was no brighter than the fire inside her. Jenna shut her eyes against the dazzle and the crash of thunder that followed close on its heels, drowning out every other sound.

"I want to be so much more than just good for you." Clay's words followed the thunder and were all the more intense in the sudden silence. "I want to be everything for you." His hands pulled Jenna into the circle of his arms, soothing and arousing her all at the same time. "I'm not saying this very well, am I?"

"I'm not asking for a commitment from you, Clay." Jenna stumbled over the words, her throat tight with emotion. Tears threatened again and she didn't care.

"I am." Clay was vehement. He pushed a hand through his hair, scattering raindrops between them. "Lord, it's hard to find the right words. I think I'm in love with you, Dr. Jenna Macklin.'' It was absurdly simple to say, after all. His indecision melted away like spun sugar in the rain. ''I love you.''

''Do I love you? Is that what this crazy, mixed-up feeling inside me is?'' Jenna asked him solemnly. ''Oh, Clay, this frightens me so,'' she whispered with a funny little catch in her voice. ''I haven't been very good at loving in the past.''

''No worse than I have.'' The wonder of seeing love for him dawning in the depths of her eyes, when they caught the light from the open door behind them, made it all worthwhile. ''But we'll learn from those mistakes, Jenna.'' Clay made it a promise and a vow. His lips found hers again, saying so much more than spoken words. His tongue slipped past her teeth mimicking a joining even more satisfying than the kiss. Her breasts were round and full, warm beneath the clinging wet cotton of her shirt. Several buttons parted under the questing of his hand. They were crazy—two fully grown, supposedly intelligent adults standing in a driving rainstorm, kissing as hungrily as a couple of youngsters in the throes of first love.

Clay lifted his head long enough to tell Jenna so and was rewarded with a wobbly echo of her delightful laughter. He strung a line of tiny, hungry kisses down the slender column of her throat, feasting his eyes as well as his lips on the velvety beginning rise of her breast.

He slid the thin covering of her bra aside, circling the pale rose tip of her breast with his tongue. Under the persuasive pressure of his gentle sucking the nipple contracted. Jenna sighed in pleasure, pulling his head back up to meet her lips. She buried her fingers deep in his hair. It was soft and dry where the rain hadn't penetrated its thick layers. He smelled good, like rain and wood smoke and sandalwood-scented soap. Jenna pushed closer, needing to be nearer to Clay's heat and vitality. Her arms slipped down over his shoulders and back, circling his waist, and her fingers pressed into the muscles of his buttocks. She pulled him closer still, letting him know she understood and shared his hunger and his need.

''We've got to get back inside, Dr. Macklin.'' Clay broke

off the kiss reluctantly and chuckled against her lips when he found the breath to speak again. Water dripped from his dark, thick lashes and from the end of his nose. "We'll drown out here." Tonight he could conquer the universe. He never wanted to stop kissing Jenna. The fire and passion of her awakening love for him was even greater than he'd imagined it could be. He wanted this moment to last forever, but not at the risk of her health. She was trembling in his arms. Passion and excitement were heady emotions, but fatigue was evident in the fine lines around her mouth and the slight frown between her brows, even when she smiled. Jenna was a brave, talented, independent woman but she needed him to take care of her as much as he needed her. "It's raining cats and dogs out here, in case you haven't noticed."

"It is?" Jenna pretended to become aware of the inclement weather for the first time. "Fancy that. We should go inside." She sighed reluctantly, resting her head against his chest. "Making love in a thunderstorm is absolutely certifiable behavior. But my grandmother would approve wholeheartedly."

"It's a novel experience, to be sure. We're definitely blowing our sober, responsible images right now," Clay agreed with another chuckle. To have Jenna to love and care for, to have her love and care for him as well, sounded a lot like heaven to the lonely man that he kept carefully bottled up deep inside himself.

"I would like to make love with you in the rain." Jenna's face was pressed against his shoulder so he couldn't see her expression.

"But not tonight, Dr. Macklin." Clay scooped Jenna high up in his arms before she could object—and before he could change his mind and help her explore her fantasy. "We can't have you getting pneumonia."

"I never get sick," Jenna came back, but she didn't demand to be lowered to the ground as he'd half thought she might. "This is very nice. I could get used to this," she murmured against his ear, following the statement with a breathy little kiss that made Clay nearly miss his step.

"I want you to get so used to me that you can't live without me."

"You don't ask for much from a woman, do you Clay?" Jenna asked quizzically as he let her feet slide down the length of his legs while he kept her upper body wrapped close in his arms. The suspension of rain beating against her skin was startling. The old-fashioned wooden screened door snapped shut behind them. The store was a shadowy impression of shelves and counters around them. Jenna shivered as the night wind came through the screen and touched the wet fabric of her shirt. No longer bathed by the unusually warm rain from the south, she felt cold and bereft.

"I'm asking for everything you have to give me," Clay said with quiet dignity. His lips found hers and Jenna closed her eyes against the rush of desire and love coming at her out of the blackness. She trembled and the shaking wouldn't stop.

"Damn!" The exclamation was rueful. "I told you you'd catch cold out there."

In a matter of minutes Jenna found herself stripped, toweled down briskly and efficiently and bundled into Clay's green pajamas once again. She made no demurrer when Clay ordered her onto the sofa and tucked a warm wool blanket around her legs, pushing first soup, then a cup of steaming brandy-laced coffee into her cold hands. She was content to be taken care of, to luxuriate in the unusual experience of being comforted and catered to. Jenna watched the fire in the small glass window of the wood-burning fireplace insert and contemplated a very rosy future.

Clay plucked the endangered coffee cup out of Jenna's slack grasp as she stared sightlessly at the dancing flames. He carried the empty dishes he'd brought from Leah's room and added Jenna's empty soup bowl as well as his own to the tray. He was glad he'd insisted that Jenna eat something. She looked better; there was a faint flush of color on her pale cheeks, and the lines had smoothed out between the delicate arch of her brows.

The house was quiet. He turned out the lamp, settling himself beside Jenna on the couch. She came into his arms unhesitatingly. "Mother and son sleeping peacefully," he reported quietly, his voice barely disturbing the silence.

"He's a beautiful baby," Jenna said, still half dreaming, her eyes never leaving the flames. "I want a son like him someday." She heard what she'd said and stiffened within the circle of his arms. The simple statement sounded intimate and erotic as she lay in Clay's embrace.

"So do I. And a little girl like Cassie, as bright as a new penny, so wonderfully happy and alive." He wanted more than anything to take Jenna in his arms, love her, perhaps give her the child she wished for; but he only held her tighter. Now, when their emotions were running so close to the surface, wouldn't be a good time to add more complications. He wanted Jenna all to himself when they first made love, with everything as perfect as he could make it. Tonight her sense of duty to Leah and the baby would preclude that special oneness. He would be patient. There was time, after all, all the time in the world.

"I could learn to love it here, Clay," Jenna said in a whisper. Her arms twined around his neck, the heat of their bodies enfolded and surrounded them in a cocoon of comfort laced with spangles of desire. Jenna locked her arms around his neck. The syncopated rhythm of their hearts softened the spatter of raindrops against the window. The rush of wind through the trees was muted by the sturdy walls of the building until it was no louder than a sigh, the rumble of thunder no more than a distant echo of their passion. "I won't have to spend very much time learning to love you. I'm almost sure I already do."

"I *do* love you, Jenna. I've been falling in love with you almost from the beginning." Their lips touched and clung together. Jenna closed her eyes and found it hard to open them again, even when Clay's mouth left hers.

"Don't stop," she pleaded. "Kiss me again."

One more kiss was all that Clay would allow himself. "I want you to get some rest, Jenna." He cleared his throat of the husky note his voice seemed to have acquired. She was almost out on her feet. "Making love to a comatose woman, even one loved almost to distraction, isn't quite what I had in mind."

"I am awfully sleepy," Jenna admitted. "I'm sorry to be such a party pooper."

"Jenna." Clay's chuckle of amusement was genuine. "You have such a way with words. I'll tuck you in, then bunk down here on the couch for the rest of the night."

"Don't leave me alone, Clay, please." Jenna played with the buttons of his shirt, her fingers brushing lightly across the dark, curling hair on his chest. "Stay with me so I can feel you close to me in the night." She was so unsettled by everything that had happened in the past few hours. "It's all so new, so confusing. But if I'm alone, I won't be able to sleep. I don't want to lie there in the dark and let it keep playing over and over in my mind."

Clay recognized the stark terror underscoring her request. He rested his hands on the curve of her shoulders, the heels of his palms heavy and exciting on the rise of her breasts. "We'll take all the time we need to get to know each other, Jenna. I won't ever rush you, you know that. But if you don't want to be alone tonight, I'll stay with you."

"Just for tonight." She sounded wistful, as if the thought made her sad.

"No, not just tonight. Always, Jenna. We have all the time in the world now."

"Do we?" Her voice was quizzical. "I hope we do." They didn't have all the time in the world, Jenna knew, but she was too tired to discuss the point. The real world was out there just beyond the silver curtain of rain that surrounded them and cut them off from reality. It would come back.

But with Clay beside her, as he'd promised to be from now on, it wouldn't be tonight. And not tomorrow, either. Jenna made herself a promise. They would find a way to have it all, and Clay would be the new center of her world.

Chapter Nine

Jenna's body curled trustingly into his. Her breasts were warm and pliant against his chest. Clay couldn't resist the urge to trace the outline of her lush curves with feather-light strokes calculated not to awaken the sleeping woman in his arms.

The long, stormy night was past. The morning sun shone in patches on the floor of his room. It was getting late; already he'd heard wakeful noises from Leah's baby in the room next door. Jenna stirred in her sleep as his pleasurable caress brought her closer to the edge of consciousness. Clay stilled his movements, not wanting to wake Jenna before she was fully rested.

Although he wanted to believe her when she said doctors learned early on to sleep twice as hard for half the length of time, he didn't intend her to get up yet. She hadn't been asleep long. He had stayed with her all night. They'd taken turns watching over Leah and the new baby, while talking and exchanging kisses till the wee hours of the morning. Before this experience he wouldn't have believed he could be this close to a woman without physically joining; but he'd been proven wrong. He wondered if Jenna would even remember some of the words, the confidences they'd shared last night. Perhaps it was best if she did not.

Now the house was coming alive. The furnace kicked on with a familiar metallic grumble before it settled down into a steady purr. Warm air rose up from the floor register to tickle the back of his neck. It was considerably colder now than it had been when he returned last night. Indian summer was gone, washed away by the steady rain and gusty wind of the past few days.

Autumn was his favorite time up here: cool mornings with frost white and thick on the grass, afternoons warm and sunny with a sky so blue that it hurt to look at it, and long cold nights, good for sleeping and dreaming dreams.

He couldn't go back to the dog-eat-dog world Jenna knew. He admitted that. He belonged here now. She seemed to think she could belong here, too. Why not? He'd made the same choice once. But would she be happy without the fast-paced, high-tech world of trauma medicine? Not every day would be like yesterday, testing her skill and her stamina, thank God. But could she feel fulfilled with only a handful of friends and relatives to treat? There were a lot of questions they still had to ask themselves, but just now he wanted to savor the wonder and joy of having Jenna all to himself. His Jenna, the woman he loved. The woman who loved him.

Jenna stretched and yawned, snuggling up against him. Clay fell to the delicious temptation of cradling her against the length of his body, placing a kiss on each of her delicately shadowed eyelids, her cheek, her temple, where the fine spun-silver hair grew soft and low. Jenna smiled in her sleep, her lips meeting his for a fraction of a second before she sighed and curled into a ball at his side.

Clay chuckled and slid out of the warm bed, his toes arching in protest against the chill of the bare wooden floor. He'd better reset the thermostat to accommodate the wiggly little visitor in Leah's room. He'd never have told her aloud, but the kid bore a distinct resemblance to that little alien critter, E.T. At least, last night he had. Possibly this morning he'd look more human. But he'd still be as wiggly as the fish Clay had compared him to, that went without saying.

Clay pulled on his socks and stuck his feet in his shoes, wandering into the kitchen as he buttoned the wrinkled, dove-gray shirt he'd worn to bed. Breakfast was next on the agenda. Thirty minutes later he'd concocted a meal fit for a queen.

Leah was already propped up in his dad's bed, devouring bacon and poached eggs, toast, jam and wild blueberries with cream and sugar, as if she hadn't eaten for a week. Soup and crackers at midnight left a lot to be desired in the way of nourishment for a grown man, or a new mother.

Clay dutifully admired the tiny bundle on the bed. Upon closer inspection, as yet swaddled in the old terry towel, he still looked like E.T. Leah appeared tired but happy as she had every right to be. After all, producing little alien creatures with no hair was hard work.

Promising to return shortly, Clay went after Jenna's breakfast. He'd heard the shower running in his bathroom, so he knew she was awake. He hoped that it was because she'd noticed he was no longer at her side and missed him.

He knocked awkwardly by banging the toe of his heavy work shoe against the bottom of the bedroom door. Frieda waited while he dealt with the doorknob, padded over to greet Jenna, then ambled down the hall to her own breakfast and the two celebratory strips of bacon that Clay had crumbled into her bowl of dry dog food.

"Good morning." His voice sounded a little tight and strained even to himself. His gaze swept Jenna from head to toe, lingering on the tightened peaks of her breasts outlined by the soft cotton fabric of his pajama top. She'd lent her last clean gown to Leah, he supposed. After the excitement of yesterday, he hated to think of anything as ordinary as doing laundry...but life went on. And new life began.

"It's cold this morning." Jenna pleated the hem of the sheet between her fingers. Her savoir faire didn't extend to the heated survey of Clay's smoky gray eyes.

"Summer blew away during the night." Clay stopped to clear his throat. Somehow bright daylight brought back the reticence he'd hoped had disappeared between him and Jenna forever. "It's fall now. Next week it's just as likely to be winter." He slid the tray over her knees. "Breakfast in bed, Madam Doctor," he pronounced with a flourish. He wished he'd taken the time to shave, or at least tuck his shirttail into his pants; their dishevelment called to mind an intimacy that wasn't yet familiar enough to be ignored.

"Thank you, sir." Jenna grinned back, as determined as he to keep the conversation on an even keel. "Have you checked on Leah and the baby yet?"

"They're fine. I scrounged up a box of disposable diapers from the store. He's dry and happy as a clam. If Locke and Cassie don't get back soon, I'll take the boat over to their place and hunt up some of the baby stuff Leah's got stored up for winter. We have to get started early bringing in supplies around here, so she's pretty well stocked on the necessities. We're cut off from the rest of the world for weeks at a time in the winter, you know."

"Don't try to scare me off with horror stories about the weather," Jenna interrupted. She picked up a strip of bacon, examining it with fierce concentration. "I won't change my mind just because it's daylight and the darkness is gone. I want to stay here. With you." The last words were barely above a whisper.

"Is that a proposal, Dr. Macklin?" Clay teased, picking up a strip of bacon from her plate. "I don't think your grandmother would accept any less formal arrangement." Damn it, why was he treating this like a joke? Was she ready to make such a lasting commitment? Was he ready to take such a chance again? Even for Jenna?

"I guess I am proposing." Jenna was surprised at her boldness, but she saw the dark reflection of pain and failure deep in the stormy gray of his eyes. She had to be very sure so that he could be. "Will you marry me, Clay Thornton?" she continued without missing a beat.

"I will marry you, Jenna Macklin," Clay repeated. This time there wasn't a trace of hesitation in his tone. "I did ask you first."

"You did? When?" Jenna was intrigued.

"Last night." Clay tilted her chin so that their eyes met and held. "I practiced the words over and over in my head. One time they just slipped out."

"And what was my answer?" Jenna reached out her hand to graze the long line of his jaw.

"The most ambiguous little snore. Now I can translate it into the affirmative." He made it just less than a question.

"You're well and truly caught. I won't be letting you off the hook." No shadows darkened the floating golden flecks in her eyes. "This time will be forever."

"Jenna, it won't be easy for us up here." Clay didn't want to keep playing the heavy, but he wasn't sure his heart could stand another loss at love. They needed to talk things out between them. "I didn't make a very good husband the first time around."

Jenna put her bacon carefully back on the blue willowware plate in the middle of the tray. She studied the pattern of steep-roofed pagodas and birds in flight for a long moment. Squaring her shoulders, she pushed the tray off to one side, far enough away so that changing her position in the big bed wouldn't overbalance it. She needed to touch Clay, to show him with physical gestures as well as words what was in her mind and heart.

Clay watched her closely while she fussed with the breakfast paraphernalia. "We've both suffered in the past from relationships that weren't strong enough to last when the going got tough," she said at last. "We can't let that stop us from loving again." He took her hands between his own, shifting his weight to bring their upper bodies closer in the quiet intimacy of his room. Jenna leaned back against the piled-up pillows on his bed. "Don't let a fear of failing in the same way come between us and what we're finding together. Please."

"I'm not that big a fool, Jenna. I'll take my chances that what we've got is strong enough to last. Even up here, away from everything you're used to. I just want you to consider what you'll be giving up to be with me."

"I don't have to give up anything, and I'll be gaining everything I want." Jenna leaned forward in her joy. "I love my parents dearly," she said, looking down at his hand covering hers. The dark hair curled tightly over his knuckles. She traced the strong line of tendons along his thumb. "But they have their lives, their love and their work. Fayette is my family. This is her home, your home. I want it to be mine." She couldn't find the words to tell him of her other dream, the one that began taking shape in her mind last night before she fell asleep. Not yet. Not while it was still so new, so fragile that it might not survive being put into words. She could practice medicine here. She'd considered becoming a general practitioner before. They treated just as many common colds, ordinary everyday illnesses in the Trauma Center as any family physician would. She was needed here, and that was the most important fact of all.

Jenna looked starry-eyed and flushed with happiness. She was saying everything he wanted to hear, but she was throwing the words at him so rapidly that they ran together with excitement. They had to be sure, very sure. Clay tried to put his fears into words. "I want us to be together more than anything in the world. But moving up here is a big decision to make on the spur of the moment. What about your practice?"

"I want to be here with you, Clay. But I'll always be a doctor. I have special skills that people need." Jenna's heart raced with a mixture of anxiety and exhilaration. Would he pick up on the opening, give her a chance to try to explain her bold new plan?

"You'll always want to make life easier and healthier for the people around you." Clay began to relax. She wasn't telling him she wanted to take on the responsibility of more than a thousand square miles in which she'd be the only source of medical treatment for a majority of the population. He'd imagined that. She wasn't obsessed with her career, as he'd seen Joann become. He wouldn't have to take second place in her life. The past was over and done with. He loved Jenna now, with all his heart and soul. She was coming here soon, to be with him always. Everything would work out fine. "It'll take a lot of work, but we'll find a way."

His words were so close to what Jenna wanted to hear. She'd wait until she found exactly the right moment to tell him her plans. Everything would work out because they had love. Clay reached over to kiss her shining face. She'd tell him just as soon as she could work out the details in her own mind. Their lips met and lingered. Her mouth opened greedily beneath the pressure of his kiss.

"You taste good, Jenna. Like toothpaste and coffee and bacon." Clay let the pent-up need he felt for her within him swell outward with the whimsical words. "We should make it a rule to wake up like this every morning for the rest of our lives."

"Clay, boy? Where are you? Still in bed at this hour of the day? Wake up, man! I know you're in there." The bedroom door had drifted shut behind Clay when he brought in the tray. Now it bounced back on its hinges with a bang that made the couple on the bed jump apart. Framed in the doorway was a small bearded man in a Black Watch plaid shirt and baggy gray cords. His hair and beard were as gray as his pants. His eyes were a bright, sparkling green. He was round, and at least eight inches shorter than Clay. But the bone structure, the similar unconscious arrogance of their stance left no doubt at all in Jenna's mind who the man was. All the questions left unanswered between her and Clay blew away in the strong current of Harmon Thornton's gale-force personality.

"Aren't you glad to see your old man come home after wandering around in the wilderness for almost two weeks?" He sounded disappointed and looked it. The green eyes were mournful, nearly hidden in folds of skin until they opened wide in momentary amazement as his gaze shifted past his son.

"Well, I'll be damned." He stared at Jenna unabashedly. "No wonder you're still in bed at ten-thirty on a weekday."

"Dad." Clay's voice was stern. "I'm not in bed. Jenna is. And lower your voice. You'll wake the baby." His tone held amusement and relief, but there was the faintest tinge of dark red above his collar. He found Jenna's hand clenched on the coverlet and folded his fingers around it. Slowly the fist relaxed. She turned her palm up, her fingers lacing through his. He squeezed gently.

"Baby? What baby?" Harmon demanded. He took his eyes off Jenna long enough to shoot Clay a piercing look.

"Leah Singer's baby. Mother and son are in your bedroom. If you'd settle down long enough to let me explain, I will. And give me a chance to introduce Jenna." Clay levered himself up off the bed in one controlled, fluid movement that brought Jenna's heart into her throat in a rush of pride and love. She tore her eyes away from the man she loved to look once again at his father.

Harmon Thornton couldn't be far from seventy. He was robust and healthy-looking, but the years were stamped indelibly on his face. Fayette had been in good hands.

Fayette!

Jenna swung her long bare legs over the side of the bed, then pulled them back again when she saw Harmon's keen green eyes fixed on them appreciatively. Like father, like son.

"Gram. Where is she?" The words came out a little thin, but Harmon picked up on them immediately. Jenna fought down an urge to pull the bedclothes up around her chin. Not because Harmon's look was lascivious, but because she'd rather have met Clay's parent in more dignified circumstances.

"Jenna? You're Faye's granddaughter, the doctor?"

"I've been trying to tell you, Dad," Clay growled in loving exasperation. He dug his hands deep in the pockets of his jeans, setting his feet wide apart as though bracing himself against the onslaught of his father's steamroller approach to conversation. Jenna felt as if she'd been buffeted by a strong wind, just hearing him talk.

"This is Jenna Macklin. She's been here over a week, helping me look for the pair of you." Clay's hands bunched into fists, pulling the denim fabric of his pants taut over slim hips and corded thighs. "Dad, damn it! I could throttle you for running off like that." His voice was gruff with relief and understandable irritation.

"Couldn't be helped, I tell you. Show some respect for your elders, boy. I can still give as good as I'll get, if you want to put on the gloves." Harmon dismissed his son's concern with a wave of his hand and a slap on the shoulder that somehow conveyed deep affection despite its offhandedness. "Faye and

I didn't have any choice. We couldn't go trumpeting our objective all over the Woods, now could we? Our contact in Warroad knew of a plane hunting outfit that was running a few preseason tours. Imagine having the gall to advertise that kind of sneaky, underhanded business...." He sputtered to a halt, shaking his grizzled head in anger. "He got us three good leads, and we started tracking them down. I'll let Faye give you the details. It's her baby, after all." He laughed loudly at his own play on words. "Now, tell me, what's this about Leah Singer having *her* baby in this house?"

Clay was explaining the previous day's events in short, succinct sentences when Jenna's eyes grew wide with pleasure and relief. A tall, incredibly thin woman appeared in the doorway behind Harmon. She gave the impression of peering over his shoulder, although she was tall enough to look directly across the top of his head. Her hair had once been almost as blond as Jenna's. Now it was a pearly-white.

Tiny half-spectacles perched on the tip of her very prominent nose. Fayette Macklin possessed little claim to traditional feminine beauty, but over the years she'd acquired a gentleness of countenance, a patina of grace and wisdom, that had softened her rawboned features.

"Is Clay decent, Harmon?" Since she was already in the room, the question was rhetorical. Fayette's voice was soft, but resonant and as imperious as ever. "Can't we talk in the kitchen? I smell bacon frying and I'm starved." She came to a halt. "Jenna?"

"Gram!"

Fayette Macklin stared unbelievingly at her only grandchild for perhaps thirty seconds without saying a word. Then her riveting gaze speared Clay right between the eyes.

"What is my granddaughter doing in your bed?" She returned her attention to Jenna, repeating the inquiry before Clay could form an answer. "Whatever are you doing here, Jenna? Are those Clay's pajamas you're wearing?"

Jenna winced and prepared to defend herself. But she was rescued by an interruption from an unexpected source.

"Hush, woman. You'll wake the baby." Harmon drew Fayette's fire unflinchingly to himself.

"Baby? Whose baby?"

Jenna was never more grateful for anything in her life than she was for Harmon's delaying tactic.

"Leah Singer's, that's whose baby." Harmon must have learned some time ago how to hold his own with Fayette's wildfire approach to life. Her questions had been as direct and devastatingly candid as Jenna remembered.

"Baby? I'm not moving a step out of this doorway until I know everything that's happened while we've been gone." Fayette wasn't going to be sidetracked so easily. Again, it was Jenna who was on the defensive, and she was certain that Clay felt the same. It didn't matter that they'd spent the past ten days being worried sick about the fate of the muckraking seniors. Now they were put on the spot to explain their own exemplary behavior.

"Gram, I can explain," Jenna began with a very real feeling of déjà vu. How often she'd had to make explanations in the past.

"You bet you will." Fayette nodded with determination. "You two men get out of this bedroom while I talk to my granddaughter. I can't believe what's happened here in the short time we've been gone." For all its softness, her voice carried the command of a Marine drill instructor. "Jenna, how in the world did you pry yourself loose from the hospital? Who even told you I was gone? You certainly have a lot of explaining to do." Jenna felt like sinking down onto the mattress and pulling the covers up over her head to make it all go away.

"Yes, Gram," she answered meekly, folding her hands on her lap, biting back a smile made up of equal parts of relief and aggravation, a twin to the one Clay gave his dad.

"And don't forget to tell me how Leah Singer came to have her baby a month early, right here in this house!"

"It's a long story, Gram." Jenna broke out laughing despite all her attempts to swallow the merriment. "It was one hell of a day and night."

"I don't doubt it was." Fayette gave Clay, and Clay's pajamas, one last calculating stare. "Out, you two! Go get us something to eat." She herded Clay and his father out the door with the skill of long practice at manipulating others to do her bidding. She turned her back on them before the door was shut.

"Now. Start at the beginning, young woman. And this had better be good."

Chapter Ten

"Yes, Sister. No, Sister. I have no problem with being back in Cincinnati bright and early Monday morning." Jenna raised her eyes from studying the dial on the phone. She tried to smile at Clay across the room, but it wasn't easy. She didn't feel like smiling. She felt a great deal more like breaking into tears. They'd had so little time for themselves during the past few hectic days, no chance at all to plan for their future. She wasn't ready to leave, to allow the real world to interfere with their growing love for each other.

But devotion to duty was strongly ingrained in Jenna's character. She squared her shoulders, turning her back on Clay's scowling countenance, and tried to pay attention to what Sister Mary Gregory was saying.

"I'm sorry to hear about Milt Wilcox's father. You're sure the attack wasn't serious?" She nodded her head at the unseen caller. Clay scuffed the toe of his shoe in the path of a sunbeam making bright, gold patterns on the floor. Dust motes rose up around him in a flurry of dancing points of light. God, he didn't want to think of Jenna's leaving him. He never wanted her out of his sight again.

"Yes." Jenna went on speaking. "My grandmother is home safe and sound. And with quite a story to tell. We're celebrating her achievement with a community get-together tonight that's in honor of another very special event that's occurred. I'll explain everything when I return. Of course, I'll drive carefully, Sister. I'll leave first thing in the morning. Your prayers will be most welcome, as always.'' Jenna turned to smile at him. Clay shifted his position, the voltage of her smile affecting him physically as well as emotionally.

"Goodbye, Sister." Jenna replaced the receiver thoughtfully. Her head lowered for a second, causing flutters of spun platinum to catch the cold, late afternoon light and shine as if with a life of their own.

"You're leaving me so soon?" Clay didn't look pleased. Jenna hardened her heart, lifting her head proudly once again, refusing to let circumstances she couldn't control or alter spoil their last few hours together.

"Yes. My assistant Milt Wilcox's father had a mild heart attack the day before yesterday. Milt wants some time off. I've been gone too long already," she added quietly, sadly. "I have to go back in the morning."

Clay held out his hands, regretting his abruptness when he saw the brightness fade from the gold flecks of her eyes. She covered the distance between them in an instant, coming into his arms so naturally, so trustingly, that he felt as if he were all at once the luckiest man alive. He propped himself against the solid bulk of the hardwood counter. He pulled Jenna closer, spreading his legs and cradling her against the hard wall of his chest.

Their bodies fit together so easily that it amazed Clay. With Joann he'd always felt as if he had to hold back, to treat her as if she were some kind of china doll. Not so with Jenna. He knew instinctively that she would return his ardor with equal abandon. His loins tightened with longing to feel her close to him without any more barriers between them. "Jenna, don't go." The words came out despite his resolve not to pressure her in any way. For a moment the stinging, desperate need to make her his before her old life claimed her again rose up to constrict the breath in his chest. "I don't think I can give you back to them so soon."

"I have to go, Clay. I don't have a choice." His intent expression mirrored her own desire. Jenna relaxed against him, luxuriating in the smell of his sandalwood-scented soap.

"Just a little longer. Please stay." His hands shaped the round curve of her bottom.

"Clay, don't," Jenna begged. "Please don't ask me for something I can't give you." She pushed against his hands, but it was less a protest at the intimacy than a petition for its continuation. Clay leaned down to brush a silencing kiss across her lips.

"I can't let you go," he repeated simply. Jenna detected an underlying note of some emotion she couldn't put a name to and it worried her.

"We have tonight." She had to make him understand. She had an obligation to St. V's. "I have no choice." She gave up her lonely struggle between duty and inclination for the moment, leaning into him, moving with delicate, natural grace in a pattern of desire known to lovers throughout time. "These past few days have gone by too quickly. I never see you alone." There was a note of desperation in her voice that she couldn't completely block out. "First, it was getting Leah and the baby checked out and settled in at home." Jenna laughed softly, shaking her head in disbelief. "I never knew there could be so much paperwork connected to a home birth."

"And it never occurred to me that I'd get caught up in the turmoil of exposing those renegade pilots," Clay explained with a doleful shake of his dark head. "That's what comes of underestimating your grandmother." His breath was warm and minty against her skin. Jenna laid her head on his shoulder, allowing his kneading fingers to work their magic on the tense muscles of her neck and shoulders. "She's been on the phone almost constantly, haranguing newsmen and legislators right and left."

"Day and night," Jenna inserted, along with a spill of her silvery laughter. "How many trips have you made to St. Paul?"

"Two in the past three days. I don't know whether I'm coming or going, but I think Faye and my dad are accomplishing what they set out to do. This ought to move those bureaucrats off dead center. We can be proud of those two, Jenna.''

Her smile agreed with him. ''It's been frantic,'' she said, placing a quick, light kiss on his lips. ''I've loved every minute of it. I'm going to miss all the excitement. Living here will never be dull. I can't wait to get back.'' It frightened her a little, this power he held over her. She'd never felt so empty, so miserable at the thought of being parted from Roger forever as she felt now that she was faced with leaving Clay even temporarily.

''How long will you have to stay in Cincinnati?''

''I don't know. Until the holidays, at least. My contract expires December twenty-third. There's a thirty-day option, but I'm sure they won't ask for it. Milt is every bit as qualified as I am. I intend to give him my recommendation. He'll jump at the chance to take my place if they offer it to him.'' Jenna raised her eyes to meet Clay's foggy gaze. ''We have so much to discuss, so many plans to make, and time is running out.''

''I need to have you all to myself for as long as we've got.'' He didn't know why the aching, irrational need to keep her with him should suddenly be so strong. In a few weeks he'd have her with him forever. He'd never been this possessive with Joann. ''We haven't had enough time.'' It was as close as he could come to explaining his anxiety.

''We'll find a way to solve everything.'' Jenna's words were a mere breath of sound. His eyes were as dark, as troubled, as a rainy sky. ''I love you, Clay.''

He smiled, the warmth of her words cascading over him like sunshine breaking through a storm cloud.

''We'll make it come out right in the end,'' he promised. His hands moved to bury themselves in the silky fineness of her hair. She was wearing it loose and free around her shoulders today. He liked it that way. It made her seem younger, more carefree, than the harsh topknot she affected when she was being Dr. Macklin and not Jenna.

She answered his smile with one of her own. Clay felt himself tighten with wanting and loving the woman in his arms.

He didn't want her to go for even a day. In less than twenty-four hours they'd be separated for far longer than that. Their relationship was new and fragile. Could it survive all the difficulties he foresaw for it? He didn't want to fail with Jenna. Already he loved her far more than he'd ever loved Joann. Still, in a short while they would have time alone together, without interference from conflicting careers and schedules, to build a lasting foundation, to strengthen this new love, to avoid the mistakes of his first marriage. To make love last.

He had trouble visualizing a future without Jenna, although she'd been in his life and his heart for less than two weeks. Yet for the time being, he must; later he'd have her all to himself with all the time he needed to learn everything there was to know about her, to make her forever his. "We'd better be going," he said reluctantly, giving her one last quick kiss. "The others will be wondering what happened to us."

JENNA LOOKED DOWN at the mug of hot mulled cider in her hand. It was definitely spiked, but delicious nonetheless. She let the aroma of spice and spirits envelop her, momentarily blocking out the scent of birch smoke and autumn leaves. She glanced over the cedar deck railing, catching a faint, satisfied grin on Horatio Gibbs's gremlin face. So he was the culprit who'd spiked her cider. Jenna shook her head in resignation, raising the mug in a mock salute. The old man returned the gesture, cackling with glee as he turned back to the small, quiet circle of men seated around the glowing remains of the cooking fire.

Harmon Thornton was holding forth in animated conversation with Fayette's old friend Walter Ericson. Clay's father was nearly as forceful a personality as his son, but far more volatile and gregarious. Clay took after his mother, "a fine, strong woman," Harmon had decreed. He favored his mother physically, too, Jenna discovered when Harmon had unearthed two big, heavy family albums for her perusal two evenings previously.

Jenna cradled her earthenware mug between her hands, one

sneakered foot swinging free as she perched on the deck railing. She was glad she'd worn the heavy, lined wool shirt Fayette had insisted on. Its muted blue-and-gray plaid suited her delicate coloring. Its practical warmth was appreciated in the chilly evening air.

Most of the other women had gone inside Leah's split-log cabin some time ago. Jenna had volunteered to remain outdoors to keep an eye on Cassie and assorted other children. Locke's sixteen-year-old brother, Jordan, was trundling his niece and two other little girls around in a wheelbarrow, skimming over the flat shelving of rock that comprised Locke and Leah's front yard.

Cassie squealed in excitement. Her white cast, resplendent with autographs signed in bright neon colors, gleamed below the cuff of her trousers. A white sock protected her toes from the cold.

Leah had been right when she said the view from every window of her home more than made up for the inconvenience of living so far from everything. The sun was going down over the horizon, but long, gold streaks of light spangled their way across the still lake. It was an unusual sunset, thick rays of light spreading out in all directions, reaching back toward the darkening eastern sky like long fingers of gold. Crafts of all sizes and descriptions bobbed gently along the length of shoreline opposite the house. Gold-crested ripples lapped at the beach.

Jenna stood up, resting both hands on the rough railing. Behind her the homey sounds of dishes being washed and small children complaining were punctuated now and again by a merry chorus of women's laughter. It was a friendly, comforting sound to Jenna. Locke and Leah's neighbors had provided everything necessary for the celebration to welcome Buffalo Point's newest resident. Now the women were busy putting Leah's house to rights. It was a demonstration of friendship and community spirit that was spontaneous and genuine.

Still, Jenna felt a little outside it all. She knew the other women would open up to her when they got to know her; yet, for now, she was an outsider, treated with respect and courtesy, but not an accepted member of the inner circle. But soon she would belong. The thought gave Jenna a pure jolt of happiness.

Clay and Locke appeared from the direction of the lake, carrying between them the huge iron kettle that had been used for the fish boil. Jenna was skeptical when she heard what was on the menu, but it had turned out to be one of the most delicious meals she'd ever eaten.

Scrubbed potatoes and onions were first put into a wire basket and lowered into the boiling springwater. About thirty minutes later, beautiful fresh fillets of walleye and whitefish were added. Then, when Locke's tall, red-faced father, the evening's unanimously elected master chef, announced that the food was done to perfection, a quart of white kerosene was poured over the logs stacked around the kettle. The fire blazed up in white-hot fury, much to the scary delight of the children watching from a safe distance. The water boiled over, taking all the fish oils and impurities along with it. What remained, covered with pure melted butter and lemon juice, was ambrosia. Combined with a bewildering variety of salads, fresh-baked bread, and topped off with Maggie Ericson's wild-blueberry pie, it had taken all the willpower Jenna possessed to limit herself to second helpings and not go back for thirds or even fourths.

She'd enjoyed the old-fashioned tenor of the get-together. The women gathered around the large wicker clothes basket that had been fitted out to hold the new baby. They kept an eye on the young children and exchanged battlefield stories of their own pregnancies and deliveries. The newest member of the Singer clan looked snug and comfortable in his gingham-lined basket. It was far easier and more practical to carry around, Leah maintained, than the elaborate bassinet her parents had shipped north by air express.

The men and boys formed their own group, arguing over sports, politics and the economy, making note of any neighbors who needed help, already well on the way to getting ready for the fast-approaching winter.

"Have you ever seen such a glorious sunset?" Jenna called. Her voice was husky and suddenly breathless when she caught sight of Clay approaching the house.

"It's a special one tonight. I'll show you why a little later, when it's dark." It had frosted hard the night before. The mosquitoes that plagued the area in summer were gone. So were the bullfrogs, but katydids still sang in the thicket behind the house. "Maybe then I can have you to myself for a few minutes."

"Soon." Jenna rested her hand alongside his on the railing, but they didn't touch. They hadn't told anyone of their love; however, Jenna planned to confide everything to Fayette that night. Events were moving so quickly that she felt she wanted to reach out and slow time down until she could assimilate all the sensations and emotions that were rushing at her with such force. "Clay…"

"No more fussing, squirt," Jordan Singer scolded, interrupting Jenna's words as he deposited a vociferously protesting Cassie on the porch. "It's bedtime for little kindergarten brats like you."

"You'll have to carry me," Cassie announced with regal grandeur. "I can't walk with this cast."

"Of course you can," Jenna reminded her small patient encouragingly. She dropped to her knees to confront Cassie's pouting little face on her own level. "I've seen you hopping up and down these steps at least half a dozen times this evening."

Cassie snorted in disdain but moved toward the door, maneuvering the lightweight walking cast with a child's unconscious ability to adapt to most situations with ease.

"Remember, save some time for me." Clay spoke to Jenna in a low, rough whisper as he turned back to the circle of men around the fire.

"Come on, Jenna. We can look at the baby if he's awake," Cassie ordered, ignoring Clay. "He's just like the Cabbage Patch dolly Grandmother Purchase sent me from Atlanta. I'm going to give him to the baby because he's a preemie, too. The doll's name is Michael Elliot. I already have Amanda Marie that Grandmother sent me for Christmas. My brother's name is even better, isn't it? Brandon Locke Purchase Singer,'' she said, rolling the syllables around on her tongue. ''I can make a *B*,'' she added proudly while Jenna was still trying to untangle all the names and identities Cassie had just tossed at her.

''That's nice,'' she replied automatically when Cassie paused.

''Of course, *I* can already write all of my own name,'' the child announced proudly. ''But Brandon is a whole different bunch of letters.'' There was a distinct edge of annoyance in her voice, as though Cassie felt that Locke and Leah had chosen her brother's name solely to put her in the position of having to learn all those new letters. Her tone implied that all five-year-olds worth their salt knew parents did such sneaky things. And Cassie, she would be the first to remind you, was a very bright five-year-old indeed.

''Learning new things can be a lot of fun.'' Jenna realized she'd made a tactical error the moment the words left her lips. Cassie looked at her long and hard. Jenna smiled sheepishly, apologizing for the pedantic utterance. She'd have to practice up on her communication skills with children. She'd be dealing with them more closely than ever in the future. Again Jenna felt the special stirring of excitement her secret dream evoked.

''I suppose you're right,'' Cassie said without much conviction.

Jenna laughed delightedly at the world-weary approach Cassie was taking to education. She'd been a lot older than the little girl before she discovered the validity of her statement. There was plenty of time. ''Where's the baby?'' Jenna asked by way of changing the subject.

''In his room,'' Cassie said as she opened the door.

''Jenna, there you are.'' Leah emerged from the hallway leading off to the bedrooms. She was wearing a pair of jeans and a loose, billowy pink top. Jenna marveled at the way some women seemed to have no trouble at all regaining their figures.

She had a dire premonition that it wouldn't be the case with her.

Locke's mother and two of his unmarried sisters, all blond, plump and pretty, were seated at the oak pedestal table in the dining room. They smiled and waved at Jenna's entrance.

"I just put Brandon down for the night," Leah explained. She looked tired but happy and far more sure of herself than she had two weeks ago.

"He's gained another three ounces since Monday," Locke's mother broke in proudly. "He'll catch up soon."

"He'll weigh over five pounds before we know it, Mrs. Singer," Jenna agreed.

"It's almost dark. I'd best be starting back home." Myrtle Langley came out of the kitchen with a freshly washed plastic bowl in her hands.

"Your three-bean salad was as good as ever, Myrtle," Fayette called, appearing behind her neighbor and wiping her hands on a terry towel.

"Thanks, Faye. Must have been tolerable. There's only a dab left. I put it in a dish in your fridge, Leah."

"Thank you, Myrtle," Leah said with a gracious nod of her dark head. "It's Locke's favorite."

"It's been nice seeing you again, Doctor…Jenna. Come back and visit us soon." Myrtle Langley's hair was still improbably red, Jenna noted, and she still wore orthopedic shoes.

"I hope to do just that, Mrs. Langley." Jenna kept her smile from breaking into a grin with some difficulty.

"I'll ask Horatio to walk you part way, Myrtle," Leah offered in her soft, musical voice.

"Well…" Myrtle hesitated a moment.

"Go ahead, Leah," Faye directed, still standing in the kitchen doorway. The thick braid of hair wound around her head glowed in the overhead light. "The exercise will do that old coot a world of good."

Myrtle sent Jenna's grandmother a withering stare while Locke's oldest sister hid a grin behind her hand. "Faye's right," the redheaded woman surprised Jenna by agreeing. "I'd be glad of the company if the 'old coot' hasn't imbibed too much of his spiked cider.''

Jenna barely restrained her smile. Locke's sister didn't fare as well, receiving an icy stare from Myrtle as she passed out of the room.

''I think I'll go take a last look at the baby,'' Jenna told the room at large.

Like every other room in the snug cabin, the nursery was richly furnished with the most expensive fabrics and accessories. Leah's parents, aware that she wouldn't accept direct financial help from them, had literally inundated their daughter with gifts, from all the latest mechanical and time-saving gadgets to elegant wall-to-wall carpeting and drapes. In the past few days the eyelet-lace-canopied bassinet, a complete layette with the labels of the most exclusive Atlanta department store, an antique-satin christening gown and hundreds of dollars worth of toys for both Brandon and Cassie had arrived by air express.

Jenna knew Leah was embarrassed by the largess, but loved her parents too much to put a halt to the gifts. She used what she needed, gave away duplicates to friends, and ignored the rest as best she could. Locke said little, as usual, but Jenna wondered just how much the conspicuous show of wealth bothered him. It seemed calculated to point out his shortcomings in providing for Leah and the children.

The couple had come a long way toward solving their problems in the short time since Brandon's birth, but they certainly didn't need additional stress from Leah's parents.

''He sounds like a little pig,'' Jenna said with a soft laugh as Leah entered the room.

''He eats like one, too,'' Leah said with a smile. ''Have I thanked you properly for bringing him into the world safe and sound?''

''All in a day's work.''

''Locke and I would like you to be godmother.''

''Oh, Leah, I'd be honored!''

''I'm sure Faye will act as proxy for you at the ceremony

next month. I realize your work won't allow you to make another trip up here this year.''

Jenna took a deep breath, her eyes shining with excitement.
"I am coming back to the Woods, Leah. I'm going to marry
Clay.''

"Jenna!'' Leah's mouth dropped open in surprise. She shut
it with a snap, recalling her manners. "Really?'' She began to
giggle, then clamped a hand over her mouth when the baby
stirred, frowning in his sleep. "That's marvelous,'' she whispered, more composed, moving forward to embrace Jenna in a
quick, hard hug. "I wish you every happiness.''

"I think it's pretty nice myself.'' Jenna knew there were
tears in her eyes. She blinked them away. "Everything's happened so quickly. But I know I'm making the right choice,
Leah. I love him so. I'm going to love it here. And I'll be able
to practice medicine the way I've really always wanted to.''

"Start your own practice? Here?'' Leah's blue eyes sparkled
with interest. "A clinic on Buffalo Point?''

"Possibly. But I think Oakhelm is better situated. We
haven't even been able to discuss wedding plans yet, not to
mention the best place to open an office. Now I have to go
back to Cincinnati first thing in the morning.''

"So soon?'' Leah looked concerned, then hurried back into
speech. "Jenna, I'll miss you. But I'll do everything I can to
help you get your practice going. Remember what I told you.
I'm a whiz at bookkeeping. And I type up a storm.''

"You don't know how much that means to me.'' This time
the detested tears threatened to overflow. "I'll write and tell
you all my plans as soon as I know them myself.'' Jenna
smoothed a trembling hand over Brandon's fuzzy skull, trying
to bring her emotions back under control. The muted ringing
of the telephone carried faintly down the hall. Moments later
Locke strode into the room.

"Leah, your parents are on the phone,'' he said shortly.

"I just spoke to them yesterday. Did you tell them we're
entertaining guests tonight?'' She held out her small hand and

Locke covered it with his own. Leah went into his arms for a brief hug.

"Yes," Locke said. His voice was strained, but his smile was full of love. "They won't take my word that you're not overdoing. They want to speak to you."

"Lordy. I have a new baby, not some dread tropical disease." Leah laughed off the interruption. The sound was muted in the quiet nursery with its Kate Greenaway wallpaper and Winnie-the-Pooh lamps. "I'll just go settle Father down, Locke." She stopped in the doorway, putting a caressing hand on her husband's arm, almost as if she couldn't get enough of touching him after the weeks of misunderstanding that had passed between them. "Jenna has the most wonderful news."

"Clay told me." He looked down at his wife and placed a quick light kiss on the tip of her nose. "Do you and Jenna think you can get along as neighbors?"

"Don't be a goose." Leah giggled and reached up to kiss him back.

"Did Clay also tell you Jenna's going to open her own practice? Imagine not having to go all the way to the clinic every time the kids have the sniffles. And Brandon's baby shots..." Leah gave a happy, exaggeratedly dramatic sigh of relief. "Jenna, you'll be a godsend."

"Practice medicine here? Clay didn't mention anything about that." Locke looked faintly troubled, but Jenna chose not to notice, blaming his frown on the low light in the nursery.

"We haven't really had time to discuss it. Everything's happened so quickly for us." Jenna knew she was blushing and didn't care. She was so happy suddenly to have these people to share her good fortune with.

"Leah, better go set your momma's mind at rest," Locke reminded her with a light proprietorial pat on the behind. "She thinks you're crazy even to be out of bed so soon." The light made his hair seem blonder than ever. Brandon resembled his father as much as Cassie resembled Leah.

"I'll just have my doctor tell her otherwise," Leah replied with a saucy toss of her dark head.

"Leave me out of this," Jenna said with a laugh, holding up a disclaiming hand.

"I won't be a minute." On the words Leah was gone.

"Are you sure you're making the right decision, Jen?" Locke reached out to tuck Brandon's blanket more comfortably around the sleeping infant. He traced the baby's cheek with the gentle touch of his big hand.

"I think I am," Jenna answered quietly.

"I do, too. Clay's a great guy. The best friend I've ever had." He rested both hands on the crib rail, avoiding her eyes to hide his own emotion. "I'm happy for both of you. Leah and I came so close to losing…Well, I'm just glad 'happily ever after' happens more than once." Locke didn't say anything else for several moments. Then he held out his arms. "Thanks for everything, Jenna." He folded her in a brief, hard hug that nearly took her breath away. "Clay's waiting for you at the back door. Fayette says to tell you she'll get a ride home with Walter and Maggie. She and Harmon are going to fill the rest of us in on their trips to the capital. She said to remind you it's going to be a long day tomorrow. Will you stop by and say goodbye to Leah before you go?"

"Of course I will. Do you think anyone will notice if Clay and I do slip away?" Again she could feel a faint tinge of color mount into her cheeks.

"No, and what if they do? You're going to make an honest man out of him, aren't you?"

"Yes, I am. Just as soon as we can manage it."

"NOW, WHAT WAS that special something you wanted me to see?" Jenna asked innocently.

Clay laughed and shook his head.

Jenna took a moment to identify the source of his amusement at her own unintentional double entendre. Or was it so very unintentional? In any case, she was glad it was dark under the stand of balsam.

"That something special is right above us." His words were indulgent. Jenna cuddled against him as they snuggled into the folds of a sleeping bag Clay kept in the back of the Jeep in case of emergency. She followed his pointing finger with her eyes. His breath was warm against her cheek, spicy with the scent of cinnamon and cider. They'd wound through the trees along the shoreline for the past several minutes of their drive, the interlocking canopy of leaves making everything as dark as midnight beyond the glow of the headlights. Now, parked along the shoreline, her eyes adjusting to the darkness, Jenna could see what Clay had been referring to.

The sky above the black, wind-ruffled lake was a shifting curtain of green and blue, with touches of gold and silver spangled along the edges. "The northern lights!" Jenna sucked in her breath in awe. "I've never seen them before. They aren't very common up here in the summer, are they?"

"Rare and unique." Clay's tone carried a deeper, more personal meaning. "Very rare and unique, like your smile. I love you, Jenna," Clay went on with quiet intensity. "I want us to be together very soon. I want to be able to hold you in my arms and make love to you over and over again."

"We could make love now," Jenna ventured, unable to meet his gaze head-on. She wanted, somehow, to let him know how much she wanted a life with him, how much she wanted to make permanent and sacred the promises they'd made to each other. Jenna wanted to show her love physically, to be as close to Clay as it was possible for a man and woman to be.

"Don't tempt me, love," Clay whispered. Her breath was hot and moist against his throat. His head whirled pleasantly, more from the heady effect of Jenna's nearness than Horatio's spiked cider. To have Jenna naked and welcoming beneath him tonight with only the moon and stars, the pines and the falling leaves to witness their act of love, was what he desired more than anything else. "I want the first time between us to be special." He found it hard to believe that she might share this particular fantasy with him, so he put it out of his mind.

"What could be more special than making love under a sky full of stars and the aurora borealis?" Jenna tried hard to sound matter-of-fact. She didn't even know enough about this man to be sure he wouldn't think she'd lost her mind in suggesting such a thing. Jenna let her hand stray nervously beneath Clay's Nordic-patterned sweater, snaking her fingers between the buttons of his shirt to rest against the warmth of his skin.

"I assumed you would want a warm bed, soft sheets and no lumps, bumps or mosquitoes," Clay replied wonderingly.

"Is that the way Joann wanted to make love?" Jenna was surprised that she could inject the other woman's name into the conversation so easily. But this shadowy figure from Clay's past was the cause of many of his misconceptions. Jenna wanted her ghost banished from between them. "I'm not your ex-wife. All I want is to be here, with you in my arms."

"Then I have a wish, Jenna."

"Wish away." She traced the outline of his collarbone beneath his shirt, anxious to have its restricting folds lifted away and slightly shocked by her own sensual longing.

"I wish for time," came the whimsical answer. "All the time in the world. Hours and hours to make you mine, for us to be alone together." Clay's lips found hers in a greedy kiss that took her breath. He tried to show Jenna with his touch, with his caress, the sense of aloneness, of oneness, he was trying to convey in words. It seemed so important to have Jenna all to himself, to make her his forever, a unity that no circumstance could separate.

"We have tonight." Boldly Jenna lifted her mouth to receive his kiss. Their tongues touched, retreated, then met to mingle for a small eternity. She nestled closer, entreating his hands to close over the soft fullness of her breast beneath the heavy wool shirt. "It's more than enough," she moaned against his mouth, her actions, her movements admitting to a hunger as great as his. Clay felt his body harden, his entire being rising up to clamor for more of Jenna, for more of her loving magic.

Still under her spell Clay felt his sweater being lifted over his head and then dropped to the ground. His fingers worked at the buttons of Jenna's shirt. Then his shirt and her bra were discarded. She tugged at the snap of his jeans and he helped slide hers over the rounded swell of her hips. Within moments they were naked, vulnerable to each other and to the cool night air. Clay pulled the sleeping bag over them but Jenna was barely aware of the chill. His warmth enveloped her, surrounding her.

Clay's hands were on her breasts tracing ever smaller circles of sensual warmth. Jenna twined her fingers with his, and his lips claimed her mouth once again. Her legs parted to allow him access to the heated center of her femininity. In only moments they were ready for love. Their joining was a quiet explosion of joy. From the first touch of his body in hers, the rhythm was established and they moved in perfect harmony through successive layers of desire and loving exchange that fused them more tightly together with each thrust of his hips and answering lift of hers.

Their sighs mingled with the call of night birds and the pounding of waves against the rocky shore. Above them the heavens moved in their ageless cycle. Clay found his wish come true in the peace of loving Jenna with his hands, his lips, his body. Desire beat around him with soft wings, shutting out the sky, the wheel of planets in their orbits, suspending them effortlessly between heaven and earth for the length of their coming together. Time stood still as he filled Jenna again and again, until they came to their peak, shattered in the elemental heat released between them, and then they were reformed, whole and renewed, to settle softly into the serenity of the north-country night.

CLAY CAME SLOWLY BACK to himself in bits and pieces. It could have been minutes, it could have been hours later. Yet it seemed as if the sensual spell still held. He shifted his body, with Jenna wrapped in his arms, so he could stare up into the sky. Above them the ever-changing, ever-shifting pattern of light in the sky had faded from green to gold, but the curtains of light continued to shimmer and dance, covering nearly the entire bowl of the heavens. He had time yet this night to hold Jenna close, to fill her again, give her the very essence of himself and take the same from her in return. She stirred in his arms, curling up to fit herself even more closely into the arch of his body.

"Jenna, when can you marry me?"

"I'd like a Christmas wedding." Her fingers glided over the sleekness of his collarbone and wandered down the tapering V of his rib cage to rest just below his waist. "Can you get away then?" She raised her head to try to catch his expression in the fading glow of the aurora lights. "I mean truly get away. I've already made plans to visit my parents in England over the holidays. It'll be a perfect time for you to meet them."

"An English country Christmas sounds fine." Clay felt a little drunk with happiness.

"You won't mind being away from your family during the holidays?"

"Not if I'm with you."

Jenna couldn't see his face, but Clay's words sent tremors of renewed longing racing down her spine. She lifted herself up on her elbow to rest her breasts against the hard slope of his chest.

"We could stop back by way of Kansas City and meet my brothers. You'll like my sisters-in-law and that assorted herd of nieces and nephews I've told you about." Clay shifted his position, catching the rapt happiness of her face. He pulled her closer as her hand moved lower and more knowledgeably along the inside of his thigh. He needed this physical contact to assure himself he wasn't dreaming, that these tranquil plans he was making for a life with Jenna, here, in the one place on earth he loved above all others, were real.

"Sounds marvelous." Jenna smiled her dazzling smile for him alone; even in the darkness he felt its voltage.

"I've found something far more marvelous." Clay bent to kiss the tip of her breast while he moved his hips against her hand. Jenna caught her breath in a ragged sigh, then answered his insistence, pulling him atop her, opening to him like a dewy rose. They didn't talk for a long time after that, allowing their bodies to speak for them. When the hurricane tide of passion had passed over them, Clay waited for Jenna's heartbeat and breathing to return to normal before he spoke.

"Where will we live?"

"Mmm." Her shoulders lifted in a shrug he felt but didn't see. "Any place will do—right here in the back of the Jeep is fine with me." Jenna sounded sleepy and contented, the way he wanted her to be.

"Might not be big enough." Clay's stomach muscles tightened with excitement as the realization came to him that he might have made Jenna pregnant already. "I keep a room at the motel in Oakhelm. The rest of the time I'm out here with Dad. It could get crowded."

"What do you mean?"

"I mean—" Clay ran his hand over the soft rise of Jenna's belly and rested his palm on the downy triangle between her legs "—you could be pregnant."

"No, not tonight." Jenna's voice was soft but certain, although slightly regretful. "The timing is all wrong for me. I'm a doctor, remember; I know. It will be lovely when it happens…but, Clay, there are a lot of things we have to work out before then."

It wasn't the response he'd expected. Frayed strands were beginning to unravel along the edges of his fantasy. "When might it be convenient?" God, weren't those the exact words Joann had used when he'd wanted to start a family with her? *It wasn't convenient.*

"When we get settled, and I've had time to look for a place to open my office." Jenna had reached out to trace the line of his jaw. "Getting a practice started will be a real hassle." Clay jerked back from her caressing hand so suddenly that she was startled. "Clay, what is it? What's wrong?" Surely he couldn't be that disappointed that there would be no baby from this first complete expression of their feelings for each other. It wasn't logical. It wasn't like him.

Clay sat up, looming over her in the pale glow of a half-moon high up in the sky. The aurora borealis was gone, its shimmering beauty only a memory. "Office? What office?"

He couldn't keep the sharpness out of his tone, although he did manage to keep his voice level. "Why do you need an office?"

"To see my patients in, naturally." Jenna laughed nervously. "We discussed it the morning after Brandon was born, remember…" But had they truly discussed it or only alluded to it? Jenna had the horrible, sinking feeling that she'd let her wishes outrun reality. Panic began to beat like frantic bird wings in her chest. She suddenly felt horribly alone, naked emotionally as well as physically. Clay remained obdurately silent. The panic grew stronger, nearly choking Jenna. She pushed it away, sitting up, winding her arms around her knees in an instinctive effort to shield herself from pain. "We talked…I thought you understood what I was trying to say, although I probably wasn't very clear in my own mind yet about what I wanted to do."

"What do you want to do, Jenna?" Clay didn't seem to mind the cold air swirling around them. He wasn't even shivering. Goose bumps popped up along Jenna's arms. Her teeth were beginning to chatter, making it harder than ever to get words out of her mouth.

"Why, practice medicine, of course. Here, in Oakhelm, I mean. Medicine means so much to me."

"It means more than being my wife and the mother of my children, obviously," Clay said tonelessly, more to himself than to her, it seemed to Jenna's heightened senses.

"That's not true." She meant the statement to come out bold and assertive, so that he couldn't misunderstand. Instead it sifted past her lips in an anguished croak. "I want to be both those things. But I want to be a doctor, too. It's my life's—"

"I want to be your life, Jenna." Clay's tone was harsh with emotion. "I thought you would be available to treat friends and relatives, even neighbors, maybe, but not the whole damned region." Clay threw out a long bare arm to encompass a thousand square miles of rocks and trees, lake water and remote settlements and scores of widely scattered human beings, all coming between him and Jenna, all making demands on her time and energy, leaving him with the crumbs. He couldn't stand loving and taking second place again. He just couldn't. Clay felt Jenna retreating from him mentally as well as physically, yet he couldn't stop the bitter rush of his own words.

"How do you intend to practice medicine when the people you'll be serving are scattered over miles and miles of wilderness? When will you have time to be a wife and a mother?" *Slow down, you're losing her, forcing her away.* But all the old worries, the fears, the jealousy he'd thought he'd conquered—all the things that had driven him apart from Joann— were there, circling just above their heads like vultures, waiting to tear them apart.

"I'll go to them," Jenna said stubbornly. She raised her chin in a touching show of bravura. *I thought we'd be partners.* A few moments before, Jenna would have said, *we* could do it together, but not anymore. Everything was coming apart. "I'll learn to fly," she said defiantly. She was already sealing off the pain, cauterizing the lacerations his words were causing even as they were inflicted. Maybe she wasn't strong enough to have it all. Maybe Roger had been right. Could she be a doctor and a wife and mother, even a real woman? Look how badly she was doing now. This was the most important argument of her life and she was mouthing platitudes that did nothing to reassure Clay, or herself, that she could succeed.

"These people will come to own you, heart and soul, I know. I can't accept the risk of not having a life to call our own. I've seen how easily it comes apart." Clay's voice had a hollow ring.

"I can separate my career and my personal life, Clay. Please don't turn away from me because Joann couldn't manage to do that. I'm not her. I won't betray your love. I can do it."

"But what if *I* can't?"

The defeat in his voice shocked Jenna even more than his anger. "Love is strong," she answered him. "We can make it last together." She loved him, that hadn't changed, but he was starting to destroy something else. He was attacking the only thing she had that was secure, her self-confidence in her ability to function as a physician. That she couldn't allow or it would tear her apart inside.

"Jenna, listen." Clay pulled her hands away from her knees, violating her cocoon of aloofness. Sometime during the past few awful minutes he'd pulled on his jeans and she hadn't noticed when. Now she felt even more unprotected because he was dressed and she wasn't. "Don't shut me out, for God's sake. We have to talk, to settle this. Now, before it's too late for us." Clay held onto her wrists, giving her a little shake. His hands trembled with the effort to keep his words and his emotions under control. "Love isn't strong. I know, to my sorrow, I know. If you don't work at it, keep renewing it constantly over and over each day of your life, it dies."

"But together we can handle everything." Jenna didn't sound very convincing, even to herself. She sounded lost and forlorn. She was trying hard not to let tears of fear and weakness seep into her words. She could do anything with Clay by her side, but she didn't know how she would get through tomorrow without him. It was that simple, but impossible to say aloud.

"I wish I could make you understand." Clay felt muddled and pulled in a dozen directions at once. He suspected that he wasn't making very much sense. "We'll talk about it in the morning." His body still vibrated with the heavy beat of fulfillment, but his nerves felt stretched as tight as guy wires. "I'll fly you into Oakhelm. I'll ride with you all the way to Cincinnati if I have to." He needed time to adjust, to work this out in his head, to learn to believe in miracles again. Couldn't Jenna see that? If he'd been thinking at all clearly using his brain instead of his heart, this past week he'd have known she wouldn't give up her medicine. She couldn't trade that kind of commitment for another at the drop of a hat. But could she make him believe they could beat the odds together?

"What's left for us to talk about, Clay?" Jenna asked wearily, reaching for her clothes. He pulled her back against him, wanting to show her with his touch, with his kisses how hard he was trying to come to terms with what she'd revealed to him. He wanted so much to believe it could work, that they did have some magic between them. But his brain kept telling him that magic, like love, was so very fragile. He'd tried to combine love and two demanding careers before, and the situation had defeated him. He couldn't live through that kind of agony again. It was that simple. For Clay, it was a matter of life and death.

But Jenna's self-isolation was almost complete. She couldn't feel the hunger, the seeking, desperate need for understanding in his kiss, only the roughness of his hand on her arms, the strength of his body willing her to do his bidding and to give up everything that she'd worked so hard for, everything that gave her life meaning before she had met him. His gray eyes were nearly black with inner pain but Jenna couldn't see anything but the blurred outline of his face through her tears, and it looked rock-hard and implacable.

"Clay, take me home." She clutched her sweater to her breasts, trying to cover herself and regain at least enough of her dignity to make it back to Faye's cabin without breaking down.

"Jen, answer me, please." Clay tried again to minimize the damage he'd inflicted on their relationship. "Give me a chance to take this all in." He was as close to begging as a proud man could come. "I need time to adjust to the idea of your wanting to become a backwoods doctor...of having to share you with all and sundry...of taking second place in your life."

It was that last telling phrase that Jenna would wish a thousand times in the long lonely nights and days that stretched ahead of her that she had answered. Clay could never take second place in her heart. Without him beside her she didn't have a heart, merely a highly efficient muscle pumping blood through a body so numbed by pain that she might have been one of the walking dead.

But she hadn't said another word.

Chapter Eleven

"Jenna! Are you listening to a word I've been saying?"

Jenna blinked twice, pulling her eyes from the moon's hypnotic gaze, trying to focus on Milt Wilcox's grinning cherub face. His stubby, square body was wedged uncomfortably into a wicker garden chair on the terrace outside the staff dining room. It was nearly the end of October; soon St. Vincent's maintenance people would take the furniture inside for the winter season. The orange and purple mums in pots at their feet would become brown and withered. The terrace would be empty and bleak like her heart.

It was hard for Jenna to concentrate on Milt's conversation. Above them the gibbous moon hung low in the sky, distracting her with its golden light. It was a beautiful Indian summer night, warm and humid, with the scent of autumn leaves and chrysanthemums heavy in the air. Off in the distance a light mist rose up from the Ohio River.

"I'm sorry, Milt. What did you say? It's been a long day." Jenna apologized for her inattention. She glanced at her wristwatch, then shuffled the jumble of legal documents lying on the table in front of her. It was seven-thirty, fully dark this late in the year, and her shift was nearly over. Luckily it was a Tuesday and fairly quiet. Uneventful Tuesdays were one of the unexplainable blessings encountered in most emergency rooms.

"I said, the new batch of first-year residents will be arriving for their orientation tomorrow.'' Milt repeated the sentence with exaggerated patience.

"Deliver us," Jenna replied in her driest imitation of Sister Mary Gregory. She smiled at her assistant and made a determined effort to focus her attention away from the hard core of unhappiness in her heart, on which she tended to dwell without constant outside stimulus to occupy her.

"It'll be a zoo until we get them settled in." Milt slouched lower in his seat. The wicker chair groaned in protest. Her colleague's outward demeanor was misleading, reminding Jenna of nothing so much as a very mischievous, redheaded boy, when, in reality, he had a mind like a steel trap and medical skills that matched her own. He'd been a year behind Jenna at the University of Cincinnati medical school, so they'd known each other for a long time.

"How many this year?" Jenna pulled her scattered wits into line. She shifted in her seat so that the moon was no longer in her line of sight over the low balcony wall. It was too close to Halloween, she decided wryly. Something in the moonlight was bewitching her, causing her to stare into its serene face and see nothing but Clay's sharply etched features staring back at her, with misery in his eyes.

"Four."

Four. Four weeks since she'd driven back into the city in a daze of fatigue and sadness. Four weeks since she'd heard Clay's voice, felt his touch. Could it truly have been so short a time? It seemed like years, or centuries, since she'd left him standing in the rain, angry and frustrated, at the dock in Oakhelm. They never discussed what had happened to them as he'd pleaded with her to do. Instead, she'd wrapped herself in stiff pride and righteous pain and shut him out of her life.

The memories were hauntingly clear. She'd spent an almost sleepless night in Fayette's spare bedroom after they'd argued following their lovemaking, going over and over it in her mind. She hadn't seen any way to alter the situation then, and when she was tired, like tonight, she still couldn't see any solution. Her fragile emotions had left her prey to paralyzing uncertainty in the darkness, and she'd come to believe that she must cling even more tightly to what was stable and familiar in her life. That next morning, just after dawn, when she heard the noisy roar of Horatio Gibbs's truck pulling into Fayette's clearing, Jenna had given up the struggle to make sense of what had happened between her and Clay and hitched a ride into town.

It was still hard to put distance between her and those painful events. Fayette had thought Jenna had lost her mind and said so. Her grandmother was hurt and confused by her rapid departure. She'd told the older woman a garbled version of the truth and promised to explain more fully when she could. She hadn't been able to do so yet, and had only sent Fayette a letter telling her she was back in Cincinnati and not to worry.

"Jenna?" Milt stood up and stretched. "I don't think your mind's on the new interns."

"You're right, it's not." Jenna didn't give any further explanation for her preoccupation.

"It's a good thing you're going off duty for the next seventy-two hours, Doctor. You're really out of it," he observed bluntly. "Is Parnelli getting to you about renewing your contract?" Elliot Parnelli was the head of personnel. He'd been increasing his pressure on Jenna to sign a new three-year contract with the Trauma Program since she'd returned from Minnesota.

"No worse than usual. I don't know what to do. Go or stay," Jenna said with an eloquent shrug of her shoulders. She tugged at the stethoscope draped around her neck. She stared down at the contract on the table before picking it up gingerly, as though it might bite. "Here's the latest edition. He's sweetened the pot. There aren't many points in here I can quibble about. It makes it hard to say no." *Especially when the rest of your life is an empty shambles,* Jenna thought. She couldn't become enthusiastic about a private practice anymore. The life she wanted, had dreamed about was in Oakhelm—with Clay. And the possibility of living that life seemed as remote as the moon tonight.

"Don't rush it," Milt advised. "And don't let them rush you." Jenna gave his hand a squeeze. Milt knew as well as she did that if she left St. V's, he would be the most likely candidate for her job. But never once had he tried to influence her decision in either direction, even though, with his growing family, Jenna knew he wanted and needed her job.

"I won't," she promised but her resolve was weakening. At the moment, the familiarity and security of the Trauma Center were all she had. "Come on, it's time we got back. I'll give you my report." She opened the glass doors that separated them from the dining room. It was past the dinner hour, and most of the tables were deserted.

"I hope it's this quiet the rest of the night." Milt obligingly changed the subject as he joined her, carrying their empty dishes to the counter. He was working the late shift on this rotation. "The baby's teething and kept me up damn near all day."

Again regret stabbed through Jenna. *Babies.* She'd never noticed how often the subject entered day-to-day conversation. She should at least send Clay a note to assure him she wasn't pregnant. But she couldn't do that, knowing full well her silence amounted to the same declaration.

Would he be disappointed?

She was. It would be wonderful to have a child of her own— Clay's son or daughter to love and cherish. And it would have taken the decision to make a move toward reconciliation out of her hands. She loved Clay. She wanted to be with him. She just couldn't see how to make the first move.

"It's peaceful now, at least," Jenna made herself comment on the relative inactivity as they came back into the unit.

"I envy you a good night's sleep." Milt was following his own train of thought.

Jenna didn't bother to explain that she probably wouldn't get it. She would be lucky to sleep at all before the small hours of the morning. Closing her eyes was tantamount to inviting Clay into her dreams. That was the hardest part, trying to keep his image, the memory of the pain he'd caused her, the guilt for

the pain she'd caused him, out of her thoughts in the darkness
of her bedroom.

The days weren't so bad. She'd thrown herself back into her
work the moment she returned to the city. That was probably
why Elliot Parnelli got the impression that she'd welcome his
early advances to renew her contract with the hospital. On her
days off she'd indulged in a frenzy of cleaning and repainting
her small two-bedroom apartment. Now she was faced with
another three days of lonely solitude.

The prospect was daunting.

JENNA PEELED OFF her lab coat, exchanging green cotton scrubs
for a plaid skirt in tones of burgundy and gray. She added a
blouse and pullover sweater that picked up the lightest shade
of each color. She was patting escaping tendrils of silvery-
blond hair back into place on top of her head when Sister Mary
Gregory poked her head around the door to the physicians'
locker room. "Thank goodness you haven't gone."

"I'm just getting ready to leave." Jenna glanced at the clock
on the wall to her left. "I stayed on after report to talk with
Milt. What is it you want, Sister?" Jenna was intrigued, despite
her fatigue and low spirits, by the look of interest on the nun's
benign countenance.

"We have a family of refugees out in the lobby asking for
you."

"Refugees? Asking for me?" Jenna parroted, a look of bewilderment on her face. She'd tried to hide the dark circles
under her eyes with an extra application of makeup, but she
suspected that the sudden predilection for cosmetics was just
as conspicuous as the physical signs of strain.

"The strangest party of lost souls I've ever encountered,"
the nun said cryptically, standing aside as Jenna settled the
sweater over her shoulders. "They arrived in a chauffeur-
driven Cadillac limousine."

"What?" Jenna rounded a corner to enter the lobby of the
Trauma Center in a rush. Her mouth formed a surprised "Oh."
On one row of uncomfortable orange plastic chairs ranged

along the far wall sat Leah Singer. Beside her was a large woven carrying basket, where Brandon lay fussing hungrily. Cassie drooped against her mother's left side. Jenna noticed that the cast was gone from the child's leg.

"Jenna! Hi, Jenna." Cassie bounced off her chair. One black pigtail was higher than the other, as though they'd been braided in a hurry. Her hooded coat was stained with fruit drink and was far too heavy a material for the warm autumn evening. "We've come for a visit," she said. Her eyes were bright with enthusiasm.

Leah didn't say anything as Jenna shot her a swift, assessing glance. She looked miserable. She was trying to smile, but her features were stiff. Her shoulders sagged under the weight of a thick wool jacket. Her lovely ebony hair was dull and pulled back into a haphazard knot at the back of her head.

"You've come for a visit? How nice. How did you find me?" Jenna managed to murmur, bending down to catch Cassie in a quick, hard hug. "How did you get here?"

"We came in a plane. Not like Clay's," the child burst out in excited speech, "but bigger. It belongs to my Grandpa Purchase. My leg is better, see?" she informed Jenna, changing the subject with the speed of a ricocheting bullet. "The cast is gone." Cassie held out the sticklike appendage for a closer inspection. "I've been ill," she added with lisping formality. "I got the chicken pox at school. I gave them to Brandon, too," she finished up proudly. "He's still got spots."

Leah was standing, holding on to the handles of the baby tote as if her life depended on it. "We don't want to put you to any trouble, Jenna. Cassie, you must slow down, you'll get Jenna all confused." She stopped speaking abruptly.

Jenna was also silent, trying to absorb and correlate all the ramifications of Leah's unexpected appearance. Sister Mary Gregory took a moment to admire the sleepy, hungry baby. Then with a total lack of curiosity that endeared her to Jenna more than ever, she advised her to get Leah and the children home and settled as quickly as possible, just as if chauffeur-driven limousines deposited distraught young women and their children on the doorstep every day.

"NOW START FROM the beginning and tell me everything," Jenna commanded, tucking her feet up under her as she curled into the overstuffed chair in her living room.

Leah stared down into her cup of tea, shifting restlessly on the tuxedo sofa placed at right angles to Jenna's chair. "I don't really know what happened. Everything just blew up." She started to cry, hiccuping little sobs she tried hard to suppress because Cassie was sleeping just beyond the thin wall that separated Jenna's living room and bedrooms. Brandon dozed in his basket on the coffee table between the two women.

"Relationships just don't blow up," Jenna said with a brittleness she couldn't keep out of her voice.

"They don't?" Leah lifted her tear-streaked face to impale Jenna with a questioning gaze. Already her spirit had reasserted itself. "What about you and Clay, for God's sake? One minute you're telling me you're going to be married and move to Oakhelm to open a practice. Eight hours later you've snuck away in the night without so much as a goodbye."

"We're not discussing my life." Jenna was on the defensive. Tears welled up despite her resolve not to cry ever again over her lost love. She blinked them back. "I tried to write to Clay, and to you and my grandmother, and to explain everything, but I just couldn't find the right words."

"Something went terribly wrong between you and Clay to have driven you away, Jenna. And just writing letters isn't going to put it right. What happened after you left our party?" Leah set her mug down on the glass tabletop, pursing her lips in a firm line. "Tell me, Jenna, for your sake."

In a few moments the tables had turned in their friendship. In Minnesota, Jenna had been the one to comfort and support Leah. She expected to be called on to do the same tonight. But Leah had changed and matured, and she was offering some of her newfound understanding to help Jenna find her way through the maze of her own conflicting emotions.

"I don't know if I'm ready to talk about it," Jenna answered with tears in her voice. She'd been holding them back for so long that it seemed they were determined to break out somewhere. Her spoon made clicking sounds against the side of the cup as she stirred her tea. The fragrant, spicy liquid reminded her of Horatio's spiked cider. The tears welled up again and spilled over her cheeks. "Clay didn't want me to open a practice in Oakhelm. We'd made plans, lovely plans. We made love..." She looked up and caught Leah's knowing gaze.

"Go on, Jen." Her low, rich voice was soothing. Sympathetic tears shone in Leah's great blue eyes and she made no effort to hide them.

"It just fell apart. He can't forget what happened in his first marriage." Jenna shook her head in helpless dejection. "He doesn't want to take second place in my life. I couldn't find the right words to reassure him, to convince him I could make our love work."

"So you ran away. As I did." Leah shook her head as if to rid herself of an unwelcome revelation. "We're both fools."

"Clay begged me to talk it out, but I couldn't get past the terror of having to choose between him and my medicine. It sounds so melodramatic now, but I panicked. When Horatio Gibbs came by the next morning, on his way into town, I hitched a ride. When Clay discovered I'd left, he followed me in his plane. My car had been sitting in the parking lot so long the battery was dead." Jenna stared past the spot where Leah had moved to stand by the window. She was unaware of the emotions, sadness and regret, that crossed her face so expressively as she reconstructed the scene in her mind's eye. "Horatio had just finished jump starting my car. He must have thought I was crazy, I was so anxious to be gone. He'd already driven off down the street when Clay landed his plane. It was very early and it was raining again."

"JENNA!" CLAY'S VOICE had been harsh. He was yelling above the engine of the Buccaneer as he tied her down alongside the boat launch just west of the pier. "Jenna, wait! Don't go. You promised to talk with me."

"No." Fumbling with the lock, Jenna had opened the hatch-back and dumped her bags and the jumper cables inside, helter-skelter. She'd missed Clay so badly during the night that she was afraid that if they talked now she'd promise him anything just so they could be together. And that would be the worst thing she could do. She had to remain true to herself. Giving in to his ultimatum that she not practice medicine would destroy their relationship as certainly as career differences had destroyed Clay's first love.

Why couldn't he see that?

Why couldn't she make him understand that he would never have to take second place to anything in her life?

And why, oh why, couldn't she put those thoughts into coherent sentences, strong logical arguments, and make him believe them?

"Jenna, stop. We have to talk." Clay's voice seemed to come to her over the miles and despite the long stretch of empty days that had passed, she could still see him coming across the gravel road at a dead run. He'd looked as defeated as she felt. He hadn't shaved. His eyes were bruised-looking and shadowed by dark circles. His clothes were wrinkled, his hair mussed, and his shirt was buttoned wrong.

"IT'S FUNNY THAT I should remember an unimportant detail so clearly, isn't it, Leah?" Jenna asked, coming out of her reverie with a sad little shake of her head. "That his shirt was buttoned wrong. I slammed the car door; the engine was already running, and I drove away. I just left him standing there in the rain. Does he hate me, Leah?" There was no way she could keep herself from asking the question.

"He says very little." Leah came back to the couch and looked down at her sleeping son in the wicker basket. "He took off after you left. He told Locke he was going into Canada to do some fishing. He stayed away almost two weeks. Frieda nearly died of loneliness. Harmon walked around like a bear with a sore paw. And Clay didn't look much better when he got back.''

"I'm so sorry," Jenna murmured cradling her cup between her hands. The tea had grown cold. The aromas of cinnamon and spice were cloying, making her stomach churn. She set the cup of cold tea down on the table. "But what happened between you and Locke? Everything seemed to be going so well...." Jenna let her words trail off.

"We had a fight," Leah answered tightly. "An awful argument over nothing of any importance." She folded her hands in her lap and leaned forward as if to convey some extra meaning in her words. "Everything was going well. Then Brandon caught the chicken pox from Cassie. They both were so cranky with those spots all over, carrying fevers and itching so badly. I was tired," she struggled to explain. "I can't even remember what started it, but before I knew what was happening we were both yelling. I was crying; the baby was crying. Locke said that he was going to call my parents to come and get me, that it was obvious I belonged with them. I told him that it was fine with me, that I wasn't going to stay up there in the middle of nowhere and be bullied for the rest of my life.''

"Leah!" Jenna couldn't repress a smile when she saw the martial light in Leah's blue eyes.

"My first big bid for independence and I blew it. Jenna, I don't want to go back to my parents and be their little Leah again. In Atlanta I'll never have a life of my own." She plucked at the folds of one of Jenna's nightgowns. "I seem to be forever borrowing your nightclothes," she said, following some memory of her own. "I don't want that country-club life. I want my husband back." She stood up, pacing the length of the Oriental rug that added splashes of vibrant color to the off-white walls and pale green carpeting. Hints of apricot and delphinium blue in its pattern were picked up in several impressionist prints on the walls and in the peach upholstery of the furniture.

"Daddy's plane set down here to pick up some important papers. I'd already made up my mind to go back to Locke. We

hadn't even left Minneapolis before I came to that decision."
She smiled. "Then we made this unscheduled stopover. It
seemed like an omen of some kind. So close to Halloween,
too." She grinned suddenly, and Jenna managed a smile in
return. The emergence of this new, more assertive Leah was a
very interesting phenomenon. "I knew my best chance of finding you was through the hospital. I needed to talk to you."

"Your parents are probably worried sick," Jenna interjected.

"They haven't stopped worrying about me since I married
Locke," Leah came back. "The only one who worries about
me more than they do is my husband." She shrugged, an eloquent lift of her shoulders. "And mark my words, Daddy's
security people will have tracked us down by now. He'll be
calling first thing in the morning."

"My phone is unlisted," Jenna informed her friend. Leah
bent to kiss the tips of Brandon's fingers as he awoke and
began to wave his little hands around, cooing and gurgling at
his mother.

"That won't stop Daddy."

"What are we going to do, Leah?" Jenna could no more
stop the words than she could stop the sun from rising. Suddenly it seemed as if Leah were in a much stronger position to
put her life to rights than Jenna would ever be.

"It's almost midnight, too late to discuss anything else tonight," Leah replied, sensing Jenna's exhaustion. There was a
calculating gleam in Leah's eye that Jenna completely missed
as she studied Brandon's slight but sturdy form in his basket.
"*I'm* putting this young man to bed. And *you* are going to
prescribe a sleeping pill for yourself. You look like you haven't
had a good night's sleep since you left the Woods."

There was no arguing with that statement. "I never take
sedatives," Jenna protested, anyway.

"Well, then tonight will be a first, won't it?" Leah sounded
an awful lot like Sister Mary Gregory or, worse yet, almost
like Fayette at her bossiest. Jenna rubbed her tired eyes with
the back of her hand to help dispel the fancy. "We both need

our rest. We have important decisions to make, and tomorrow morning is as good a time as any to start.''

At 11:45 A.M. the phone rang. Leah didn't hesitate. She answered on the second peal. ''Yes, Daddy, it's Leah.'' She gave Jenna an I-told-you-so smile over the receiver. It was amazing what twelve hours of uninterrupted sleep had done for her. Unfortunately, it hadn't worked quite the same magic for Jenna. ''We're all fine. I know I shouldn't have walked off the plane that way. You'll apologize to Captain Morris for me, won't you? It won't happen again, I promise.'' Leah listened patiently for a few moments.

''The baby is fine, and Cassie, too. She's looking forward to seeing you. Dinner? I'd love to, Daddy. Where are you staying? The Orchid Room at the Clarion is fine. Seven?'' Another pause.

''No, perhaps it would be best if Cassie and Brandon stayed here with Jenna.'' She asked permission with her eyes, and Jenna nodded without hesitation. The Orchid Room was no place for a small child and an infant. ''It will be nice to have some time alone together with you and Mother. After dinner we can come back here to see Cassie and the baby.'' Leah hesitated fractionally, then hurried on. ''Daddy, there's something else I want to discuss with you.''

Jenna was feeding Brandon at the kitchen table. She settled the baby on her shoulder, patting his back, paying as much attention to the marvelous, soft baby feel and powdery scent of him as she was paying to Leah's phone conversation. Brandon gave a healthy, satisfied burp, wiggled like a fish and settled down to sucking lazily on his fist. Jenna dropped a kiss on the top of his fuzzy skull. Leah's next words brought her head up with a snap.

''I'm not coming home to Atlanta with you and Mother. I'm going back to Oakhelm and my husband.'' Leah's eyes were sparkling with excitement, but the set of her jaw was stubborn. ''I intend to make Jenna an offer she can't refuse. She wants to practice medicine up there. And I'm going to build her a clinic.''

"THINK ABOUT IT, JENNA. Just think about it." The words had become Leah's battle cry, and Jenna didn't need a lot of prompting in any case.

A clinic. A practice of her own, with Leah to look after the business end of the arrangement. Freedom for Jenna to deal with her patients one-on-one. It was an opportunity to make a dream come true—at least part of her dream.

The afternoon passed all too quickly. Jenna still couldn't quite believe what Leah was proposing. It was more unreal still to be discussing so important a decision, involving both their futures, in the midst of a whirlwind shopping spree at a nearby mall.

"Where will you get the money?"

Leah held up a red designer sheath, shook her head over the drape of the fabric and returned it to the hovering saleswoman. "From the trust fund my Grandmother Purchase left me. I haven't touched a cent of it since Locke and I were married. The interest alone will get us started. I'm going to look into some grant proposals, too. There are ways, Jenna. Trust me. I'm not Jason Purchase's daughter for nothing. I'll take this one," she told the clerk and indicated a jade-green sheath in the same style as the red one. "And would you be so kind as to pick out a pair of shoes to go with it? I wear a six, narrow." She handed the woman the dress with a brilliant smile. "Let's go over to the children's department, Jenna." Leah had walked off her father's jet with nothing but her purse and Brandon's tote.

"You'll have to handle all the business aspects of the partnership," Jenna repeated dazedly for at least the tenth time as they chose jeans and cotton shirts for Cassie before heading to the infant section to outfit Brandon for the flight home.

"I told you at the very beginning, that's one thing I'm good at—paperwork. And my father will bend the rules of the Purchase Foundation a little to get us some seed money. After all, Jenna, you saved my life. And Brandon's." She was deadly serious when she spoke those words. "I want everyone in Oakhelm to have the benefit of your expertise. Think about it, Jenna, please.''

A clinic of her own.

But to go back to Oakhelm—with Clay there, where she would have to see him, speak to him, perhaps someday treat him? Later in the long twilight, with shadows filling the kitchen, that scenario was frighteningly bleak.

What's the alternative? Jenna scolded herself. She got up to switch on lights all over the apartment. Sign her contract with St. V's, dedicate her life to the Trauma Center and grow old and stale and distant in heart as well as body and spirit? That prospect was very nearly as terrifying as facing Clay again and seeing nothing but cold disinterest in his gray eyes.

Cassie wandered into the cheery yellow-and-white kitchen. She was scrubbed and happy, in a fleecy purple-and-white sleeper with feet. Her piping voice cut into Jenna's whirling thoughts. "The cartoons are over. Brandon needs his diaper changed. And I'm hungry. What is there to eat?"

Domestic responsibility came to Jenna's rescue, turning her thoughts to happier things. She changed the baby, propped him on his side on the couch, pushed a chair up as a precaution against his wiggling over the edge, and fixed Cassie a burger and fries.

"This is almost as good as a Big Mac," Cassie told her with a child's devastating candor.

"Thank you, young lady." Jenna accepted the compliment in the spirit in which it was offered.

"Aren't you hungry, Jenna?"

Jenna shook her head. "I'll have something later."

"Good. I really don't want to share my french fries, but Momma says I should always ask." Cassie squirted catsup fastidiously onto the plate alongside her potatoes. "I'm glad we're going back home. I'm missing a new story at nap time in kindergarten."

"You'll be back in school in no time," Jenna assured the child.

"'Course I want to see my grandpa and grandma, too," Cassie added conscientiously.

"They'll be here shortly. You can wait up for them if you like."

"Thanks! Are you sure you don't want some of my french fries?" Cassie's grin was as wide and sunny as a summer sky.

Cassie wanted to go back to Oakhelm as badly as Leah did. And—Jenna had to admit it—as badly as she herself wanted to return. It was time to take control of her life. If she couldn't have Clay, couldn't make him believe that she could be everything he wanted her to be, she would still have the joy of her work.

She was a mature, reasonable adult, wasn't she? So was Clay. Why wouldn't it be possible for them to live in the same area and still be friends?

Friends. Every time she closed her eyes, Jenna could see the misery on Clay's face, the anger and disbelief in his eyes when she'd slammed the car door and pulled away from him. How could he ever forgive her? She had faith that she could do everything she wanted to do with her life and still find all the love she needed for him, but she'd behaved in such a stupid, irrational manner, running away, refusing to talk things out like a reasonable adult. Clay would never admit just how badly his failed marriage had scarred his heart, but Jenna knew, and she should have stayed and fought for her happiness.

Leah was going to take her life into her own hands and mold it to her design. There was no reason that Jenna couldn't do the same. Here was the opportunity she'd been praying for: a practice of her own, to be near Fayette, to be back on Lake of the Woods and to see Clay again—to risk it all on the gamble that she could make Clay love her again.

Chapter Twelve

"Where the hell have you two been?" Harmon Thornton
glared at his errant son and the staggering, bleary-eyed form
of Locke Singer stumbling into the kitchen. Fayette Macklin
clucked in mild disapproval as she looked up from the letter
she was typing at the kitchen table in the cozy living quarters
behind the store.

"You are drunk, Locke Singer," she said accusingly with a
shake of her white head. Clay brushed light flakes of winter's
first snowfall off the shoulders of his coat before pulling a chair
up to the table. He pushed his friend toward it. Locke was
already suffering from the effects of a few too many beers on
an empty stomach. He'd be even more uncomfortable when
Fayette's sharp tongue was through with him.

"Yes, ma'am," Locke answered contritely. "Never could
hold my liquor. Ask anyone in Oakhelm. My good buddy Clay
here brought me home from Mike's."

"He's pretty far gone," Clay said. His gray eyes were grim,
but softened as he regarded his friend slouched in his seat.
Lines of fatigue carved deep grooves from his nose to his chin,
giving Clay's face an added dimension of light and shadow.
"He's been at Mike's since he put Leah and the kids on the
plane to Minneapolis."

"House is too damn quiet." Locke's words were little more
than a self-pitying groan. "Like a mausoleum over there, a
monument to everything they could give her and I can't."

Clay shrugged off the last maudlin observation, but he knew exactly what Locke meant about the house being too quiet. He kept finding traces of Jenna everywhere he looked. Even her scent seemed to linger in the air of his bedroom, assaulting him with bittersweet memories in the sleepless hours before dawn. He'd driven himself hard these past few weeks, trying to get Jenna out of his mind, but it hadn't worked.

He'd even taken off by himself in the Buccaneer to rough it in Canada, fishing for pike during the short, cold days and, at night, dreaming of achingly sweet encounters with a silent, smiling woman possessed of Jenna's hazel eyes and starlit hair—fantasies that were wholly erotic and more than half nightmare because they always ended with her leaving him.

Clay didn't need a psychiatrist to interpret those dreams for him. He'd never forget Jenna's car pulling away from him in Oakhelm that morning while he stood in the rain like a damn fool. Rain that hadn't seemed to let up for more than a day or so in the four weeks since she'd been gone, and then only to turn to snow.

"Oh, for heaven's sake, Locke, cut it out." Fayette pushed back her chair, shuffling the drafts of her column that she'd been working on with Harmon's assistance into a stack beside the electric typewriter. She switched off the machine. The abrupt silence that followed was startling. She glanced sharply at Clay, catching his black look at being included in the admonition; she allowed her sternness to soften, regarding Locke with a look of impatience mingled with warmth and sympathy for his predicament. "Harmon, get him some coffee. And you'd better bring some for Clay, too."

"I could use a cup." Clay straddled the seat of one of the high-backed chairs and rested his chin on his folded arms. "It's getting nasty outside." As if to verify his statement, a gust of wind sidled around the corner of the building and rattled the windowpane.

"Can't spend a whole damn winter alone up here," Locke mumbled with his head in his hands.

"Good grief." Fayette rolled her eyes in exasperation. She stood up and opened her mouth to speak.

"Here's the coffee." Harmon plunked the steaming cup down on the table with enough force to bring Locke's head up. A look of extreme discomfort crossed his face. There was a tight white line around his mouth. He swallowed hard. "Drink that, boy. But I think what we have to tell you will sober you up quick enough. Right, Faye?"

"Tell me? Is Leah all right? Has something happened to the baby?" Locke tried to stand up, then shook his head in bewilderment and sat down abruptly. "Is Cassie sick?"

"They're all fine as cat's hair." Faye finally took pity on his misery as Harmon shoved a second cup of strong black coffee in front of Clay. "We heard from them this morning."

"It was Leah's father who called," Harmon said in clarification. "Drink your coffee, son."

"Come on, Dad, I'm not drunk. You know as well as I do, alcohol and airplanes don't mix." Clay felt irritation rise like bile in his throat. He hadn't had much patience for anything but his own anguish these past weeks. He didn't like the way he was acting, but it hadn't made it any easier to live with himself. He'd put the limitations on his relationship with Jenna. When she couldn't accept his strictures on her career, she'd gotten out. There was no one to blame but Clay Thornton. It was as simple as that, but it didn't heal the pain.

"I know you're not drunk. But I think what I have to tell will hit you damn near as hard as it will Locke." Harmon chortled as he turned back to the coffee maker. Clay wasn't sure he liked the sound.

"Leah's parents called from Cincinnati." Fayette spoke as if that piece of information should explain everything. Clay pushed his chair back on two legs, trying to keep both seniors in view. They were definitely up to something. He could recognize the signs.

"From where?" Locke pushed his broad, rough hands through his thinning hair. "Why Cincinnati?"

"Leah never went home to Atlanta." Harmon couldn't keep

quiet any longer. He shot Clay an arch look from beneath his gray beetle brows. "She's in Ohio with Jenna."

"They're planning on coming back to the Woods. My granddaughter, too," Fayette added with the triumphant air of a woman having the last word. Clay's amusement at the couple's verbal antics faded abruptly. All of a sudden his heart was beating in a funny, choppy sort of rhythm.

"What the hell for?" Three heads twisted around to stare at him with varying degrees of speculation.

"Don't snap my head off, Clay Thornton. It's not my fault you and Jenna had some kind of silly argument," Faye came back so quickly that Clay knew she'd been waiting for an opening to pounce on the subject. "Jenna is perfectly capable of running her own life." Her expression suggested that she didn't grant him the same ability. "If she wants to come and live near her poor old granny, it's not for any of us to stand in her way." Her tone left no room for disagreement.

"Leah's coming back to me." Locke homed in on the words he wanted to hear. A smile broke out at the corners of his mouth.

"Not necessarily," Harmon qualified with a glance at Clay. "Jason Purchase didn't say anything about…Leah's personal plans when she returns."

Clay watched his friend absorb the information like a blow. "Do you think she's planning on living by herself in Oakhelm?" He shook his head as if he couldn't believe what he'd heard.

"And Jenna?" Clay couldn't stop himself from asking. He wrapped his hands around the coffee cup to hide the sudden tremor in his fingers. He didn't trust himself to raise the cup to his lips. Jenna was coming back. But…

Harmon shrugged, having no answer. "If you stubborn, lovesick fools—" he made it very clear that he included his son in the category "—have any sense at all, you'll go down there and talk to those women before they come to the possibly valid conclusion that they can get along very well without you."

Fayette nodded in agreement. "Personally and profession-ally. They're going to open a clinic for Jenna."

"The hell they are?" This time the three sets of eyes turned on Clay were openly skeptical of his carefully neutral state-ment.

"With Leah's money, I'll bet." Locke grinned sheepishly, but there was a glimmer of pride in his brown eyes. "Well, I'll be damned. She must have sweet-talked her daddy into that one."

"A clinic for Jenna?" Clay felt as muddled as Locke sounded, although he hadn't had a single beer back at Mike's. That was why Jenna was coming back—a clinic of her own. But would she be willing to give him another chance? Was it possible that his selfish, unsympathetic behavior that last night they were together hadn't killed all her feelings for him?

"I don't know." Fayette sounded genuinely worried. "She has such a promising future at St. Vincent's, but she wants to practice here." She appeared to want to say a great deal more on the subject of Jenna's return, but for once kept her opinions to herself.

Fayette was more upset about Jenna's abrupt departure from the Woods than she'd let on. And Clay couldn't help her un-derstand. He saw from the way her eyes sparkled when she mentioned Jenna's return that she hoped the problems between them would be solved. It was a logical deduction—that they'd quarreled because Jenna hadn't wanted to leave her life in Cin-cinnati. He wondered what Fayette would say if he told her that it was far more complicated than that. That it wasn't Jenna's dedication to medicine that had caused the rift, but his inability to see past his own bad experiences, his failure to combine marriage and careers successfully.

"Leah's mother is beside herself, poor old girl," Harmon added self-righteously. "She wants you to help squelch this scheme before it goes any farther." He paused. "I think it's a great idea myself."

"And I'll tell you something else," Fayette broke in. "In my opinion, you'd better go make your peace with those two women—'' Fayette's sharp tongue got the better of her discretion as it usually did ''—or they're just liable to figure out they're better off without two such stubborn, moonstruck imbeciles in the first place.''

"THIS IS IT, BUDDY." Clay stretched his arms over his head, banging his wrist on the low ceiling of the rental car. "According to the directions Faye gave me, Jenna's apartment is the corner one in this building." He looked out over the well-kept, still-green landscape with detached interest.

Cincinnati lay spread out over the hills in the distance, basking in the genial warmth of a late October afternoon. Fatigue tugged at Clay's brain; apprehension made his palms sweat. He rubbed them down the side of his pant leg. He closed his eyes, and a mirror image of the view that was spread out before him danced behind his eyelids. He and Locke had flown non-stop from Lake of the Woods, leaving at dawn, setting down just long enough to refuel at a small field south of Chicago. He'd radioed ahead for a rental car to meet them at a private strip an old airline buddy owned west of the city, near the Indiana line.

"I don't know what to say to her." Locke swiveled to face Clay. His face was drawn, his eyes dulled by anxiety. His arm rested along the back of the front seat, fingers clenched into a fist. "I'm afraid she's not up to this clinic project."

Clay made a real effort to put aside his own worries about Jenna's reaction to his showing up uninvited on her doorstep. "She's up to it. Haven't the changes we've both seen in Leah these past weeks proved that to you?"

"I guess you're right. Her parents' interfering and the kids' getting sick just made it too easy to drop back into those same old patterns." Locke ran a hand over the stubble on his chin. "I want Leah back. I want my kids back. I'll take them on any terms I can get them. I don't care if she wants to move the whole damn Mayo Clinic up there."

"I don't think they've set their sights quite that high." Clay switched off the ignition and opened the car door. The scent of burning leaves drifted in on a light afternoon breeze. It was an older, settled neighborhood, and if the city had a prohibition against open burning, it evidently wasn't always followed. It smelled good, like home. Clay took a deep breath. "Leah will need to have you behind her all the way or it will never work."

"Advice from the master?" Locke's tone held more sympathy than censure. He watched Clay's reaction closely.

"I never claimed to be an expert." Clay's words were bitter. He didn't have any secrets from Locke. "Look, old buddy, just do as I say, not as I do, all right?" He got out of the car feeling stiff and sore, and every one of his thirty-seven years.

"Clay." Locke stretched a hand across the roof of the sedan. "You have to be willing to change to keep a relationship growing. I'm damned slow to pick up on some things, but I'm learning. Leah's one special woman. So is Jenna. I was stupid as hell to send my wife away for whatever reasons. If I get her back, I'll never let her go again."

"Are you giving me advice now?"

"Maybe I am." Locke lifted his hand, palm-up, in a gesture of uncertainty. "If Leah wants to build this clinic, I'm going to hear her plan out." He grinned suddenly, brown eyes crinkling against the sun bouncing off the car roof. "I'm going to do things differently from here on. Leah's a grown woman, not the girl-child I thought I married. She's rich to boot. I'm tired of being alone with my stiff-necked pride. I think I can get used to helping her spend that money. And as for her parents…well, time will tell. However things turn out, I'm not going back home to make all the same mistakes again."

"Sounds like you're on the right track." Clay touched his finger to his forehead in salute to his friend, then gestured toward the apartment building with more assurance than he felt. "Let's go."

IT SOUNDED AS IF a three-ring circus was going on inside her apartment. Jenna could barely hear the chime of the doorbell over the roaring cries resounding from the TV, where Cassie was ensconced on a floor pillow, avidly following the adventures of *He-Man and the Masters of the Universe*. Jenna had always assumed that little girls would be more interested in pretty, fantasy animals and fairy-tale characters flitting from one video adventure to the next. Evidently she'd been laboring under a sexist stereotype. Cassie was as bloodthirsty as any little boy in the world.

"Just a moment," Jenna called, giving her hair a shake over her shoulder. She knew it was only rationalizing, but she couldn't forget her wish that nature had taken the decision to broach a reconciliation with Clay out of her hands on that night they spent together. To be carrying his child would be wonderful. But, of course, reality was far more complicated than daydreams. It was becoming more apparent to Jenna with each passing hour that she would have to go back to Oakhelm and prove to Clay that she could be true to her profession and also to her heart. She was never going to be whole and content until she had them both.

The doorbell pealed again with an insistent note. It must be the paperboy, Jenna decided, with a wry grin. She tucked her pink-and-rose-striped blouse into her slacks and gave the belt a pat to make sure it was straight. She swung the door open, expecting to see an impatient twelve-year-old, eager to finish his route and join the touch-football game in the vacant lot two doors down. Locke Singer was just reaching up to use the brass knocker when she swung open the heavy metal door.

"I thought the bell might be out of order," he explained, lowering his upraised hand.

"Locke, what are you doing here?" Jenna regretted the abruptness of her statement immediately.

"I came to get Leah and my children." The effect of her tone showed in the tight set of his jaw, the stubborn tilt of his chin.

"Leah's changing the baby.... I'll go get her." Jenna stopped talking as Clay stepped out of the shadow of the big arborvitae that acted as a privacy screen outside her front door. The rest of the world shifted out of focus. She wasn't sure if Locke actually stepped aside or only faded out of her vision, because she couldn't take in any figure but Clay's. He looked older, sadder, tired and somehow unsure of himself. His expression was a mirror of her own uncertainty.

"Clay." His name came out faint and strangled; Jenna was mortified at the weakness in her voice. She couldn't keep from staring at him. So often she'd ached to see him since she'd returned to Cincinnati. Yet, each time, her fantasy of a happy reunion was overwhelmed by frustration both of body and of spirit.

"May I come in, too, Jenna?" She looked as troubled as he felt. Somehow that made it easier for Clay. Then Cassie caught sight of Locke and exploded toward him like a small heat-seeking missile, causing a diversion that allowed him to drink his fill of Jenna under cover of its distraction.

"Daddy! Did you come to take me to the zoo? Jenna says there are tigers there that are white."

"Sure, sweetie. If you want to go to the zoo, we'll arrange it." Locke gathered the child into his arms, lifting her high off the floor. He buried his face in her soft black hair, rocking back and forth. As Clay watched, tears filled Jenna's eyes. She blinked them away with characteristic fierceness, but she was smiling all the while. She turned her head and their gazes met and locked with a magnetism that Clay felt almost as a physical force. His body tightened with longing and desire. He had to set things right between them.

"I've missed you, Daddy. I want to go home," Cassie piped up as her arms squeezed tight around her stepfather's neck.

"So do I, Locke." Leah stood in the bedroom doorway. Her face was pale but composed. Her great blue eyes dominated her features. "I know my parents called you. Have you come to try and talk me out of building the clinic?" She shifted Brandon's weight to her left arm, patting him on the back, smoothing his blue terry sleeper across his shoulders with trembling fingers.

"I want you to come home with me and to forgive me once more for treating you as less than the woman you are. I love you, Leah, and I'll back you all the way."

It was all Leah needed to hear. She flew across the room to nestle in his arms. "I've missed you so badly. It's been the longest four days of my life."

"Mine, too." Locke lowered his head to kiss his wife. Cassie clung to them both, giggling at the show of affection between her parents. Brandon was rooted on Leah's shoulder, trying to lift his head to bring the new voice into focus. Locke dropped a kiss on the top of his son's head. "Let's go home, Leah."

"As soon as we've talked to my parents." Leah looked radiant but adamant, and Locke shrugged.

"You're Jason Purchase's daughter, all right." He didn't look completely reconciled to that unfolding trait in his wife's personality. "Where are they staying? At the Clarion?"

"Always. Daddy owns stock in the company." Leah's eyes twinkled mischievously.

"Then we'd better get over there." Locke's voice was resigned.

Taking his cue, Clay handed Locke the keys to the rental car with an exaggerated bow. "Don't worry about me. I'll take a cab to a motel."

"I imagine we'll end up staying at the hotel with Leah's parents. They never take anything less than a three-room suite." His eyes held Leah's.

"Are you going to refuse to stay?" She cocked her head and waited for a response to her challenging question. She was beginning to exercise her feminine powers with more assurance.

"No," Locke said as he ran a finger lightly over the soft, stubborn line of her jaw. "I told you I'm turning over a new leaf. Your parents can look after Cassie and Brandon for us tonight." Locke and Leah had eyes only for each other. They had shut the rest of the world out. Jenna couldn't find the willpower to turn her head and meet Clay's eyes. It was a very private moment for her two friends. Locke spoke quietly. "I intend to have you all to myself this evening, Leah Singer. We have a lot of…business…to discuss.''

Leah's answer was equally soft and rich with excitement. ''Indeed we do.''

Chapter Thirteen

"I hope Locke remembers to unload my duffel from the trunk," Clay remarked dryly as he craned his neck to watch the rented sedan pull away from the curb and disappear past the window.

"We'd better stop him." Jenna welcomed the chance to take action, any action, to keep from standing there gaping at Clay with her heart shining in her eyes. "Maybe I can catch—" She threw open the door, only to come within inches of stumbling over Clay's bag, which was sitting on the doorstep. His hand shot out to steady her from behind. For a moment Jenna allowed herself to rest against his lean, hard body. Recovering her balance and her senses, she pulled away. "He didn't leave you stranded, after all." Jenna could have bitten off her tongue, but it was too late to take the inane comment back.

"Good. I'd hate to check into a motel without even a toothbrush to my name. A guy's got to consider his reputation." Clay's nonchalance was strained. The touch of Jenna's body against his own had set off a chain reaction of nerves and desire that beat through his body in mounting waves of unease. What the hell was he doing here? He'd made the first move by coming to her, but how would she respond? He shouldn't have just appeared in the doorway that way without a warning. He pushed his hand through his hair with a gesture of uncertainty.

Clay's features looked strained. Dark waves of hair stood on end. Jenna's palm itched to smooth them down again. Oddly, his uncertainty gave her new courage. "You're welcome to stay here tonight, Clay. I have to go on duty at midnight," she hurried to add, so that he wouldn't feel any obligation to decline the invitation. Jenna found that she was holding her breath, willing his acceptance, and she deliberately relaxed, letting the air sift out in a soft sigh. She couldn't quite bring herself to meet his eyes head-on. She fidgeted with the fringe of her tie belt. What would she see if she did look up into those reflecting gray depths? What emotions would be visible in the shifting patterns of light swirling below the surface? Was he making the first overture toward resolving their problems? Or had he come only to support his friend Locke?

Jenna was afraid, and she needed to conceal her vulnerability for that reason. She compromised by focusing her attention at a point just past Clay's left shoulder. "You really are welcome to stay here, Clay. I don't want hard feelings between us, believe me. I'm so ashamed of the way I acted...."

Clay wondered at the moment if she could see him standing there at all. She certainly couldn't see the effort it took for him to answer levelly. He stuffed his hands in the pockets of his flannel slacks and balled them into fists. "I don't want to intrude." *Hard feelings.* That phrase didn't cover the half of it. He wanted to drag Jenna into his arms and kiss her, caress her and shake her until she agreed never to leave him again. He didn't like these conflicting emotions that fluctuated so alarmingly between tenderness and anger. "I'll manage, Jenna, don't worry."

"But I will." He hadn't made any response to her halting apology and Jenna's spirits fell, her confidence dwindled and her words drifted off into silence. Clay looked thoughtful, she decided, glancing fleetingly at him from the corner of her eye. Was he still angry? Or was it possible that he was recalling the first night they had met, when she insisted he sleep on Fayette's couch and not risk the trek back across the Point in the rain? He'd listened to her then; perhaps she could persuade him again. "It's no trouble, truly."

"Maybe Locke will remember he left me stranded here."

Jenna tried hard to hide the sorrow caused by his careless remark. "I think Locke and Leah have a good—"

"Looks like those two will…"

Again silence reigned in the room. After the bustle and confusion of the past few days, the quiet was magnified many times. Jenna wished she hadn't turned the TV set off. She didn't like the hushed atmosphere; it intensified the beating of her pulse in her ears. She took a deep breath to slow her careening heart. She didn't dare think of the empty stretch of years ahead of her. The man she loved was here with her. Why couldn't she find the courage, the words to make right what had gone wrong between them? He must still care, or he wouldn't have come, even for Locke and Leah's sake. She clung to that certainty like a lifeline. Fate was giving her a second chance to clear up the misunderstanding between them.

Jenna couldn't quite find the best way to begin. Panic threatened to render her speechless. She had to say something, she thought, or Clay would turn on his heel and leave the apartment. "Thanks for bringing Locke down here. It was important for Leah to have him with her." She twisted her hands together, then willed herself to relax. "We've been on a merry-go-round ever since Leah and the children arrived. This has all happened so quickly. I can't quite believe it myself yet."

"We didn't get any of the details of your plans for the clinic, only Leah's parents' call," Clay prompted. His heart was beating in strange, painful jerks whenever he looked in her direction. She did appear a little shell-shocked, tired and unusually fragile, and so very, very desirable. Clay's heartbeat accelerated. "Anyway, it isn't any of my business at this point."

"Oh, but it is." Jenna couldn't keep the excitement out of her voice. "It's going to involve everybody in Oakhelm sooner or later." She wanted to share her plans with Clay. She *could* make him understand—she knew she could. She reached out and took his hand impulsively. "We all have to pull together or Leah will never get the clinic off the ground."

"You think that will be enough?" Clay felt exhilaration rise within him, only faintly tempered by the old anxiety. The hope that Jenna still cared for him had refused to be snuffed out, no matter how often he'd attempted to do just that. Now it insisted on flaring into new life. "Are you sure she isn't taking on more than one woman can handle?" Clay made the words deliberately provoking. He needed to see Jenna's hidden passion spark into brilliance like dry tinder to his flint and steel.

"Leah isn't alone. She has Locke. She'll also have her family's backing before she leaves Cincinnati. And she has me," Jenna insisted. She'd detected the slightly patronizing tone of his words and she didn't like it.

"Mmm. If everyone involved doesn't pull together, she'll never get it off the ground." This time the condescension was more pronounced. Clay remained standing, towering over Jenna, willing her to stand up and fight for what she believed in, to make him believe in it, too.

Jenna rose to the bait. "We will make it. We've got every chance in the world for the clinic to succeed." Her cheeks were flushed, her eyes sparkled with zeal. She moved closer, meeting him toe to toe, eye to eye. "She already has the two most important things she needs. Access to funding. And me." Jenna stabbed a pearl-tipped finger at her own chest. "A doctor, and a damn good one, if I do say so myself. I'm a member of the American College of Emergency Physicians. I'm licensed by the American Board of Emergency Medicine. I'm in charge of a trauma unit that handles twenty thousand patients a year." Was that a slight twist of a smile lurking at the corners of his mouth? Jenna came down off her high horse in a rush. "You're baiting me, Clay Thornton," she accused him, shaking her finger under his nose.

"No, I'm *listening* to you, Jenna. I'm trying to take it all in, to understand what it is you and Leah are dreaming of doing." Clay was suddenly very serious. He was more certain each moment that he would never be pushed out of Jenna's life, but he needed to know that she needed him as badly as he needed her.

"Oh, God," tears threatened once again and Jenna fought

them back. "And I'm standing here sounding so pompous and defensive."

The amusement left his features. "You sound marvelously competent, knowledgeable and determined."

"I'm scared to death," Jenna admitted without any hesitation. "I can't do it without you." The words came of their own accord, as though in answer to a spoken request. Jenna didn't question the intensity of the urge. Was that what he wanted to hear her say? Now if she could only tell Clay how much she loved him, how sorry she was that they had quarreled. But doubts kept her silent. Admitting how much she needed him was one thing. Finding that the love he'd felt for her was irrevocably gone was something else entirely. "Obstetrics is one of the specialties I'm going to have to take a crash course in before I leave for Oakhelm." Jenna caught her lip between her teeth as she waited for Clay to take the initiative.

"You're determined to go through with it? To leave the city—" he gestured in a sweeping circle around them "—to leave the Trauma Center and to cast your lot with the citizens of Oakhelm?"

"Yes." She put all the conviction she could muster into the affirmative.

"Good." Clay gave a short whistle of relief. "Then I won't need to go hat in hand back to the airline and beg for my old job back." His words were low, but distinct. For a moment the room spun in a slow spiral around Jenna. She took a shaky step forward, holding out her hands to brace herself. Clay took both of them between his strong, warm hands.

"What did you say?" Jenna needed the reassurance of hearing his words repeated.

"I said I was prepared to stay here, to work for the airline again, if that's what it takes for us to be together." Clay swallowed hard against the sudden dryness in his throat. His heart hammered against his chest wall. Had he confused her with his roundabout proposal? Did she understand that he'd be willing to come back to this world, where he no longer belonged, if that was what it took for them to be together?

Jenna didn't say anything for another long march of seconds, only watched him with fathomless eyes. Faint sparks of gold ignited in their depths.

"That's the loveliest thing anyone's ever said to me." Suddenly she burst into tears. For the first time since he'd known her, Jenna did nothing to hide the crystal drops running down her cheeks. Clay pulled her against his hard body and held her tightly, stunned by her reaction.

"Jenna, love, don't cry." The words were almost a groan as he buried his face in her hair.

"You're the one who's always telling me not to hide my feelings."

"That's true, but I can't bear to see you unhappy." Clay smoothed away a tear from her cheek with his thumb.

"I'm not unhappy. I thought I'd lost you forever." It had taken her several moments to understand what he was telling her. He loved her still. He wouldn't voluntarily suggest returning to a life so demanding and stress-filled that he considered it responsible for the breakup of his first marriage if he didn't believe their love was strong enough to survive.

Jenna clung to him, savoring his closeness and the feel of the hard muscles of his arms beneath her fingers. The scent of wood smoke and pine woods still clung to his jacket. "I love you, Clay, with all my heart and soul." Cupping her face in his hands, Clay bent his head and their lips met, lingered, retreated, and then returned to taste of each other's mouth a second time. Jenna welcomed him with parted lips, their tongues mingling in the dark warmth of their mouths. "I've wanted to tell you how sorry I am for all the things I said to you the night of Locke and Leah's party. I tried to write. I picked up the phone to call you again and again...but I just couldn't find the courage."

Clay placed a finger on her lips. "Don't apologize, Jenna. I ought to get some kind of award for being the world's oldest adolescent. You just threw me so off balance. I'd never thought I'd find love again...then to face what seemed like an instant replay of my marriage to Joann—" Clay shook his head regretfully. He lowered his forehead to rest against the top of Jenna's head. "Please don't run away from me like that again. Promise me, Jenna." Suddenly Clay felt that he couldn't possibly get close enough to her. The terrible loneliness of the past few weeks of solitary days and nights welled up in him like a horde of stinging insects.

"I promise." Jenna pressed against him tightly. "I'll stay with you always."

"At least until midnight." Clay hugged her close, then chuckled, but the laughter ended in a throaty sigh. "Isn't that when you said you have to go back on duty?"

"Midnight," Jenna confirmed. She shivered now in anticipation of feeling his body against her bare skin. There was an urgency now, a fever in her blood, to pledge a renewal of their love.

"Midnight," Clay repeated. A line formed between his dark brows. "Well, I'll have to get used to you running off in the middle of the night, won't I?"

"Afraid so. But remember, it's even harder to get out of a warm bed at three in the morning than it is to be left alone in one." This time Clay's laughter was full and unrestrained.

"Jenna, you're so good for me." There was a dancing fire of passion in the stormy gray of his eyes.

"Only for you." Jenna held her breath. The erotic suggestion hung heavy in the air between them. Clay seemed to be waiting for something, too. Jenna took his hand, leading the way toward her bedroom. It was absurdly easy, after all. Sometimes you just didn't need words.

Her bedroom was small and simply furnished. Clay stood in the doorway for a long moment, watching Jenna as she moved across the room to pull the shade down over the casement window. The walls were cream-colored. Her bed was narrow, and he anticipated how closely he could hold her throughout the hours ahead. The bed was topped with a green gingham comforter, and the sheets were cream-and-green-striped, with lace along the edges. The furniture was warm golden oak, and there was a thick green carpet covering the floor.

He dropped his jacket across the top of a lowboy inside the door. Jenna watched him, her hand still on the ruffled curtain. He began unbuttoning his shirt, anxious to be on the bed, under the cool sheets and buried deep within Jenna's warmth. Clay guessed that his thoughts were plain to read on his face, for Jenna blushed slightly, the faintest tinge of rose covering her neck and rising to her cheeks.

Never taking her eyes from him, she began to unbutton her blouse. Clay stopped to watch her soft shoulders and the rise of her breasts as the garment slipped to the floor. He couldn't stand still any longer. With two quick strides he was beside her, reaching behind to unfasten her bra, while Jenna pulled his shirttail from the waistband of his slacks. The bra joined her blouse on the floor and he pulled her close.

"I will trust in our love, Jenna. It's already so much more than I felt for Joann. I let her go without a backward glance." He moved his head against her hair wonderingly. "I didn't care enough to try and keep that love alive."

"You're already beginning to understand the difference between that and our love." Jenna reached up to kiss him again. The rest of their clothes came off with a minimum of fuss. Jenna slid under the sheets. Clay followed. She liked the way the mattress moved under his added weight, the way the heat of his skin enfolded her in warmth. Their bodies fit together nicely. He was sleek and hard, the perfect complement to her softer feminine curves. The easy familiarity of their bodies together banished Jenna's nervousness. She gave herself up to the pleasure of their passion. It would never make up for the agony of separation, but it soothed the scars almost into forgetfulness.

In only moments they were both ready for love. Clay's voice was a low rumble as he whispered endearments and promises for her ears alone. As he entered the welcoming softness of her body, the last barriers of restraint came crashing down around them.

Jenna knew the serenity of unity.

Clay threw off the last constrictions of lost love. He'd never be alone again.

"DID YOU TRULY MEAN you'd come back to live in the city and go back to flying commercial jets?" Jenna drew patterns with her fingertip through the crisp, dark hair on Clay's chest.

"Stop that, it tickles," he commanded, grabbing her hand and carrying it to his lips. He was propped against the pillows of her bed, looking very masculine and out of place in the apple-green-and-cream room. "Why do you ask now, woman?"

"I suppose it was another way of saying you love me." Jenna cocked her head, watching him from beneath her lashes, enjoying this small exercise of feminine power.

"You suppose correctly." Clay caught her hand and kissed the tip of each finger in turn. He held her thumb against his lips for a long, emotion-charged second. Jenna couldn't help but trace the outline of his mouth with the edge of her nail. "I was willing to stay here and go back to commercial flying, if that's what you wanted."

"No." Jenna shook her blond head in vehement denial.

"But I hoped you'd call my bluff." Clay looked a great deal like the Cheshire cat just before he faded away.

"That's what I thought." Jenna snorted inelegantly. "I never knew you were such a cold-blooded gambler, Clay Thornton." She looked severe, as if it were a character flaw of great magnitude. "What if I told you that's what I want you to do?"

"I only gamble on sure things. We're going back north." He pulled her down possessively into his arms, but there was the merest hint of a question in his voice. Jenna's skin was still damp from her shower. Only a towel separated the soft peaks of her breasts from his chest. Clay ached to feel himself within her yet again. They had made love over and over as the short afternoon faded into night, but he would never have his fill of her. "How soon do you have to leave for the hospital?" He thought he kept the reluctance to allow her to leave him out of his voice very well. Jenna was watching him closely, and he had to make her sure of his love.

She glanced at the bedside clock with a faint frown between her brows. "I imagine Milt will give me a few minutes grace. About twenty minutes or so. I'm sorry Clay—" She broke off and Clay cursed his own slight hesitancy in asking. Tonight had to be perfect—no complications, no more problems. Solutions would come first with their bodies and their hearts, then tomorrow and every day after that with their minds and souls. "Clay?"

"I'm trying to decide if that's long enough," he answered with exaggerated concern.

"That depends on what you have in mind." He could feel Jenna relax against him. A mischievously contented smile tugged at her lips, still soft and pouting from his kisses.

"Something I'm going to have to learn to squeeze into twenty minutes, if I'm going to spend the rest of my life married to a busy G.P." Clay grunted in satisfaction as he gave the towel a tug that parted the loose knot between her breasts. He stared boldly at the soft curve of her breasts, lifting her slightly to kiss each rosy upthrust peak in turn. Jenna shifted her weight to straddle his lower body.

She bent her head to kiss his mouth when he settled her back on top of him. With her recently acquired awareness of his needs, she sensed that Clay was only half teasing. He needed her reassurance that their love could withstand the stresses they'd encounter. She could only show him now with her hands and her body that he was the most important thing in her life and her heart.

"I have a suggestion," Jenna said, her voice thready with building desire. She looked down into Clay's passion-dark gray eyes as his hands traced erotic patterns along her spine to the curve of her buttocks, positioning her more intimately atop him.

"What's that?" He nibbled at her collarbone, moving his hands lower to meet between her thighs.

"It's just something that came to me a few moments ago."

Jenna swallowed to control the tremors in her voice that his seeking caresses had produced. "But I seem to be losing the thread of the conversation."

"I'm going to have to improve on my technique if your mind is going to wander off the subject during such intimate moments." Clay grinned devilishly as he moved to enter her with carefully controlled power. Jenna moaned, reaching up to curl her arms around his neck and answer each thrust of his passion with one of her own.

"I think I remember now." Jenna's fingers clenched in his hair as his lips moved lower to tease the satiny rise of her breasts.

"Go on, Jenna, I'm listening." Clay lifted his head to watch with purely masculine satisfaction as her eyes drifted shut in pleasured response. "It occurred to me—" she kissed him back, murmuring the words in his ear, glorying in her turn at the immediate and fierce reaction of his body "—that this will be the perfect activity for those winter nights when the wind's been blowing for five days straight and the snow is up to the eaves."

Clay didn't waste precious time with a reply. He rolled her over, burying himself still deeper in her softness. The teasing banter halted abruptly. Jenna lifted her face to his kiss, opening her body for his loving possession in wordless reaffirmation of her love. She would be his; he would be hers. No matter how busy they were with their separate lives, they would always find time for private moments together. But those words were too strong, too magical to be spoken aloud—they passed from her heart to his in silence.

Epilogue

Jenna watched her husband prowl around the muddy excavation for the foundation of the clinic. Behind him, the feathery tips of new growth on the pines matched the spring-green of unfolding leaves on maple and birch. Clay stepped off the area recently staked out at the rear of the building. He stopped, pushed the ball cap he was wearing back on his dark head, turned and paced off the distance once again. Jenna's heart gave a quick beat, then settled back into a steady cadence. As she watched, Clay stuck his hands in the pockets of his dark blue jacket and kicked at a two-by-four half buried in the sandy mud.

He was very close to discovering her secret. Jenna didn't want anyone else around when she told him. She took a step in his direction.

"Dr. Thornton." Jenna blinked in surprise at the reporter who'd materialized at her elbow, tape recorder in hand. She opened and closed her mouth soundlessly, looking a lot like one of her goldfish, she suspected. Thank heaven he wasn't the TV reporter, video cameraman in tow, who was prowling around what had been, until a few short days ago, nothing more than an empty lot smack in the middle of downtown Oakhelm. "You seem to be the nucleus around which the citizens of Oakhelm are planning to build a medical future."

Jenna tore her eyes away from the dark, lean, preoccupied

figure of her husband. "I'm sorry, I didn't hear your question,"
she stalled with a shy, enchanting smile.

"Dr. Thornton is indeed the key to our plans." Leah, in her
turn, appeared at Jenna's side, clipboard and press releases in
hand. She handed one to the reporter. The two women exchanged a conspiratorial glance in which Leah clearly said,
This is business, not medical; I'll handle it.

Jenna took her cue. "Mrs. Singer is our public relations of-
ficer. She will be able to tell you everything you want to
know." Jenna's smile was gracious as she gestured to her petite
friend. "And if you'll excuse me, please..."

"In the near future we have every hope of bringing a second
qualified physician to the area," Leah began in her soft, cultured voice, which seemed capable of hypnotizing funding
committees and newspeople alike.

The sounds of their conversation faded away as Jenna hurried around the corner of the double-wide mobile home that
had been her temporary office headquarters since she and Clay
returned to Oakhelm early in February. She stationed herself
at an angle to the clearing that was swarming with people.

Clay had disappeared from view during the momentary distraction, and Jenna scanned the crowd of town officials taking
their places on the truck bed that was serving as a temporary
platform. His tall figure wasn't among them. To her right a
tight knot of citizens huddled together for warmth. A regional
news team from a St. Paul TV station was taking the opportunity to interview Fayette, now a familiar figure in legislative
circles, on what she thought were the chances of her hunting
bill being passed in this session.

Walter Ericson was fiddling with the PA system supplied by
the volunteer fire department. It squealed with mechanical
shrillness and Locke nearly dropped the microphone he was
adjusting in front of the speaker's stand. Good-natured laughter
and ribbing swirled through the crowd and floated faintly to
Jenna's sheltered location on a fitful May breeze.

Her husband still wasn't in sight, but, not far away, his father
had collared two newspaper stringers assigned to the ceremony

and proceeded to harangue them about his idea for establishing small satellite clinics at several locations around the lake. Jenna didn't need the one or two words she overheard to pinpoint the gist of the conversation. It had been the only thing on Harmon's mind for the past two weeks. He had a workable suggestion. She planned to spend half a day at each of the two pilot locations, thereby eliminating the need for outlying residents to make the long journey to Oakhelm, except in emergency situations, and allowing her far more efficient use of her time.

Everything seemed to be falling into place. Just last week a dentist had written requesting information on the feasibility of opening a practice, after he read about the project in a Milwaukee paper. Leah, whose powers of organization and fundraising expertise had turned out to be formidable, was investigating the possibility of luring a young optometrist to Oakhelm also.

And Jenna, for reasons of her own, was interested in finding a partner to share her medical duties. She hoped the doctor might even be one of the group of bright, dedicated young interns that she'd worked with during her last few weeks in Cincinnati. But that was some distance in the future, and she brought her thoughts back to the present.

"Pssst. Hey, Doc, come here." Jenna looked around. There seemed to be no one close enough to have reached her with that gravelly whisper but Catherine Martin. Jenna laughed inwardly and shook her head. Small, fair and fortyish, the woman had appeared on the heels of the last depressing heavy April snowfall and asked for a job. Her credentials were excellent. Her references were most impressive and, miracle of miracles, she was a certified nurse-midwife—the answer to Jenna's most heartfelt prayers. She'd immediately taken charge of what promised to be a sizable obstetrics practice. Catherine was a pearl of great price, but one thing she didn't possess was a sexy baritone voice.

Jenna swung around, searching the underbrush of jack pine and saplings for the source of the summons. "Hey, Dr. Thorn-

ton, come here." Clay stepped out of the concealing screen of
new foliage and beckoned her to him. He turned up the collar
of his jacket to ward off the chill wind that refused to acknowledge that it was spring.

"Come on," Clay repeated, waving her over with exaggerated stealth. "Before anybody sees you hiding there." The
hazy sunshine of late May glinted through the budding leaves
of maple trees that marched down the slope to within yards of
the building site. A stray beam of golden light reflected off the
plain gold band on Clay's left hand.

"What's up?" she asked brightly, picking her way through
the rocks and pieces of scrap lumber littering the construction
site.

"I'm tired of sharing you with the media blitz."

"I'd hardly call three or four reporters a media blitz," Jenna
said with a laugh, coming into his arms. She slipped her hands
into the pockets of his jacket to warm them.

"In Oakhelm it is," Clay reminded her dryly.

"Point well taken."

"There's something odd about the placement of those
marker stakes," Clay went on, looking over Jenna's shoulder
while his fingers worked soothing magic on the tense muscles
at the back of her neck. Jenna held herself very still. She'd
hoped to put this discussion off until they could be alone that
night. "I'll show you." Clay pulled her hands out of his pockets firmly and bent to pick up a roll of architect's drawings that
Jenna hadn't noticed lying on a nearby rock. "They aren't following the blueprints correctly."

Jenna stuck her chilled hands deep into the pockets of her
own coat as she searched for the right words to explain the
discrepancy. The sudden rush of pink to her cheeks complemented the rosy hues of the jacket and slacks she wore.
"We've made a few adjustments to the plans," she ventured
at last.

"Looks like you've added another room. More storage?"
Clay was clearly mystified as he stared down at the line draw-
ing of a rustic-looking, steep-roofed, split cedar building.

"You might say that." Jenna smiled a secret woman's smile. "I'll explain all the...details...later, when we have time alone." She'd wanted to tell him her news in that lovely and private time they shared together before going to sleep at night. It was her favorite time of the day. "Come on, everybody's ready for the ground breaking. If we don't hurry, someone will come down with frostbite, for sure. When does spring get here anyway? It's nearly the first of June." She shivered theatrically and grabbed for his hand, heading in the general direction of the speaker's platform.

"I still don't understand why we need to add another room. I'm not moving another step until you tell me what's going on." Clay swung her around in time to catch the last of that special smile. The look on his angled face was speculative. He planted his feet firmly in the slippery layer of last year's leaves on the forest floor and stood his ground.

Jenna couldn't keep her precious secret a moment longer. "It's going to be a nur—" The squeal of tires on the gravel road leading to the clinic drowned out her words.

"What the hell?" Clay stepped out of the concealing trees, still holding Jenna's hand. "That's Wiley Geer's pickup." A long-limbed, roughly-dressed man careened out of the beat-up cab. His grizzled head and long, bony face swiveled on his neck until he spied Jenna standing there with Clay.

"Doc! Come quick! That damned fool Myron Walker's gone and nearly cut his leg off with a chain saw. He's bleedin' like a stuck pig all over the back of my truck." He waved at Jenna, and the crowd turned with a single movement as if they'd been choreographed by an expert hand. The TV cameraman stuck his camera in Wiley's face and got an angry scowl for his pains. "Come on, Doc Jenna, he's a mess." The cameraman swung to focus on Jenna running across the clearing, but she never even spared him a glance.

Not for the first time, Clay felt a spurt of irritation at the demands others made on Jenna's life jump into his throat and clamor to be voiced in words. But he'd learned something of patience and plenty about love and commitment this past winter. His wife was a doctor first, now, at this moment, because she was needed. Later she would be wife and lover, all his as he would be all hers. The impatience faded away to be replaced by throat-tightening pride as he watched Jenna move purposefully through the crowd.

"My bag's in the trailer," Jenna called over her shoulder. She didn't even have to look back to know Clay was following her. He was always there for her.

"We'll finish this discussion later." His voice told her that he was close enough to touch; his tone made the words a promise as he veered off to do what she asked.

"Yes, later, tonight." She smiled to herself. "I'll need some help getting Myron on a stretcher." For the first time, she noticed the hovering newsmen who were bent on making the most of an opportunity to beef up what had been, at best, a thirty-second spot in the regional news to a possible lead on the six o'clock report.

"She's turning out to be damn near as good copy as her grandmother," Clay heard one reporter crow as he shoved past with Jenna's medical bag.

"I'll have the examining table ready by the time she gets there," Catherine Martin shouted, moving swiftly in the opposite direction. Clay nodded and shouldered past a gawking bystander.

In a matter of moments they had the injured man inside the trailer. Jenna cleared away the extra helping hands with a few quick words as she praised her crew of six E.M.T.'s, recently trained at the county clinic seventy-five miles away. The quarters were too cramped to allow anyone other than Catherine and Jenna to be with Myron. Clay stayed long enough to hear his wife's evaluation of the injury, then he disappeared to ready the Buccaneer for duty as an air ambulance.

Locke and Leah moved to block the doorway as the newspeople pushed into the void. Leah's cultured tones could be heard urging the media and the rest of the hangers-on toward the tent that held coffee urns and refreshments. Jenna registered all those events with a sixth sense that filtered out the distractions while allowing her to keep abreast of developments as she worked. It was suddenly very quiet in the trailer; only the sound of Myron Walker's labored breathing broke the silence.

"I hit a spike or something in that log. Bounced the damn saw right back at me. Hang it, Doc, am I going to lose my leg?" He propped himself on his elbows as Catherine cut away his pant leg and Jenna pulled on a pair of sterile gloves.

"No way." Jenna grinned. "It looks a lot worse than it is. You're lucky you weren't alone out there." With grace and efficiency of motion she cleaned and then stitched the long, ragged wound. She administered tetanus antitoxin, antibiotics and pain medication, all the while listening to Myron's excited recounting of the accident.

Less than thirty minutes later Jenna left Catherine to clean up the treatment room and to deal with the temperamental autoclave while she followed the stretcher, carried by willing volunteers, toward the pier where Clay waited. The TV and press reporters were still inside the tent, and Jenna was grateful for the reprieve.

"I'll be back as soon as I get Myron settled in at the clinic," Clay said. "You go ahead and start the ceremony while you've got everybody's attention." Clay smiled, but his eyes were serious. "Walter and the other town fathers are going to be disappointed if they don't get to make their speeches." He stood close but he didn't touch her.

"They'll let me know how he is on evening rounds." Jenna had already established a good working relationship with the four young doctors who ran the county clinic. She sent her patients to them with complete confidence and none of the old, sad feeling of being only important to them for a brief moment of need.

One of the newspaper reporters stuck his head out of the tent flap. Clay caught the movement out of the corner of his eye and pulled Jenna close. "Before we were interrupted back there, were you about to tell me the extra room is going to be a nursery?" Blood pounded through his veins, making it hard to draw a deep breath. The glory of Jenna's smile was all the answer Clay needed. Oblivious to the people converging upon them, the roar of the plane's push-prop engine overhead, he pulled her into his embrace. "Are you pregnant, Jenna?"

"I think so. Clay, don't squeeze me so hard." Jenna held on for dear life as Clay whirled her around in a great arc.

"You *think* so? Don't you know, Doctor Thornton?"

"It's a little too soon to be positive. But, yes, I'm sure. Are you happy?" Would he worry that there wasn't enough love, that there wouldn't be enough time for all of them? Had the healing he'd experienced, the strengthening of their love that had occurred these past few months worked its miracle?

"Another adjustment to make in our schedules, right? This kid of ours is going to have one hell of an unconventional childhood. He'll turn out to be as ornery as Cassie and Brandon," Clay warned, with a teasing, exalted glint in his gray eyes that couldn't disguise for a moment the pride he felt.

Jenna's chin came up. "Locke and Leah seem to be managing very well." Locke occasionally still had a tendency to treat his wife like the fragile hothouse flower she resembled, but Leah had learned to stand up for herself, and they were growing together into a stable, happy relationship. "You're right. Leah will turn this day into a real publicity coup. What do you want to bet we get the funding for the new ambulance out of this?" Jenna was regaining her equilibrium, but her eyes sparkled with suppressed desire. Her fingers stroked gently over the back of his hand as Clay prepared to climb into the cockpit of the Buccaneer, standing where he'd taxied it on the paved drive leading to the community boat launch.

"You're right on the money there, Jenna. And I'll never doubt you again." Clay was serious now. "You told me we could have it all and you were right." He looked deep into her eyes, the intensity of his gaze and his feelings reaching out to encompass them in a private world that momentarily blocked out the distractions of their busy lives and reaffirmed their bond of love.

"I feel as if I can do anything...when we're together." Jenna turned her head to see a crowd of people crossing the road to where they stood. "I want to kiss you." There was impatience in her tone, but only love and joy were reflected in the depths of her eyes. A faint blush rose to her cheeks as Clay regarded her with an answering passion in his gaze.

"Our kids are going to be as lucky as their old man, know why?"

"Why?" Jenna whispered, as if the silence surrounding them was indeed real.

"Because you've got enough love for both of us, for all of us."

"But especially for you." Jenna lifted her mouth for a quick, light kiss that, as always, said far more for them than words.

The momentary renewal of their commitment was all they needed. Indeed, from the sound of shouts and pounding feet coming closer, Clay knew that it was all they would be granted until they could come together in the warm darkness of the night.

Their lips touched, savored each other and clung together for a precious second before the world came noisily back into focus around them. Clay felt himself pulled once more from the serenity of their private paradise at the eye of the storm, back into the whirlwind of the loving, caring life-style that was Jenna's choice.

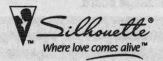

Silhouette® —

where love comes alive—online...

eHARLEQUIN.com

your romantic life

─Romance 101─
♥ Guides to romance, dating and flirting.

─Dr. Romance ─
♥ Get romance advice and tips from our expert, Dr. Romance.

─Recipes for Romance─
♥ How to plan romantic meals for you and your sweetie.

─Daily Love Dose─
♥ Tips on how to keep the romance alive every day.

─Tales from the Heart─
♥ Discuss romantic dilemmas with other members in our Tales from the Heart message board.

SINTL1R